I looked back. Alane was right. No one was there. "There was a guy standing there," I said. My voice sounded as tinny as the bell. "I saw him."

"It was probably just someone running late," she said. "Maybe a teacher. Lucy, seriously, come on!"

I nodded. Again, I couldn't speak. That hadn't been a teacher running late. I knew that man.

Or, rather, Julia Vann had known that man.

Also by Amanda Panitch

Never Missing, Never Found

DAMAGE DONE

AMANDA PANITCH

EMBER

Text copyright © 2015 by Amanda Panitch
Front cover photograph copyright © by Roy Botterell/Fuse/Getty Images;
back cover photograph copyright © by Cultura Creative (RF)/Alamy

All rights reserved. Published in the United States by Ember, an imprint of Random House Children's Books, a division of Penguin Random House LLC, New York. Originally published in hardcover in the United States by Random House Children's Books, New York, in 2015.

Ember and the E colophon are registered trademarks of Penguin Random House LLC.

Visit us on the Web! randomhouseteens.com

Educators and librarians, for a variety of teaching tools, visit us at RHTeachersLibrarians.com

The Library of Congress has cataloged the hardcover edition of this work as follows:
Panitch, Amanda.
Damage Done / Amanda Panitch.—First edition.
pages cm.
Summary: "Julia Vann has a new identity after being forced to leave town because of her twin brother's terrible crime. Julia is the only survivor but she can't remember what happened—at least, that's what she tells the police." —Provided by publisher
ISBN 978-0-553-50749-2 (trade) — ISBN 978-0-553-50751-5 (lib. bdg.) —
ISBN 978-0-553-50750-8 (ebook)
[1. Brothers and sisters—Fiction. 2. Twins—Fiction. 3. Secrets—Fiction.
4. Murder—Fiction.] I. Title.
PZ7.P18933Dam 2015 [Fic]—dc23 2013050070

ISBN 978-0-553-50752-2 (pbk.)

Printed in the United States of America
10 9 8 7 6 5 4 3 2 1
First Ember Edition 2016

For my parents,
Beth and Elliot Panitch,
who believed in me
when I didn't believe in myself

DAMAGE DONE

ONE

I have one picture left of my brother. I used to keep it in my underwear drawer with the other photos I'd hidden from my parents, confident that my lacy unmentionables, at least, would be safe from my dad's searching hands. I was wrong. The picture survived only because it'd slipped behind the drawer.

It's a good picture. The taker, long forgotten, managed to catch us both midlaugh, dark curls flying around our faces, arms draped over each other's shoulders. We were thirteen, maybe fourteen. Young. Innocent. Or at least I was.

The picture is the last thing of my brother I have left, period. My parents' preliminary sweep, right after the incident, took his notebooks and papers but left me with more: his varsity swimming jacket, which still smelled like chlorine and sweat and Axe, and some of his books, big, fat fantasies with page corners so creased and worn they fluttered to the ground like frenzied moths when I flipped through them.

I lost the jacket and books when we moved, right before my parents sold the house and I became Lucy Black. I'd gone out for a run, still Julia Vann, and returned to find my things all in boxes, my clothes crammed into garbage bags that smelled like tar. I sank to my knees in the doorway, suddenly dizzy, wondering if I'd pulled a Rip van Winkle and fallen into a trance, running for what felt like forty-five minutes but was actually forty-five days.

"Mom?" I said hesitantly. She stood up from behind a stack of boxes. "What's going on?"

She swiped at her cheek with the back of her hand. "There was a reporter in the bushes when I went to take out the trash," she said. "Everybody stares when I leave the house. I can't do it anymore, Julia. I just can't."

So that's how we disappeared from Elkton, leaving behind bags of trash, our old names crumpled on the floor like dirty tissues, and the eleven skull-sized bloodstains on the floor of my high school band room—my brother's goodbye.

It took me a good three weeks to learn to respond when people called me Lucy. That was my new name, though I hadn't officially changed it; it wasn't like we were in witness protection or anything. Anyone who really, really wanted to track us down probably could have—Lucy is my middle name, and Black is my mom's maiden name. But the public's memory is short, and it's a long way from the top of California to the bottom, and so nobody had called me anything but Lucy in over a year. Not *Julia,* not *bitch,* not *murderer.* It was quite refreshing.

So when Alane called out "Lucy!" my head turned automatically. I wondered, as I usually did, whether I'd still turn if she yelled "Julia!" I didn't feel much like a Julia anymore. I'd left Julia behind when I carved her name into the music stand I later hid behind as my brother sprayed the room with bullets. An obituary in C minor.

"I'm coming!" I yelled from my front stoop, hoisting my books higher in my arms. Six classes today meant five books to keep track of. They strained my shoulders as I ran down the driveway to Alane's truck. I slid into the passenger seat and dumped the stack into the well. "Sorry. I dropped all my stuff looking for my keys."

She snorted and stepped on the gas. The truck lurched forward, scattering my books and uncovering the quarter-sized hole in the passenger-side well under my feet. I usually loved peering through it when we stopped at red lights and parking spots, where I'd seen all sorts of cool stuff. Loose change. Dead things ground into the pavement. "Maybe you should get a backpack like a normal person."

My brother had borrowed my backpack that day. He'd looked so ridiculous, barreling into the band room with my old neon-pink-and-purple bag, that my mouth had still been open in a laugh when he pulled out the gun.

I pushed my books into a neat stack and clenched them between my calves. "Maybe your face should get a backpack."

"Ouch." She rolled her eyes. "Good one. I might need a skin graft for that burn."

The ride to school was bumpy. Physically. Every ride was bumpy in Alane's truck, or, as I affectionately called it, Alane's heap of scrap metal. I kept a running account of everything I thought (or pretended) I saw through the hole. "A dime. Part of a hubcap. Something rubber. Ooh! Gold doubloons!"

"*Arr*, matey," Alane snarled. She squinched one eye shut as if she were wearing an eye patch. Which was not a good idea, if you think about it, because she was driving. "If you do really be finding gold doubloons, *arr*, you could buy your own ship and sail your own self around."

I stiffened. "I don't drive. You know that." My voice came out colder than I'd intended, and Alane's face fell. "Besides," I quickly added, "you know you love being my chauffeur. You should just let me call you Jeeves."

"Jeeves is for butlers," she said, but her shoulders had relaxed and there was a smile twitching at the corners of her lips. My own shoulders relaxed in turn.

Any tension in the truck fizzled out as we pulled into the student parking lot. We were on the late side of on time thanks to my book-dropping mishap (and also my hitting-snooze-too-many-times mishap, and my oatmeal-burning mishap—it had been a morning full of mishaps), and so the lot was nearly empty, students mostly inside, leaving their cars gleaming iridescently in the sunlight like beetle shells.

"We're going to be late," Alane observed.

"Not if we run."

She frowned at me. "Running is bad for you."

"Running is good for your heart."

"It's bad for your spirit. And you can't survive without spirit."

"But you can without a heart?" Her frown deepened, and fear shot through me. I might have gone too far—I didn't want to make her mad. I slung an arm around her shoulders and leaned in. "Kidding. Just look at the Tin Man. He survived quite well without a heart."

She smiled. "Just look at most of the kids in our class. They survive without a brain."

I laughed and pulled away as we began our walk across the parking lot. Heat still rose from the cars' hoods; some of their engines were still pinging. Unless they all jumped to life and piled upon one another to form some kind of giant Transformer car ready to take over the world, we would probably hit our desks before the late bell rang.

Halfway across the parking lot, I could hear the tinny ringing of the homeroom bell inside. We had a full three minutes to make it. No problem. I stretched my free arm and cracked my neck, and the laughter died in my throat.

There was a man standing at the distant edge of the parking lot, his arms crossed, his face lean and tan. Trendy glasses, large squares, covered what I knew were dark eyes. He was squinting in our direction like he was staring directly into the sun. Even from this far away I could tell his suit was wrinkled and his tie askew. I turned away. Looking at him was like staring directly into the sun, too. Dangerous.

"Alane," I said, or tried to say. It didn't come out. My throat had turned to stone. I coughed, breaking the stone into a hundred pebbles that rattled down my neck and settled in my stomach with the weight of a boulder. "Alane, do you see that guy over there?"

She'd pulled slightly ahead of me when I'd stopped to look, and now she paused and sighed. "Come on, Lucy. If we don't hurry, we'll be late, and I really don't want to have to tell Mrs. Corey her lead soprano won't be at show choir practice today because she has detention."

"Just one second," I said. "Please."

She turned slowly and glanced behind me. "I don't see anything," she said. "Now will you come on?"

I looked back. She was right. No one was there. "There was a guy standing there," I said. My voice sounded as tinny as the bell. "I saw him."

"It was probably just someone running late," she said abruptly. "Maybe a teacher. Lucy, seriously, come on!"

I nodded. Again, I couldn't speak. That hadn't been a teacher running late. I knew that man.

Or, rather, Julia Vann had known that man.

TWO

I let Alane lead me into the building, the force of her walk pulling me along at a near-run. We slid into our seats just as the late bell unleashed its war cry through the halls.

"You okay?" she asked once we were safely seated. I was staring at the surface of my desk, trying to find some sense in the grains of fake wood. "You look like you just swallowed a squirming puppy."

That was an oddly descriptive way to say, *Lucy, you look crazy.* Because that was how I must have looked. I couldn't have seen that man, not here. This was it. I'd finally cracked.

The teacher began calling attendance, and I gestured toward the teacher and then at my lips. *Can't talk now.* Alane's eyes washed over me with one of her concerned looks, but she turned her attention to the front all the same. I raised my hand when I heard "Black, Lucy" and then let myself disappear into my head.

Once upon a time I'd had a squirming puppy. No, Julia Vann had had a squirming puppy. A yappy little thing, more fur than sense, with a pink rhinestone collar that proclaimed FLUFFY in big bubble letters. (Julia had been ten—cut her some slack.) For two months, Julia loved that dog like it was a baby, or like how a ten-year-old imagined someone would love a baby. Then one day Julia went out into the backyard and found the dog sans fur, its organs on the wrong side of its skin, its tail missing. And there was Ryan, holding the knife.

You have to understand, my brother and I were born hand in hand. As in, we literally had our fingers entwined inside the womb. My mom and dad had been all set for a natural birth: no drugs, certified midwife, pool in the living room. They ended up having to rush to the hospital for an emergency C-section because the two of us just wouldn't let go. My dad said we didn't cry as they lifted us out and exposed us to this bright, cold new world. We didn't cry until they wrenched us apart. Our parents tried making us sleep in separate bassinets, one on either side of their bed, but they quickly learned neither of us would sleep without the warmth of the other curled alongside.

And so that was why I didn't scream. Of course it was also because Ryan had glanced between me and my beloved dog, unconsciously insinuating that the same thing could quite easily happen to me. I'd backed away slowly, still retching, until my mom poked her head out at the noise.

Ryan assured me later as I cried that I must have been

imagining that glance, because he was my twin, my other half, and he would never do anything to hurt me. I was a female version of him, after all. We shared the same genes. Had been tied together before we were even born. I had to bite my tongue to keep from telling him how very different I was. But still I pleaded on Ryan's behalf, saying that it must have been an accident, it wasn't as bad as it looked, and so instead of sending him away, my parents made him start biweekly sessions with a psychologist, Dr. Atlas Spence. Dr. Spence wore a perpetually wrinkled suit and hipster glasses that didn't suit his solemn demeanor. I never spotted him without either during the months Ryan saw him, or later, during the few weeks I saw him before my family fled Elkton.

After the incident, my parents and I became modern-day Medusas—nobody would look us in the face. Neighbors we'd once shared potluck dinners with—whose kids I'd babysat—lost the ability to knock on a door or ring a doorbell. The friends I'd had who were still above the dirt suddenly weren't answering their phones. Even the people who were supposed to sympathize with us—the police—tended to be brusque and stare at their notes rather than look me in the eye.

Dr. Spence was no exception. The week after the shooting, which I'd mostly spent cocooned in blankets, my parents summoned him to our house, ushering me and the good doctor into the living room and shutting the door behind us. I took the armchair, leaving Dr. Spence to take the couch. I wasn't going to be one of those people who stretched out and yawned and let all their secrets float away like dandelion fluff.

"Julia," he said. He perched on the edge of the cushion, notebook and pen on his lap, his legs crossed. One foot jittered hypnotically. I couldn't look away. "How are you feeling?"

I wrenched my eyes away from his jiggling foot and stared at the fireplace. A week ago, the mantel had been cluttered with family photos in crystal frames: me and my brother as toddlers with gap-toothed grins; me and my brother dressed up as Aladdin and Jasmine for Halloween in fourth grade; me and my brother holding our instruments high, clarinet and trumpet, respectively, when we started band in middle school. They weren't there anymore. I would've settled for smashed frames, bits of crystal everywhere, or even having them tipped over, bowing, like they were as devastated as we were. But they were just gone, as if they'd never been there at all.

"Wonderful," I said, my voice heavy with sarcasm. "How do you think?"

He lowered his head and scribbled something on his pad. "Sometimes we use sarcasm as a way of masking our true feelings," he said gravely. "It sounds like that's what you're doing here."

"Really?" I said. "Does it? I hadn't realized."

"It does," he said, and then furrowed his brow. "You're being sarcastic again."

"Way to earn that PhD, Doc."

He wrote something else down, then leaned back and met my eyes. His were big, doleful behind the pair of blocky black frames. "You sound angry," he said. "Nobody would blame you. I would be angry, too."

"Would you?"

"It's not your fault, what happened," he said. "You are not your brother. You did not do this, and people should not blame you."

I looked him hard in the eye, and I almost believed him.

And then he flinched. A tiny, nearly imperceptible flinch, one I probably wouldn't have noticed if I hadn't been looking for it. To his credit, he continued staring me in the face, even if he was afraid I'd go for a gun or a knife, or jam his pen through his eye while he was looking at me. Or that my brother would burst through my skin, laughing maniacally, wearing our almost identical dark curls and hazel eyes and permanently rosy cheeks.

"It was nice to see you again, Doc," I said, and then fled. That was the good thing about a house call: your nest of blankets was never too far away.

I'd done all I could to leave Dr. Spence behind in Elkton, and I wanted him to stay there. As soon as homeroom ended, I rushed out without a goodbye to Alane and charged through the hallways, elbowing my way through the streams of people surrounding me, and locked myself in the handicapped bathroom on the second floor.

Once safely ensconced in my disinfectant-smelling haven,

I sat on the closed lid of the toilet and pulled out my phone. The cold porcelain chilled me through my jeans, and I wrapped one arm around myself as I tapped away with the other. Dr. Spence shouldn't be here. He shouldn't know my new name. I was probably just crazy—probably just seeing things—but I would feel a whole lot safer if I knew he was back in Elkton, where he belonged.

Just as I was about to press the green CALL button, to send my voice beaming over the waves or wires or whatever across the state, I laid my phone back on my lap. What if they somehow traced my number? If they—and by *they*, I wasn't even sure who I meant—found out where I was?

So I clicked over to the Web and Googled him instead: *Atlas Spence psychologist Elkton*. I skimmed the list of results. Most were familiar: he'd appeared in a few articles about the shooting (though he never granted an interview), and then there were the general listings for his practice, a boxy brick building at the edge of town he shared with a few other psychologists and one misplaced chiropractor.

Nothing, notably, about a mysterious disappearance. But he didn't have to have disappeared. He could just be taking a trip.

I sighed and realized my hands were shaking. I had to call. It wasn't like the police had a wiretap on his phone. It wasn't like anyone was actually looking for me.

Still, I had to hold my phone against my shoulder as it rang to keep it from slipping through my sweaty fingers.

"Good Help Clinic, how may I help you?"

"Hi," I said breathlessly. Today was Tuesday. Dr. Spence should be in his office today. Unless his schedule had changed. Everything had changed—why not that? "I'm looking for Dr. Spence?"

"Dr. Spence can't come to the phone right now. Can I take a message for him?"

"It's kind of an emergency. Is he with another patient? Or will he be in at all today?"

"Dr. Spence is actually out of the office for a few weeks." The receptionist's voice had softened. "If it's an emergency, I can get you in today with Dr. Fischbach. Do you—"

My finger missed the screen three times before I was able to hang up. I lowered my phone back to my lap, my hands shaking again. *Out of the office* could mean anything, I told myself. It could mean he was sick. He could be visiting family out of state. He could be reclining on a beach somewhere in the Bahamas, snapping his fingers for someone to bring him martinis.

Or he could be here. In Sunny Vale, looking for me.

But why? It didn't make sense. Everybody in Elkton had been glad to be rid of my family. Or at least it seemed like everybody. I'd forgotten what my neighbors looked like; all I saw for weeks on end were their silhouettes behind drawn curtains. Reporters were everywhere; so many had popped out from behind bushes I was paranoid my mom would one day peel off a mask and announce she was from the *New*

York Times. And every so often a few people would gather out front and just glare at our house, as if the power of their disapproval would cause it to crumble and trap us inside.

Sometimes I knew them. That was the worst.

A couple weeks after the incident, I'd finally pushed myself to start leaving the house, usually just running—because what else did I have to leave the house for?—and was always mobbed by reporters throwing questions at me. *Julia, how are you feeling? What happened in the band room? Tell the world your story, Julia! The world deserves to know!* As far as I was concerned, the world didn't deserve anything from me.

One day, on the way home, I just couldn't do it. I rounded the corner of my block and I couldn't face the thought of elbowing through the reporters again, of feeling their hot spit on my cheeks as they yelled. So I jogged a few steps backward and slunk against my neighbor's fence.

"Excuse me, hi."

My head whipped toward the voice. All my muscles clenched when I saw who it was—one of the many reporters who'd knocked on my door after it happened. This one was short and curvy in a way that stretched the seams of her pantsuit, and she held her notepad and pen under her arm. A blotch circled the paper where her pit sweat had seeped into the pad. Gross.

"I'm Jennifer," she continued. "It's nice to meet you. I hope you're well. Well—as well as you can be." She tittered nervously.

I eyed her warily. I could turn and run away, but I was so exhausted. Of this. Of everything. I could stand here and refuse to speak, but that would say more than any interview could. I could jump her and paper-cut her to death with her notepad. No. That was a terrible idea.

"Call me Julie," I said. Nobody called me Julie.

"Julie," she said. A savage sort of triumph welled in my belly. Now this would be okay. She might pretend she knew me, she might sympathize with me, but every time she said *Julie,* she'd remind me she was just some stranger I could paper-cut to death at any time. "Julie, how are you doing?"

"That's a stupid question," I said. No, more like spat. The flash of shock in her eyes fanned my triumph into glee. "You don't care how I'm doing. You want to know what happened in the band room." The glee or triumph, or whatever it was, was beginning to burn, and I swallowed hard, hoping to quell it. I hoped it worked before I started to cry.

Jennifer pursed her lips and chewed on the inside of her cheek as if she was trying to figure out whether she should take the bait. "Fine," she said finally, biting so hard the hook jutted through her upper lip. "What happened in the band room, Julie?"

I pulled back my lips, trying hard not to cry. I had to scare her. I had to freak her out so much she'd never come back. "Can't help you there, Jennifer," I said. "Or is it Jenny? I'll call you Jenny." Her smile tightened. "Jenny, I remember nothing. I remember sitting in the band room, my clarinet on my lap, carving my name into my music stand as the band director worked with one of the freshmen. My brother burst through the door. And then"—I gave a dramatic pause—"nothing. The last thing I remember is blinking and everybody was dead. Is that what you wanted to hear, Jenny?"

"I'm so sorry for your loss." Her words had a rote, memorized quality to them, like the greeting on an answering machine. "You knew most of the people in the room, didn't you?"

"Eleven people died," I said. "One was my boyfriend. One was my best friend. One was my teacher. I knew the others, but not super well."

"I'm so sorry," she repeated. I just hoped she didn't ask me to repeat myself. I'd lied so many times over the course of our conversation I was having a hard time keeping track of all I'd said. My stomach squirmed. "Julie, you really don't remember anything?"

"Not a thing," I said. Add another one to the list.

She chewed on her lip again, and she tapped her pen against her notepad. "Twenty-two minutes passed between your brother entering the room and you walking out, alone," she said. "You're saying you remember nothing?"

"The doctors say it's fairly common," I said. "Some kind of amnesia. Surely you've heard of amnesia, Jenny?"

I read the article the next day. She quoted everything I said, and added some tears shimmering in my eyes, sobs gulping in my throat. The implication was that I'd confided in her, that I'd cried on her shoulder. And the conclusion she reached? That I was angry. That I was troubled. That it was only a matter of time before I followed in my brother's footsteps.

My mother had clucked her tongue, reading it, and talked to my father in a murmur she thought I couldn't hear. "We have to leave. For Julia. For our child. I'll tell her it's for us. For me. That I can't handle the reporters and the social isolation."

I became Lucy Black two weeks later.

THREE

I don't remember, obviously, coming into the world with my brother's hand in mine, or sleeping side by side in our cradle. But I do remember when we got our bunk beds.

There had never been any question about the two of us having our own rooms; it had always been a fact that we'd share, like how the sky is blue or the grass is green. Something we'd never doubted. We slept on twin beds for a while, his bedding blue and mine green, but he was always too far away, all the way on the other side of the room. What about when I had nightmares and needed someone to cry on? It wasn't like we could depend on our parents for that. When we were six, we decided we needed bunk beds, and our parents said okay.

It took our dad nearly four hours to put them together, sweating and swearing and once, memorably, nearly taking his thumb off with a hammer. This was probably the first time he'd spent this many hours with us in one sitting, and so it felt more like four minutes than four hours. My brother and I stood there rapt, our eyes following each pound of a nail, each of us afraid to speak, as if we might spook him back into the bush like a startled gazelle.

"Julia, Ryan," our dad said when he'd finally hoisted the second mattress up top. "Who's taking which bed?"

"I get the top," we said in unison, then turned and blinked at each other. This was a new thing: disagreement. It tasted bitter on my tongue.

"I really want the top," I said. I would be like a princess waving down at her subjects from the top of her tower, or an astronaut staring down at the earth from the moon, depending on how I felt that day.

Ryan cocked his head and surveyed our future kingdom. I could see his mind working. His cheek worked, too; he was chewing on the inside of his mouth.

"I really want the top, too." His voice was even, but I shrank away from it. I don't particularly remember thinking anything was off, but I must have known even then.

"You can have it," I said mournfully. "I guess the bottom will be fun, too. I can pretend it's an underground cave, and every time you move, it'll be like an earthquake."

He chewed on his lip. Again, I could see his mind working. Earthquakes and caves were cool. Super cool. "I want the bottom now," he said. "You can have the top if you really want it, Julia."

My shoulders slumped. "But I really wanted the bottom."

I could see Ryan's thoughts congeal, solidify. "Well, the bottom is mine now," he said. "But you'll like the top."

I sighed and made myself smile. "Okay. I guess."

And that night I was the princess in her tower on the moon.

Somewhere far away, from the land outside my world, which had shrunk to the size of the handicapped bathroom, I heard the bell ring. I took a few deep breaths and stood. I had Spanish second period. Spanish was my worst subject, partially because I had a hard time wrapping my brain around the fact that other people actually put these nonsensical strings of syllables together and they sounded right to them, like proper talking, and partially because I sat next to Michael Silverman, the Michael Silverman of the Greek-god legs and Olympus-blue eyes.

I raised my arms above my head, and my shoulders popped. It had taken a few months for me to be able to stand that sound again. The first time my dad had cracked his knuckles in front of me, a few days after the band room, I had actually passed out and hit my head on the fridge door.

I didn't like how it felt, popping my joints, but now I did it just because I could. It hurt, but the pain felt like victory. I was strong now. Strong enough to hear popping and not immediately think of gunshots.

Again, I slid into my seat just before the late bell rang.

"Close one," Michael Silverman said just as our teacher started taking attendance. I looked over to see him smiling at me, but that smile slid off his face as I turned. "You okay?"

I cleared my throat and raised my hand for "Black, Lucy." "I'm okay," I whispered. "Thanks."

"You just look kind of sick. Like you might be coming down with something. There's a nasty cold going around. Half the swim team has it."

"I don't really get sick," I said. Wonderful. He thought I looked sick. "I hope you don't get it."

He smiled at me again, and it was as if the sun shone through his teeth. "I don't really get sick, either," he said, and raised his hand for "Silverman, Michael."

This was my chance. I could turn this into a conversation about the swim team and then what he did for fun, and then transition into him potentially doing *me* for fun, except for some strange reason the words got stuck in my throat, and then Mr.—excuse me, *Señor*—Goldfarb was calling attention and talking about tenses or something, and I looked over and Michael was focused on the board. Maybe later.

But I ran out as soon as the bell rang, and without Michael Silverman's legs there to keep me focused on something, I spent the rest of the day in a daze. Faces blurred around me, and voices all sounded like Charlie Brown's teacher: *Mwah mwah mwah. Mwah mwah mwah mwah.* If you'd asked me what I'd learned that afternoon, I would say

I'd completed a vigorous study of the colors on the inside of my eyelids: a shifting and strangely beautiful array of grays and purples, with the occasional blast of orange.

Alane finally caught up with me at the end of the day. Well, she didn't so much catch up to me as find me waiting for her outside the chorus room after she'd finished leading show choir. She was, after all, my ride home.

"Well, well," she said. "If it isn't Lucy Black."

I didn't have patience for her games, and besides, I wasn't really Lucy Black. "Let's just go home," I said dully, shrugging my books higher in my grip. They felt especially heavy today, pulling me toward the ground with every step.

"We"—Alane slung her arm around my shoulders, pushing me even farther down—"are not going home."

Alane hadn't had many friends before I moved here. I remember showing up on my first day, my heart thumping nervously, and surveying the crowds of kids laughing and chatting and judging. I'd braced myself for the inevitable rejection, for them to see my past playing out in my eyes like a filmstrip and back away in horror, but I'd actually been welcomed. Sure, people had their established groups of friends, and sure, it was late for me to try to butt in, but I'd stretched my lips in what I hoped was an approximation of a smile and asked people questions about themselves—it turns out people love talking about themselves—and by lunch, three tables had invited me to sit with them. Violet Norris had even asked me to be her bio partner, and Violet Norris, my new friend Ella assured me in a breathless whisper, was one of the most popular girls in school.

And yet, all of lunch, even as Violet and Ella chattered away in my ear, my eyes kept straying to a table in the corner where a girl sat alone. She nibbled at a sandwich, huge dark eyes trained on the table in front of her. Curls, the most extraordinary I'd ever seen, tumbled down past her waist like doll hair. "Who's that?" I asked.

Violet rolled her eyes. "That's Alane Howard," she said. "Nothing against her—she's perfectly nice and everything—but she's just weird, you know?"

"Yeah," I said, and ate another cafeteria French fry. It was cold. Violet and Ella kept talking, and some boy threw a French fry at some girl and apparently it was a big deal, but I couldn't stop looking at Alane.

I knew what it was like to be that person sitting all by herself.

I gave it a few weeks, of course. I wanted to be nice, but I wasn't stupid; I knew I had to take the time to cement my social standing and make sure my relationships with Violet and Ella were solid enough to withstand a little shaking. Once I'd gotten to the point where Violet's grade in bio was dependent upon my knowledge of anatomy and my ability to slice into a frog or a fetal pig without fainting or throwing up, I marched over to Alane's table. "Hey," I said. "I'm Lucy."

She looked at me warily. Her eyes shone against her dark skin. "I'm Alane."

I jerked my head at my usual table. "Do you want to come sit with us?"

If I were a queen, I would have dubbed her the Knight of Wariness. "Why?"

I shrugged. "Why not?" That didn't seem to be enough for her. "I'm new here. I'm still getting to know everyone. Come sit with us."

Something in my face must have convinced her I wasn't playing some sort of joke. "They know you're asking me to sit there?"

"Sure," I said. They didn't, but they'd be okay with it. They had to be, or Violet would be stuck stringing out formaldehyde-soaked intestines and pinning tiny livers to sheets of cardboard all on her own.

And so somehow Alane was absorbed into our group. The next semester, Violet and I got placed in different chemistry classes and drifted apart, and Ella started hanging out more with the girls on the swim team, but Alane and I stuck. I told her to go out for show choir after I heard her singing under her breath, and the chorus teacher was so stunned by Alane's voice that she made Alane lead soprano.

So I was willing to risk my social standing for Alane, but I wasn't going wherever she wanted to go right now. The only place I wanted to go was my bedroom. Spence wouldn't be there. He couldn't.

"I"—I stopped for a dramatic pause of my own, fully worthy of the one Alane had just given me—"want to go home."

"You," she said, "do not want to go home. I know you're not having a good day, and I'm going to cheer you up."

"You can cheer me up by taking me home."

"No, the boys' swimming practice is just about ending. On Tuesdays after practice, they stop off at Crazy Elliot's for coffee and scones." She paused and considered. "Well, probably not scones. Meat or something. Giant plates of meat. Whatever boys eat.

"And of course," she continued, "you know who's on the boys' swimming team. That's right. Michael Silverman."

My feet stuttered to a halt. Banging erupted in the hallway, echoing against the lockers that lined the sides, and I shrank into myself, cringing, before I realized I'd just dropped my books.

"See?" Alane said wisely. "That's why you need a backpack."

I knelt to gather my things. Alane crouched beside me, her arm still on my shoulder.

"I don't even know Michael Silverman," I said. "I've spoken to him, like, once." I'd actually spoken to him four and a half times including today, if you counted our teacher-mandated interactions. "And it was in mangled Spanish, because that's the only class we have together. And it was about tacos. And today he thinks I'm sick. So I just want to go home."

"You might not know him, but you loooove him," Alane said, her voice a singsong.

I was glad I'd dropped my books. It left both my hands free to smack her.

"Okay, I deserved that," Alane said, wincing and rubbing her shoulder. "But seriously, we're going and I'm not going to take no for an answer."

"Would you take me hitting you again as an answer?" I asked. "Because I'm serious. I can't do the whole social-with-other-people thing right now."

"You're being social with me."

"You don't count as a person," I said. "I mean that in the most affectionate way possible."

"How do you expect to fall deeply in love and have his babies if you won't even talk to him?" she said, pouting.

"I have talked to him." Four and a half times. "We've had some great conversations." He'd seemed especially excited and cheerful at the idea of eating tacos with dog meat, *perro* being the only animal word I could think of at the time. "And who said anything about having his babies? I don't want to have anyone's babies right now."

"God, Lucy, it was just an expression."

I took a step forward, and she followed. Good. We were on our way to the parking lot. Each step was a step closer to being home, where I would have a chance to obsess about Spence and my brother, and whether I had, in fact, cracked right down the middle and spewed a giant fountain of crazy all over the school day.

"The only babies I'd want to have right now are yours, baby," I said, waggling my eyebrows.

She rolled her eyes, but she was smiling. "God, Lucy, you're such a loser."

We crossed over the doorway and outside, and I instinctively breathed in the sun. SoCal sunshine had a different smell than NorCal sunshine; the former was bright and clean, almost tangy, while the latter had been stuffier, mustier. Foggier.

"I really want to go home. I can probably find another ride if you really want to go to Crazy Elliot's," I said.

She gave me a mock slap on the shoulder. "I'm proud to be your Jeeves," she said. "And your future baby-daddy. Let's get you home."

We were five minutes into the ride when the smell drifted in through the open window, and I froze. "Do you smell that?" I said, hardly breathing.

She took a sniff. "Yeah. Smoky. Someone's probably burning leaves. Or having a barbecue." She glanced at me from the corner of her eye. "What's up with you today? First you had that panic attack this morning, and you look like you're going to have one now. Should I pull over?"

My chest was tight, as if someone had wrapped me in rubber bands. "No," I managed to say. I took quick, shallow breaths through my mouth. Not through my nose. Not with the smoke in the air.

I could feel her concern burning my left cheek. "Are you sure you're okay?"

"Fine," I said. "I won't puke on your upholstery. Don't worry."

"I'm not worried," she said. "My upholstery's had plenty of puke on it already." Gross. Suddenly my butt, my legs, everything touching the seat felt itchy. "But are you okay? You can tell me. If you don't, what sort of example are you setting for our future children?"

I barked something I hoped sounded like a laugh. "It's just the smell of smoke," I said. "And fire. It brings back bad memories. From before I moved." That was vague enough, I thought.

The truth was anything but vague. After poor Fluffy, there had been squirrels and mice and a few cats. The cats' MISSING posters still haunted me with their desperate appeals and flashy rewards.

And then there had been a fire.

"I'm sorry," she said. "Do you want to talk about it?"

"No," I said flatly. Her face fell, and I realized my answer had come out more harshly than I'd intended. "I mean, sorry. I just . . . don't want to. It doesn't matter anyway. The person who set the fire is dead."

"Oh," she said, her tone abnormally subdued. "I'm sorry. If you ever want to talk about it, you know I'm always here."

"Thanks," I said, and meant it. We drove in silence for the rest of the ride, with Alane occasionally sneaking a glance at me when she thought I wasn't looking, and she bid me goodbye with a hug tighter than the rubber bands around my chest. I waved as she pulled away.

I had lied to her. I had lied to myself.

My brother wasn't dead.

FOUR

If the public had their way—and if my old classmates had *their* way—my brother would be rotting in his grave, or, alternatively, rotting in a jail cell before getting a needle stuck into his arm that would stop his heart and send him to that grave just a little bit later. Even if my brother had had his way, he would be dead. He'd turned the gun on himself after he shot all those other people, but it hadn't killed him.

He might as well have been dead. The doctors had had to put him into a medically induced coma, drilling into his skull to relieve the pressure and keep his swelling brain from becoming irreversibly damaged. As if his brain wasn't already irreversibly damaged. I still remember my parents sitting me down in our old living room and telling me he'd never wake up and the howl that had escaped my throat when I realized I'd never talk to him again. Sometimes I wondered if it might have been a kindness on the doctors' part rather than a medical decision.

I think that might have been why the world was so angry. Because he wasn't really dead and he wasn't really alive. He'd taken the coward's way out in attempting suicide, and he hadn't even succeeded. He couldn't face justice, and he wasn't sharing the oblivion of his victims—or burning in hell, depending on your religion. There was no other outlet for the public's fury, and so the outlet became me— his twin.

I had been to visit him exactly twice, both in the week after the shooting. He'd become progressively gray-faced and hollow-cheeked. The only sound in the room was the *beep-beep-beep* of the heart monitor. There were always a couple of cops, their sides bulging with guns, hovering around his bed or the doorway. I'd tried just about everything I could think of to be alone with him, to lean over and whisper into his ear and wait for his eyes to pop open for me, because I was his twin, his other half, and I was the only one who might possibly understand, just a little, but they never left, not even when I set off the fire alarm to try to get the ward evacuated.

I wasn't allowed to visit after that.

A week after the shooting, the state police transported him to a more secure ICU. They talked to my parents, and my parents talked to me: Ryan would never wake up. Every month or so, my father would disappear for a few days. My mother would say he was on a business trip, but once I'd found his flight itinerary. I knew business wasn't why he was in NorCal. I knew love had nothing to do with it, either: he never spent this much time with Ryan when he was awake. My father was a lawyer; he'd probably been in the hospital examining every drip of medication going into his son's veins, sniffing as hard as he could for a lawsuit.

Back in the safety of my Sunny Vale living room, I tried calling Spence's office again; I got the same patient receptionist telling me he was out of the office for the next few weeks. I hung up on her midsentence and paced around the room for a good ten minutes, wiping my sweaty palms on my shirt so many times it clung to my skin with wetness. I needed to calm down.

"What would Lucy do?" I asked myself. I should really have that printed on a bracelet, like the rubber WWJD bands the kids in the Purity Club wore to school. What would Lucy Black do—WWLBD? What would a *normal* person do? "Normal girls eat chocolate and ice cream when they're upset. So Lucy should eat some chocolate or ice cream. Or chocolate ice cream. That's even better. Now stop talking, because normal people don't talk to themselves."

We didn't have any chocolate or ice cream in the house, only green things like kale and broccoli. Those wouldn't do. Luckily there was a convenience store within walking distance. Walking was good. Walking would give Lucy a chance to burn off some of her excess energy.

I set off down the road, my heart still leaping and flailing in my chest like a frog in boiling water. Cars whooshed by me as I plodded along through the scrappy grass on the roadside, kicking the occasional flattened can glittering under the dying sunlight. I found a sort of calm in the walk, in putting one foot in front of the other, in knowing I wasn't actually a crazy person, because a crazy person would do something crazy, like throw herself in front of a car or dance in the middle of the road, not plod, plod, plod like Lucy Black.

I don't know what made me turn and squint into the sunset behind me. Maybe I heard, faintly, the faraway crunch of shoes over the dying grass, or maybe I was seized by the urge to admire the melting colors of the California sky. Whatever it was, it made me turn and see the man strolling behind me. Not behind me in an about-to-reach-out-and-strangle-me kind of way, but behind me in a half-the-length-of-a-football-field kind of way. On the other side of the road, too, so my view kept breaking up thanks to the cars whizzing past. I stopped short, squinting harder, trying to make out anything besides the suit he was wearing, and he paused. And waved.

The lump rose from my stomach back into my throat. "Hey," I called weakly. "Hey!"

What, had he been waiting to get me alone? Well, I was alone. And I was ready to duke it out. I wasn't going to let him pop up and ruin my life again. No, not *my* life. *Lucy's* life. Lucy's life was a precious thing.

"Hey!" I shouted, and launched myself after him. Into

the middle of the road. Where there was a car bearing down on me.

Panic wrapped itself around my head like a scarf, blinding me. I threw myself backward and felt the car whoosh past, so close I could feel its heat.

When I blinked, I found myself on the ground at the side of the road, my heart beating so hard against the dirt it felt as if there were a herd of horses galloping over me. At some point, I became aware that some of the hoof beats weren't just my heart—they were another person's footsteps running toward me.

"Lucy?" someone was saying. "Lucy Black, are you okay?"

I looked up. It was Michael Silverman.

Naturally.

At least it wasn't Spence. I licked my lips and propped myself up on an elbow, then immediately gave up on trying to look even remotely attractive. I was soaked in sweat and caked with dirt, and there was something wet that I hoped was water dripping down my leg. I took a big sniff under pretense of taking a deep breath. I'd just landed in a puddle. Thank God. "Michael," I said. "Fancy meeting you here."

He crouched down beside me. "Are you okay? God, I'm so sorry. I take my eyes off the road for a second and . . ."

So he hadn't seen me wander into the road. He thought *he* was the one who'd messed up. "I'll live," I said, rotating my joints just to make sure. My right ankle creaked a little bit in protest, but thanks to an old sprain, that one had always been a temperamental little bastard anyway.

"Did you see that man? Across the street? By the side of the road?"

Michael shaded his eyes and peered around. "I don't see anyone. Don't tell me I hit someone else."

I pushed myself to my knees, then stood, tottering just a little bit. "You didn't hit me. I got out of the way just in time."

"You have good reflexes," he said. He stuck his hands in his pockets and squinted into the setting sun. Its last rays poured over him, turning flyaway hairs to gold. "What were you doing out here? It's dangerous, without any sidewalks."

"It was an ice cream emergency," I said. "As in, I didn't have any in the freezer. The store's right down the road." Someone like Lucy would need ice cream even more after this whole mishap. She would probably eat a whole pint on the couch, in sweatpants, watching a Nicholas Sparks movie.

"Let me drive you," he said. "It's the least I can do after running you down."

"The least you could've done is leave me lying there. At least you stopped." I turned again and craned my neck. Spence had vanished, almost like he'd never been there at all. Maybe he hadn't. Maybe this was it: I was officially seeing people who weren't there. Maybe my brother had been seeing people who weren't there that day, too.

Then again, maybe Spence *was* real, and he was out to get me, and if I turned around and went home, he'd follow me there. I certainly did not want him coming across my parents. It would be best for everyone, I decided, if I got into Michael's car.

"Thanks," I said, and climbed into the passenger seat. "It's been one of those days."

"I can tell," he said, climbing in himself. "First you were dying of a cold in Spanish, and then you were almost run over by some maniac driver."

I laughed as he pulled away. It tasted unexpected and sweet. "Thank goodness you were there to rescue me from that maniac," I said. "Were you coming from Crazy Elliot's?" I regretted the words as soon as they left my mouth. Only a creepy stalker would know he went to Crazy Elliot's after school with the swim team. "I mean, or swim practice, or school, or home, or wherever you went." Nice save, Lucy.

"Nah, I usually go to Crazy's after swim, but I didn't feel like going today." I couldn't help but notice he was driving ten miles under the speed limit, like being hit at forty miles per hour instead of fifty would make somebody any less dead. "I can only take so much of the guys. You still don't look great, by the way."

"Thanks," I said drily. "Way to win a girl's heart."

He rolled his eyes. He smelled so strongly of chlorine he was practically giving off waves. Wasn't he supposed to shower after practice? My brother always did, though the smell of chlorine was never quite scrubbed from his skin.

"I didn't mean it like that," Michael said. "You just look like you've seen a ghost. I think you're wrong and that you do get sick and that you're breathing germs all over my dashboard and I'm going to get sick, too, and miss Friday's meet."

"I'm not sick. I promise." I squinted out the front window, watching the yards and yards of asphalt disappear beneath our tires. I was anonymous, blank as that road. No matter how much I wanted to talk about Spence, about the idea that I was being followed, about the frightening and all-too-possible idea that I was seeing things that weren't there, I couldn't. Because all that belonged to Julia, and I was Lucy, and our two minds couldn't meet or the world would probably explode on a quantum level.

But maybe I could say something. "I'm worried I'm being followed," I said. "I saw him this morning in the school parking lot, and then just now on the side of the road. But I might just be seeing things."

Michael risked a look away from the road. "Followed by who?"

I sighed. "I don't even know why I feel like I can tell you this. I barely know you."

He leaned toward me, almost imperceptibly. "I'm a good listener."

I sighed again, stalling. I had to come up with something quickly. Obviously I couldn't tell him the truth. "For some reason I feel like I can trust you," I said. "I can trust you, right? Not to tell anyone? I don't want it to get around."

"Of course," he said. "I swear. You can trust me."

Voilà. The perfect lie popped into my head. "My ex," I

said. I could lie with the best of them—it had always been one of my talents. My clincher was the strategic hesitation. It wasn't a skill I'd enjoyed honing, understand, but over the past year, lying had become a necessity. "From where I used to live. He was . . . not a nice person. It was . . . one of the reasons we moved."

His knuckles whitened on the steering wheel. "My dad's a cop," he said. "Should I talk to him?"

"No, no." I waved at the window as if the idea were preposterous. It just made his knuckles whiter. I had him, I thought. I knew his type: the white knight. He wanted to save the princess, to kiss her awake after her bite of poisoned apple.

Well, I couldn't be saved. I was beyond saving. "I don't think it was him," I said. "He doesn't even know I moved down here. I think I was just seeing things. It just freaked me out. You know, all the memories." I put a hand to my upper arm as if I were unconsciously tracing a bruise. Strategic hesitation and body language. "But thank you."

"Of course, Lucy. Just let me know." The lights of the convenience store glowed ahead; Michael pulled into the parking lot and turned off his ignition. The *ting, ting, ting* of the engine winding down reverberated through the car. "I'll come in with you," he said. "I have to pick up some stuff, and then I'll take you home."

"You don't have to do that," I said as I climbed out.

"It's almost dark," he said. "And you were already almost killed by a crazy driver today."

37

I snorted as we entered the store. "And you had nothing to do with that."

He paused in the doorway. "As if," he said, sounding greatly affronted. "I'm a great driver."

"Either come in or stay out!" someone called from inside the store. "You're letting out all the cold air!"

I shot a nasty look at the clerk, who shot one right back, and rolled my eyes at Michael. "Of course you are," I said, and stepped into the store. Michael followed me in, and the door eased closed behind him.

He had said he needed to pick some stuff up, but he trailed me to the freezer. "Don't you have to go get stuff?"

"No," he said. "I just wanted to come in with you."

"Oh," I said. Tenderness swept over me, as soft and warm as the Southern California sun. "What's your favorite flavor?"

"What?"

I gestured to the shelves and shelves of ice cream. "Your favorite flavor," I said. "What is it?"

He scanned the shelves. "Chocolate," he said decisively.

"Chocolate? Just plain chocolate?" I said. "How boring." His face tensed, so I added quickly, "Kidding. Just kidding. Chocolate is my favorite, too." It wasn't.

I stepped up to the register to pay. "Two spoons," I told the cashier. He didn't deserve a *please*. He'd yelled at us. "And a plastic bag."

"Two spoons?" Michael said.

I strode purposefully out the automatic doors and braced

myself against the front of his car, sliding back across the warm hood with a squeak of flesh on metal. I threw a spoon at him. He caught it. I popped open the ice cream and patted the space beside me.

"Sit down and eat."

He did, and we ate in silence, our faces glowing in the harsh glare of the store's lights, and the chocolate melting over the plastic spoon's sharp edges tasted so sweet it made my molars ache.

Re: Ryan Vann, age 10

Ryan Vann presents as a ten-year-old white male in the fifth grade at Elkton Elementary School. He lives in a single-family home with his father, a real estate lawyer; his mother, a part-time computer science instructor at the local community college; and his twin sister, Julia. The client maintains an especially close relationship with his sister.

Ryan was sent to me by his parents, who first referred to something they called a "little incident." When pushed, they admitted that Ryan had killed and mutilated his sister's dog. At this point, the mother had to leave the room to vomit, and the sister burst into tears. The client betrayed no affect; he did, however, put his arm around his sister as if to comfort her. The father admitted that there had been other "incidents": a neighbor's cat, a few squirrels, several mice.

The family then left to sit in the waiting room while I spoke with Ryan alone. We sat in silence for a few minutes, staring at each other. I felt almost as if the boy was sizing me up. "Ryan," I said, "did you kill your sister's dog?"

The client stared at me and did not speak for another few minutes. "Yes," he finally said. "And the cat. And the squirrels. And the mice. I killed all of them."

Hearing something like this in a child's high voice is

unsettling, to say the least, but I kept my composure. As police psychologists must. Though I wouldn't know, as they didn't accept me into their behavior analysis program. "And how did that make you feel?"

His eyes were as flat as his affect. "Good," he said. "I liked it."

A chill ran down my spine. "Did you show any of your friends?" I asked.

"No," he said, and paused. "I did it all by myself."

"Your sister, Julia, saw the dog, though. Isn't that correct?"

"I wasn't lying," Ryan said. He blinked at me slowly, lazily. "I didn't show her. And she's my sister, not my friend."

A hollow had opened in the pit of my stomach, but I must admit I did feel a bit excited. Not by what the boy was describing, obviously—by the thought of helping him. Though I hadn't spoken with him and his family long, he seemed to be presenting with conduct disorder, the precursor to antisocial personality disorder, or sociopathy. Here I have the opportunity to treat someone who might otherwise grow up to be a murderer. To make a difference.

The most effective course of treatment, I feel, will be Multisystemic Therapy (MST), and I will speak to the family and teachers about management techniques they can integrate into the client's daily life. I will also recommend that he continue therapy with me so that I can best track his progress.

I will make a difference.

FIVE

The next morning, I threw open Alane's passenger-side door, tossed my books into the well, and slammed the door behind me with a sense of great purpose. "I spent last night eating ice cream with Michael Silverman outside the 7-Eleven," I announced.

"Good morning to you, too," Alane said.

"He'd skipped out on Crazy Elliot's, so it was good we didn't go," I said. "We talked about nothing for, like, an hour and I got to stare at his legs. It was wonderful."

"Babies wonderful?" she said gravely.

"You know no one can replace you in my heart," I said.

"That's right," she said. "Now tell me everything."

I told her almost everything: my walk to the store, Michael nearly running me down, all the highlights of our conversation. I didn't tell her about Spence, or about my fake ex-boyfriend. She was too close, somehow. I couldn't stand the thought of her judging me.

I tensed as we pulled into the parking lot, fully expecting to see Spence lurking behind one of the rows of cars or hunched inside the truck next to us, but he was nowhere to be seen. It wasn't surprising, really; we were on time today, so the lot was packed with chattering kids. Spence could've been two rows over, and I would never have seen him.

If he was even here. If he was even real.

The beginning of the day passed quickly, and I walked to Spanish even more quickly, each breath heavy with anticipation. Michael and I arrived at the same time; he bowed in the doorway, sweeping me through. "After you, *señorita*," he said.

"*Gracias, señor*," I said, feigning shyness. He smiled. "*¿Cómo estás?*"

"*Bien*," he said, and then, as we sat down at our side-by-side desks, in English, "I had fun last night."

I didn't have to feign my blush. "I did, too."

"Are you feeling any better?"

"I haven't seen him since, so yeah," I said. *Just being next to you makes me feel better,* I didn't say. "Chocolate heals all wounds."

He laughed. "What are you doing after school today?"

"I don't know," I said. "What are *you* doing after school today?"

"Swim practice, then I'm actually going to Crazy Elliot's," he said. "If you're there, I could buy you a coffee."

"I hate coffee," I said. "Hot chocolate, on the other hand . . ."

Before he could respond, our teacher clapped his hands for silence. *"Silencio, por favor,"* he said. Despite what he claimed was fluency, I had a hard time taking Señor Goldfarb's expertise seriously. He might have studied for a college semester or two in Barcelona, but the man had a Brooklyn accent. "That means you, Señorita Black."

Michael scrunched up his face at me, a fair imitation of Señor Goldfarb's permanent lemon-lips. I snorted with laughter. "Señorita Black," Señor Goldfarb said, his voice flashing warning lights. *"¡Silencio!"*

I waited for him to look away, then turned back to Michael. *Hot chocolate or bust,* I mouthed.

The rest of the day crawled by. Band practice finally rolled around, which was the only part of the day that moved at its normal speed. I just closed my eyes and let the notes flowing from the bell of my clarinet join the tide of the saxes and flutes and oboes and sweep me away.

As usual, I met Alane outside the chorus room. "Guess where we're going right now," I said in greeting.

"Home?" she said hopefully. "I have mountains of homework to climb."

"That's what experienced Sherpa tour guides are for," I said. "No. Today we're going to Crazy Elliot's so Michael Silverman can buy me a hot chocolate."

"I have homework," she said. "Can you get a ride with Ella? I think she's going."

I forced my lower lip into a pout. "But I want you there," I said. "Ella is a terrible wingwoman."

She hoisted her backpack higher on her shoulders. "Ella's never winged for you," she said, but she looked pleased. "You'll be fine without me. If you miss me, just stare at Michael's legs and you'll feel better."

I rested my head on her shoulder. "Please? I won't have any fun without you."

She sighed. "Fine," she said. "If you insist."

Inside, I smiled.

Crazy Elliot's was owned by a woman named Alicia. Her ex-husband's name was Elliot. Put the pieces together yourself.

Whatever its origin story, Crazy Elliot's was the central gathering place of Sunny Vale High School. It was a fifteen-minute walk off campus for the freshmen and sophomores who couldn't drive, and a five-minute ride for the rest of us. The inside was big and homey, scattered with squashy arm-chairs in assorted clashing patterns and little round tables, and a bar wound around the inside wall, though obviously the place didn't serve alcohol. It did, however, serve pretty much everything else: coffee, tea, cupcakes, hamburgers, protein shakes. Everybody went there to see and be seen.

Alane took a spot right in front, her tires squealing on the pavement as her pickup shuddered to a halt. I clenched my jaw, worrying, as always, that today would be the day it just gave up and collapsed into a pile of gears and rust.

"I look okay?" I asked.

I could feel the tickle of her eyes take me in from bottom to top. I'd changed from my T-shirt and jeans (now stuffed in Alane's backseat) to one of the flowered dresses she kept in her car for emergencies such as these. It was a bit big on me and hung around my waist, but I'd corrected the worst of it with a strategically tied ribbon. "You look perfect," she said.

Easing myself out of the truck, I swore I heard the soles of my flip-flops sizzle as they touched the pavement. Outside smelled like tar, and my heart did a funny sort of flutter for a second as I thought of garbage bags and boxes and disappearing. I was done disappearing, though.

"Come on," Alane said. "I have to lock up."

Nobody would steal that truck if you paid them, but I bit my tongue.

As soon as we pushed open the double doors, an explosion of sound blasted us in the face: people shouting food orders, the buzz and whirr of assorted fancy coffee machines, the low roar of thirty to fifty people talking at once. The booths and couches and even the bar were all packed, with kids sitting on one another's laps for space, and backpacks and books were piled on every available surface. Light streamed through skylights every few feet in the ceiling, which kept the crowded room from inching over the line into claustrophobic.

I grabbed Alane's hand, soft and sweaty, and trailed behind her as she expertly weaved her way through the crowd. She raised her hand and shouted when she saw Ella, who had taken over a circle of chairs and was snarling—quite literally baring her teeth—at anyone who tried to take one. Fortunately the baristas were quick today, and it didn't take long for me to get my hot chocolate with caramel sauce and whipped cream, so sugary it made my teeth rot just looking at it. We made it over to Ella and claimed our places before she actually bit somebody.

Once my hot chocolate had cooled enough for me to take a casual sip, I turned to look for the boys' swim team. I didn't have to look far. They'd taken over a bunch of chairs nearby. Michael sat maybe ten feet away in an armchair directly beneath a heavenly ray of light. Of course. The sunlight draped over him and turned his blond curls gold, the pale hairs coating his upper lip to glitter. You could chisel his biceps out of marble. He glanced over at me and blinked, then his lips turned up in a smile as he looked me up and down. My cheeks went pleasantly hot as I lifted my hand in a wave. I wasn't getting up, though. He could come to me.

"Lucy? Hey, Lucy." Alane waved her hand in front of my face. "Ella said hi."

I blinked and turned back to Ella, whose half-lidded eyes, strong under her black pixie cut, suggested she'd been imbibing something other than coffee or cinnamon buns. Looking at her made me feel almost as if a fog had lifted from my vision. "Hi, Ella."

She blinked back. Her lips twitched. "Michael, huh?"

I blushed. "Am I that obvious?" I squeezed Alane's hand, silently thanking her for bringing me here. She squeezed back, saying *You're welcome* better than any words ever could. "He promised to buy me a hot chocolate. Another one. When he's done gossiping like a little old lady, that is."

"Ah," Ella said. The smile that flashed onto her face came too quickly, looked almost plastic. "Want me to call him over? We've been friends since we were little. He lives right down the street from me."

I didn't want to look desperate, and besides, I got the feeling she hadn't been entirely sincere. Maybe she had a crush on him herself. Poor her. I certainly wasn't going to step aside. "No," I said. "I'm happy with just looking, for now."

To illustrate my point, I looked again. Michael was smiling wide. I couldn't help but smile back. From the corner of my eye, I saw Ella's smile falter. Michael's smile stretched even wider, and I tingled from the crown of my head to the tips of my fingers.

But he wasn't the only person staring at me. My smile dropped from my face and landed with a sick thud on the floor between my feet. Over Michael's shoulder I saw a trendy pair of glasses (man attached) dressed in a rumpled suit enter Crazy Elliot's and fix his eyes on me. Spence.

I glanced down at my feet, convinced—hoping—I was imagining it, then looked back up. He was still there. Still staring. Worms wriggled in my stomach.

I nudged Alane. "Does that guy look like he's staring at me?" *Does he exist?* I didn't say.

She glanced over and shrugged. "He just looks like he's looking around," she said, and winked. "Maybe he is staring at you. You do look awfully stunning in my dress."

My breath froze in my throat, and I gradually became aware my entire body was shaking so hard my chair was practically vibrating. It *was* Spence. For some reason Spence was following me, and now he was here, staring at me. Any minute he could scream "Julia Vann is in this very room!" and someone would recognize my name, and then the reporters would be back, and Michael would avert his eyes every time I came near, and Alane would never talk to me again. Best friends and boyfriends? Didn't fare well around me.

Spence had to be trying to get me alone. Otherwise he would've approached me in the parking lot or caught up to me on the side of the road. Each time he'd fled once he saw I was with someone else.

Well, if he wanted me alone, he'd get me alone. He'd get me telling him to get the hell away from me and my new life.

I swallowed hard and balanced my drink on my armrest. Despite all the hot chocolate I'd downed, my mouth was dry and dusty. "You guys, I'll be right back. I have to pee." I stood and, naturally, knocked over my drink. Alane gasped, but I barely felt the heat soaking my dress, the swamp of hot chocolate squishing between my toes.

"Lucy, I'll come with you. Help you clean up." She stood, too, but I shook my head. All my attention was focused on Spence.

"Stay here. I'll be right back." She looked skeptical, so I raised my eyebrows. "Seriously. I'm fine."

Alane sat back down with a thump. "Fine, whatever."

I'd have to apologize for that later, but I didn't care. I was too busy trying to look casual and unconcerned as I walked across the coffee shop.

Or, to be more accurate, shoved my way across the coffee shop. People pressed against me from all sides, and backpacks littered the floor like land mines. I shouldered through them, using my blessedly sharp elbows and long legs to their full advantage; my throat was too dry to shout out an "Excuse me" or a "Coming through." Scowls glanced off me, and muttered curses zipped right past my ears. I could not possibly have cared less.

Spence's eyes were darting back and forth at the growing buzz and commotion. He clearly hadn't expected me to charge right for him. Good. Spence began to back toward the door, his eyes on me, but I was gaining on him. I was thirty feet away . . . twenty feet away. . . .

A guy loomed before me, scowling, coffee dripping down the front of his T-shirt. "Haven't you ever heard of manners?" he said.

I must have been the source of that spilled coffee. "Sorry," I said breathlessly, trying to do a half-twirl, half-skip around him, but he moved to block me. "Dude, seriously, I'll buy

you a new cup. I have to get out or"—inspiration struck—
"I'm going to puke."

That did it; he leapt out of the way so quickly and
gracefully I wondered if he'd ever done ballet. I searched
the crowd as I continued on, but I was too late. Spence was
gone. Again.

By the time I burst through the front doors and into the
parking lot, it was as quiet and still as a graveyard. Spence
was gone. Really gone, this time.

But he'd be back. I could feel it deep down in my bones.
He clearly wasn't going to give up until he got whatever
he'd come for.

"Miss, are you okay?" asked a Crazy Elliot's employee
leaning against the building on a smoke break. A thin trail
of smoke whirled up from the cigarette pinched between
her fingers. "Can I get you a glass of water or something?"

"Lucy? Lucy, are you okay?"

It took Alane saying "Lucy!" three more times before I
collected myself enough to turn. Seeing Spence's face and
knowing he was real—and here—had snapped me back into
Julia, flooding her mind with memories of Ryan. But, as I
reminded myself when Alane's hand landed on my shoulder,
I wasn't Julia anymore. And Lucy didn't have a brother.

"Lucy, are you okay?" Alane repeated. I closed my
eyes and tried to take a deep breath, but it shuddered and
squeaked on its way down, as if I had a mouse stuck in
my throat. "Lucy. Lucy." She enveloped me in a hug. Once
her warmth and her familiar smell, something between

potpourri and cinnamon, had calmed me enough that I could breathe again, she hooked me firmly by the elbow. Somehow we'd gotten back inside the building, though I didn't remember walking there. "Let's go sit down. People are staring."

People *were* staring. It brought back that last walk from my high school in Elkton, where two police officers had propped me between them because otherwise I would have toppled over, and where wailing students and white-faced parents had lined the police barricades out front. My boyfriend's mother, whose soda I had drunk after school and whose vodka I had drunk in secret when she was sleeping, had broken through the barricade and shouldered aside the cops the way I had shouldered through the crowd in Crazy Elliot's. "Julia!" she'd screamed, her voice a high, unbroken wail. "Where is he? Where is he?"

"Are you okay?" Alane steered me back to our little gathering in the corner, her stooped shoulders and fluttering hands shielding me from the crowd. The guy whose coffee I'd spilled was still scowling and looming, like he was going to release a thundercloud of rage, but Alane stopped him with a *look*. "Here. Sit. Ella, get up."

Ella stood and left me enough space to collapse into the armchair. A shadow materialized overhead, and I looked up to see, to my surprise, Michael Silverman, outlined in gold against the light overhead. "I brought you some water," he said. "Replacement hot chocolate to come?"

My throat was dry as paper. I wanted so badly to make

some witty quip, but I took the water and gulped instead. My throat stayed scratchy. "Sorry for being so crazy," I said. I couldn't tell the truth. I couldn't tell anything approaching the truth. If I said I freaked out over some guy staring at me because of my nonexistent brother, everybody would think I was crazy-pants. "I thought I saw a rat," I invented. "Near the bathroom."

"A rat," Ella said, her voice heavy with skepticism.

"Lucy hates rats," Alane said. "She's terrified of them." I shot her a grateful look. "She grew up in a house where rats would nibble on her toes every night and she worried they'd eat her." My grateful look collapsed into a warning. "To this day she only has eight toes."

I couldn't help it: I burst into a laugh. A slightly hysterical laugh, true, but a laugh. "She's joking," I said. "I'm sorry if I freaked you out. I just . . . think I should go home." My insides were churning; I couldn't decide whether to feel sick or excited or humiliated. "Rain check, Michael?"

Michael looked like he wanted to say something, but he only nodded. Alane looped her arm around my back and steered me toward the exit. The paper cup of water crumpled in my hand; I looked for a garbage can and didn't see one, so I held it, soggy and limp, the whole way home.

Re: Ryan Vann, age 10

I was reprimanded by the head of the practice after the last session for including a personal note with my session notes. As I don't believe I can properly assess this patient and keep a full set of records without consideration of my subjective experience, I have therefore decided to keep two separate accounts of the patient. I will keep one set of strictly clinical notes as well as this journal, which will contain my clinical notes as well as my personal thoughts and considerations. In this way, I will be better able to treat this patient.

I will, after all, need a full record of everything that happened when I join the behavior analysis unit. I may have failed the state's first "test," but once I have a record of treating and fixing the most problematic sociopaths-to-be, they'll need *me* more than I need *them*. Ryan Vann is merely the first of many steps.

Ryan has now been undergoing MST for two full weeks. I met with him eager to hear how the therapy was going. Maybe to get some emotion out of him, but probably not. Too soon.

"Good afternoon, Ryan," I said once we were alone. "How was school today?"

"Fine," he muttered. "I had a test."

"A test," I said. "In what subject?"

"Spelling," he said, scowling. "I hate spelling. I got five wrong."

Here I felt my first glimmer of empathy for the client. I, too, had never been much of a speller. My teachers and mother hadn't figured out I was dyslexic until I was eleven. I didn't ask him how many questions those five were out of.

"And my sister and I asked if we could go to Six Flags with our friends next weekend, and our mom said yes," he said. "Roller coasters are cool. I like to sit up front."

The sister again. I made a mental note. She might be able to help with the client, should I need it.

"Very cool," I said. "So, how have the talks been going with your parents and your guidance counselor?"

"Stupid," he said. He didn't elaborate.

"How so?" I asked.

"So stupid I didn't do any of it," he said. "It's a waste of time. I could be playing football with my friends instead."

I had to take a moment to swallow hard. *He could quite easily be lying,* I reminded myself. Children with conduct disorder are often pathological liars. "I'm sorry to hear that," I said. "How can I make it better for you?"

He kicked at the leg of the couch. "I killed another squirrel yesterday. I cut open its belly," he said, peeking at me through his curls, almost as if he were daring me to react. "It smelled really bad."

My stomach roiled, though I didn't let it show on my face. At least, I hoped I didn't. Kids like this would take the slightest hint of discomfort and run with it. "I can imagine," I said. "So over these last two weeks you killed a squirrel, made plans to go to Six Flags with your sister, and didn't do as well on a spelling test as you would have liked. What else did you do?"

"I can tell you what I didn't do," he said. "I didn't go see the guidance counselor. Not once. Or the school therapist. And my parents didn't make me do anything, either."

He's probably lying, I told myself again. I found it hard to believe that these parents would turn a blind eye to such behaviors, especially given what I'd warned them about—that if these behaviors weren't corrected, they would set. Rotten dough would make for spoiled bread. A boy with unworked-upon conduct disorder might very well grow up to display strong psychopathic tendencies.

And kill more than a squirrel.

SIX

My brother and I slept in our bunk beds, aka our tower and our lair, until we were ten. The big double digits. I'd already befriended Liv—Olivia Liang—who was the second to die in the band room. Liv would come over and perch with me atop my bed, where we'd dangle our legs over the side so that our feet swung in my brother's space. If he happened to be there, he'd swat at our toes and growl and pretend to snap at them. I'd giggle and pretend-scream, but Liv would just frown at me.

One day, as my brother and I were just getting to school, Liv caught me and pulled me away from him. We hadn't been walking hand in hand, but our fingers might have been brushing each other's as we walked. "Julia, I'm your friend," she said. "You know I'm your best friend, right? That I 'love you like a sister'?"

"LYLAS," I said automatically. My eyes strayed over her

shoulder to my brother, who was tapping his foot impatiently as he waited. We were in the same class, and we always walked into school together. On days I was sick, he'd stay home, too.

"I'm telling you this because I love you," she said. "Everybody is talking about you, you know. They're laughing at you. Because of the whole thing with Gabriella at recess."

My back stiffened. I didn't want to think about what Gabriella had done at recess. "People are laughing at me?" I'd seen the side glances, seen snickers sucked back into throats as I walked by, but I hadn't spared them much more than a passing thought. At least, until Gabriella. "Why?"

"Because of you and your brother," she said. "Gabriella was right. It's weird. You guys, like, hold hands. You sleep in the same room. You're always together. It's creepy. It's like you're in love or something."

"I do love him," I said, but my mind was already racing. People talking about me behind my back? People saying mean things about me? People *laughing* at me? The very thought made me itch like I had bedbugs.

"Not love," she said. "Of course you love him. I mean, like, *in* love. Like you want to marry him."

I hadn't ever really thought about it, but I could tell by the way she wrinkled her nose and spat the words that I was supposed to be disgusted. "Ew, gross," I said. "No way."

She linked her arm with mine. "So you need to stop hanging out with him so much," she said. "Get your own room. And I'll tell everyone you're not a total weirdo."

The itching settled into a sick feeling in the pit of my stomach. I couldn't be laughed at. I just couldn't. "Okay," I said. I held her arm tight, like it was the only thing anchoring me to the earth. "Let's walk in together."

She smiled. "Okay."

Liv and I marched right past my brother and into the school. My brother didn't show up for class that day. I found out later that he had gone home sick, but I didn't care. Even if I knew I'd pay for it later. I wasn't being stared at, for once.

When I got off the bus, he was waiting for me at our stop, his arms crossed and a stormy expression on his face. "You don't look sick," I greeted him.

"You went in without me." Far from sounding mad, he sounded sad. "Now the Demetros will never see their cat again."

I lifted my chin, fighting back the wave of nausea that came when I pictured the cat's fate. I felt sorry for it, and sickened by what had surely happened, but I couldn't build my life around that mangy old thing. Also, it had scratched me once. "I had to," I said. "People were talking after what Gabriella said." Might as well dump the whole load on him at once. "And I want my own room, too."

Our dad got home late that night and told us he would unscrew our beds and move mine to the spare room the next day. We'd have to spend one more night in bunk beds. I laid on mine, my eyes closed, and tried to breathe evenly through all the sniffling going on beneath me in the lair.

When I simply couldn't take it anymore, I dropped from the top to the bottom. "Are you crying?" I asked, though I knew he was, and that it wasn't over the Demetros' cat.

He sniffled. "No."

I crawled into bed beside him and snuggled up against his back and breathed into his hair. Curls tickled my nose, and he grew very still. "People think we're weird," I said. I hoped this would soothe him and maybe save the neighborhood's other cats. "We need to have more friends. But you're still my favorite."

I could feel him relax. "Okay," he said.

He stayed home from school the next day, and the next day, and the next. But then on Monday he met up with his friend Eddie Meyer, the third to die in the band room, and the two marched together through the front door before Liv and I had even said hello.

Alane and I escaped the coffee shop with no further Spence-related incidents, but she only dropped me off when I promised her, cross my heart and hope to die, that both of my parents were inside, waiting patiently for me at the dinner table with a full roast turkey and platter of stuffing. None of this, of course, was true. (I might have gone a little overboard with the turkey and stuffing.)

"Call me if you need me," she said, her eyes searching.

I nodded. I might need her, but I knew I wouldn't call.

Inside I found my mother busy with her new favorite

activity: cleaning. Every surface and nook and cranny in our house positively sparkled. You could eat soup out of the toilet bowl or brush on mascara in the reflection from the kitchen tiles. I couldn't remember the last time I'd seen dust. I wasn't sure if I remembered what it looked like. "Hi, Mom," I said, dropping my books on the coffee table.

She turned to me with a tremulous smile, which collapsed when she saw the hot chocolate stains down my front. Her hands twitched; she wrung them together in what looked like an effort not to race over and scrub me where I stood. "Lucy, you're a mess," she said. "Give me your dress. I'll wash it out for you."

"I spilled my hot chocolate," I said. Shoot. Alane's dress. I'd have to remember to apologize later, offer to buy her a new one, though I knew she'd never take my money. I hesitated and focused back on my mom. "Can I tell you something weird?"

Her eyes skittered down to my feet; her shoulders visibly relaxed when she saw I'd removed my shoes. She probably would've fainted if I'd left chocolate footprints on the rug. "What is it?"

I swallowed hard. "I think I'm being followed, and that it might have something to do with Ryan. With Elkton. Do you remember Ryan's old psychologist? My old psychologist? Dr. Spence? I've seen him three times now," I said, and braced myself for her to tell me it was ridiculous, that obviously I'd made a mistake, that all I needed was a hug and all would be okay. That it was okay to talk about Ryan.

I should have known better. Her quivering lip was the only indication I'd said his name. "That's ridiculous. Julia Vann no longer exists," she said. *Ridiculous.* Score one point, at least. It was a hollow victory. "We aren't from that place anymore. And I'll thank you never to mention that name in this house ever again." Her eyes darted again at the stain down my front.

"I'll say his name if I want to," I said. "He's my brother."

"Lucy Black doesn't have a brother," she said coldly. Inside I prodded myself, waiting to feel something, but I just felt cold. Empty. As soon as I realized that, I was swept by a rush of wanting. I wanted so badly to feel something. Why didn't I feel something? "Now give me your dress."

Afraid she'd rip it off me if I didn't comply, I grudgingly changed into sweats and then made a turkey sandwich. It tasted like chalk with mustard, but I didn't want to be a total liar to Alane.

I was halfway through when the doorbell rang. My mother was probably knee-deep in soap suds or whatever, so I opened the door to find Michael Silverman standing there, shifting from foot to glorious foot.

"Oh," I greeted him. Ugh, ugh, ugh. "I mean, hey. *Hola.*"

"Hey, Lucy." Michael had his hands in his pockets and his shoulders hunched forward. I would've thought he was cold if it wasn't eighty-something degrees out. "I just wanted to make sure you were okay. With . . . I didn't want to say anything there, but did you think you saw your ex? At Crazy's?"

I leaned against the doorway and put my hands in my pockets, too. "I thought I saw him. But it wasn't him. It just freaked me out. Again." I tried to smile brightly. "I'm fine. I'm okay. Thanks."

Michael tilted his head back and smiled; his molars winked at me from the back of his mouth. "You think I'm going to let you off that easy? I brought this. I figured you might need it." He produced a plastic bag. I drew the handle aside with a crackling sound to see a container of chocolate ice cream, and I let out a surprised laugh.

"Oh," I said. "Thank you." I took the bag of ice cream and stepped back. "Want to come in? I was just eating dinner."

"I don't want to interrupt your dinner," he said. "I just . . . your sweatshirt. Did you go there?"

My sweatshirt. I was wearing an old band hoodie, one of the few I'd managed to sneak to Sunny Vale. It might as well have announced in glaring neon lights that I'd gone to Elkton High, Home of the Fighting Elks and the crazy-pants shooter who had gone off the wall and slaughtered eleven people.

"I went to a school nearby," I said. This was the story my parents and I had agreed on. "Before I moved here. I had a . . . boyfriend who went to Elkton. An ex-boyfriend. A different ex-boyfriend," I was hasty to add. "This is his old sweatshirt. I just wear it at home because it's comfortable and I didn't think anyone would see me and . . ." Whoa, there, Lucy. Talking too much.

"Cool," he said. "Was he involved in . . . what happened?"

I stiffened. The sweatshirt's tag scraped against my neck. Why had I even put it on? I'd never liked this sweatshirt. "Maybe you shouldn't come in," I said.

"No, hey . . ." He took one of his hands out of his pocket and rubbed the back of his neck. "I'm sorry. It must have been awful. I mean, it was awful watching it on TV and reading about it online, but it's not the same thing as going to school right near where it happened."

I relaxed and considered just melting into the door frame. This conversation would be so much less stressful if I could just disappear. "Yeah," I said. "Well, I was just eating dinner. . . ."

"What are you having?" He was moving past me and into the kitchen before I could reply. So much for not wanting to interrupt my dinner. "That? *That's* your dinner?"

I followed to find him staring at my sandwich with an expression somewhere between horror and disgust. "Yes," I said defensively, considering running over and shielding it with my body. It was just a sandwich, I reminded myself. And not even a very good one.

Michael shook his head. "We can't have that," he said. "As an apology for asking you about Elkton and as an apology for nearly running you down with my car, let me make you dinner."

"What?" If I listened hard, I could hear the ghostly vibrations of my mother's scrubbing somewhere above me. At least she'd moved upstairs. My father probably wouldn't be home for another few hours, if he came home at all. "Really? You already apologized with ice cream." I held it up in case he'd forgotten.

"Yes. Really." After a brief scan of the fridge and the pantry, he began assembling kitchen things. A sauté pan, a grater, a chopping block and giant knife, a block of some kind of cheese (white? Was it called white cheese? I didn't think so), some onion, garlic, mushrooms, peppers, eggs. "Do you like eggs?" he asked, almost as an afterthought.

"I'm allergic to eggs."

His face cracked right down the middle in disappointment. "Really?"

"No. I like eggs." I stood and went to go survey the ingredients on the counter. "Omelet? Are you making omelets?"

"Yes. I figured I'd start small the first time." The first time? That would seem to suggest there were going to be more times. "Go sit down."

I went and sat at the kitchen table. "Are you into cooking?" I asked. My brother would cook for me sometimes. Not eggs, thankfully; he actually had been allergic. He'd been into Asian food. He'd make me stir-fries with baby corn, which we both loved when we were little because it made us feel like giants, and fried Chinese noodles. He'd make tempura and frightfully inauthentic bibimbap, and even once attempted hand-rolled sushi that began in sticky rice and ended in food poisoning. All of this in our old kitchen, which had been straight from the seventies with its

65

avocado-green furnishings. My heart twanged like a guitar string. He would have loved our new kitchen, where all the furnishings were stainless steel, the walls tiled blue.

"Kind of," Michael said. He chopped garlic and onion so fast his hand was practically a blur.

"Kind of?" I asked. "I can barely see your hand move."

He scooped everything up on the blade of his knife and tossed it in the pan, which sizzled and spat. Tiny drops of oil hit his arms, but he didn't flinch. "I was super into the Food Network when I was little," he said. "All my parents made were casseroles. I kind of took over out of necessity."

I nodded gravely, then realized I was just nodding to his back. "Casserole Overload is a very serious illness," I said.

"Indeed." He cracked the eggs so deftly and surely against the counter he was like an . . . I don't know, an egg ninja. "Symptoms include getting fat, high blood pressure, and an irreversible blandness of personality." He shot me a look I couldn't quite read. "Fortunately, I saved myself that much."

So he was a little conceited. We'd fit well together, considering I'd been spending the past few minutes wondering if it would be too obvious to run upstairs and change out of my sweats. Yes, I decided, it would be too obvious to go change. Plus then there was the chance of running into my mother, and Mother's Knowledge of Boys in the House was an even more deadly condition than Casserole Overload— symptoms included immediate evacuation of the premises.

"Too bad the fat already set in," I kidded.

He turned, his eyebrows raised in mock hurt. He clapped a hand to his chest. "Right here, Black," he said. "That hit me right here."

I shook my head sadly. "Right in the high blood pressure," I said. I wiped a smear of egg off my cheek. "Now, now, Señor Silverman. That was not very gentlemanly."

The omelet might have been the most delicious thing I'd ever eaten, and I wasn't shy about telling him so. And showing him so—all conversation ceased as I wolfed down my entire omelet and then half of his. "You weren't hungry, were you?" I asked. I shifted in my seat; my waistline felt a full size bigger than it had this morning. Look who was experiencing symptoms of Casserole Overload now.

"I'm just glad you liked it," Michael said. "So are you sure you're okay? Because you don't look okay."

"I'm fine," I said emphatically. "Besides, how would you know whether I look okay or not? Before yesterday we'd only talked, like, once."

His smile was wide and warm. "Four times," he said. "And a half, if you count the time we were paired up to talk about tacos. I counted."

Blood rushed to my cheeks. "Oh."

"Yeah." He leaned toward me. Our faces were no more than a foot apart; I could feel the garlicky heat of his breath on my cheek. "I will need you to take back that comment about the fat—"

The front door opened. "Lucy," my father's voice boomed.

My own voice jumped an octave. "Hi, Dad!"

His footsteps thudded through the entryway. "Your mother called me earlier. She was very upset." Of course she'd called my dad. It wasn't like she would ever dare to talk to me herself. "She said you told her you think someone is—" His voice died as he entered the kitchen and saw Michael. "You have a guest," he said. His words were stiff. "Who's this?"

I patted Michael on the arm and stood. "This is my friend Michael," I said. "He was just leaving."

Michael glanced over his shoulder. "I don't want to leave you with the dishes," he said. He stuck out his hand. "It's nice to meet you, Mr. Black."

"You too," my father said. He didn't stick out his own hand, and I knew he wasn't going to; as the realization dawned over Michael's face, his own hand fell back to his side. "Shall I show you to the door?"

"The dishes," Michael said. "I was going to wash them. I don't want to leave you with the—"

"It's fine," my father and I said at once. I coughed to cover up the annoyance in his tone.

"I actually kind of like doing the dishes," I said. "It's . . . fun?"

"Okay." I couldn't read Michael's face. "If you're okay, Lucy, then I'll go."

"I'm okay." Lines settled into his face: creases in his forehead, indentations at the corners of his mouth. Worry. He was worried. "Really, I'm okay! I'll see you tomorrow at school."

"Count on it." He glanced at my father, then away, then gave an awkward shrug-wave and headed out, his hands back in his pockets. My heart twinged to see him go, but I'd see him tomorrow. Spence was a more immediate concern.

My father waited until the door closed to speak. "Your mother told me you said you thought someone was following you and that it has something to do with . . ." He paused and swallowed hard. "Ryan." His suit was too small, I noticed; his shoulders were straining at the seams of his jacket. "Do you really think this is true? That the psychiatrist is following you?"

"Psychologist," I said. "And yes. I saw him. Three times."

My father shook his head. "Nobody is following you, *Lucy.*" He emphasized my new name. "Don't start trouble. We've had enough trouble for a lifetime."

"But I saw—"

"And this is the last we're going to speak of this. Do you understand?" He talked over me, and my voice trailed off into nothing. "If you think you're seeing someone from our old life, we'll have to call Dr. Ferro."

"No." Dr. Ferro was the only person in Sunny Vale who knew who we really were. My parents had brought me to her soon after the move. I'd talked myself out after eight months and convinced my parents I didn't need to go back. Talking to her wasn't going to bring my brother back, or change what had happened in the band room. "Don't call Dr. Ferro."

After I did the dishes under my father's watchful eye,

I escaped upstairs, closing my bedroom door against the sound of my mother's scrubbing. My father's mention of Dr. Ferro had brought back some old memories I'd rather not unearth. It wasn't that she didn't help me. She did. I always left her sessions feeling physically lighter, as if she were actually a plastic surgeon. It was more that she'd gotten me to say too much.

She was the only person who knew that, at the time of the shooting, exactly zero of the eleven kids in that band room had been my friend.

SEVEN

My dead boyfriend—ex-boyfriend? Does someone automatically become an ex when he dies, or will he technically be my boyfriend until we're both dead?—Evan Wilde was a football player. Aside from my brother and my best friend, it was his name that probably saw the most coverage. The news couldn't resist the whole "small-town football hero tragically cut down before his prime playing years" thing.

I know that sounds cavalier. I'm sorry. It's just that, at this point, I was so done with tragedy. If I had to feel heavy and sad and bow my head every single time any of the victims crossed my mind, I would probably have to follow them into the ground.

Evan and I were star-crossed lovers: a tall, strong football player and a band geek. Once he asked me to climb on his hands, and then he lifted me over his head; I was so nervous I fell off and hit my head on a fence post. (There might have been tequila involved.) He let me wear his varsity jacket, which smelled like boy sweat and dirt and grass, totally different from my brother's, until he was done and wanted nothing more to do with me. I gave it back. We didn't officially break up, though. That was the afternoon he died.

And that's all I have to say about him.

Word of my spaz attack at Crazy Elliot's had clearly gotten around school by the time Alane and I pulled in the next day. I could tell from her shifty eyes and the way she flexed her hands the whole ride, like she really wanted to give me a pat on the shoulder, that something wasn't quite right. I didn't receive confirmation, though, until I saw all the stares in the parking lot. As soon as I stepped out of the truck, whispers rushed over me in a cool wave.

"I see everyone knows what happened," I said.

Apparently that was all Alane needed to set herself off; she turned to me and wrapped me in a hug so tight it might as well have been a straitjacket. "I didn't tell anyone," she said into my shoulder. "I don't think Michael would, either. It was probably Ella."

Ella, or the tens of other kids who were there that day. Whatever. As long as it didn't progress beyond stares and whispers, I could do this. I'd done much worse. I lifted my chin. "Just don't tell that weird story where rats ate my toes, okay?"

Her body sagged in relief. "Okay. I won't."

It only took one period for Michael to catch up with me. Well, it wasn't so much catching up with me as it was sitting down at his desk in Spanish. "You okay?" he asked.

"Fine," I said, and racked my brain for something witty and fun to say next. Maybe I could make a joke about rats. No, enough with the rats.

Before I thought of something clever enough, he had turned to the guy to his other side, another swimmer, and they were talking about butterfly times. The glow inside me flared into something ferocious and then dimmed, like a candle caught in the wind, and I tapped the girl in front of me on her shoulder. She turned, her eyebrow raised, and then I realized I didn't know her name. "Hey . . . there," I said.

She blinked at me. "Hi."

"I really like your earrings," I said. I didn't. They were hideous and they had feathers on them, two things that are never mutually exclusive.

A smile crept across her face. "Thanks," she said, touching one so that it spun gently in the air. "I made them."

Out of dirty bird feathers? They probably had disease crawling all over them. "Oh," I said dubiously. "That's cool."

She leaned back, resting her elbow on the edge of my desk. Oh, good. Now there would be disease crawling all over my desk, too. "I have a bird feeder in my backyard," she said. "And the birds shed all the time, and I figured I might as well do something with the feathers, right? So I—"

Señor Goldfarb clapped his hands at the front of the room. *"¡Silencio, por favor!"* he shouted, and then continued in Spanish. "Let's go over the homework. We'll start with number one. Ava?"

The girl in front of me—Ava—began to speak, her feather earrings wobbling with every rolled *r* and nasal *n*. I settled back in my chair, relieved our conversation was over.

Something hit me on the arm. I turned, scowling, to see Michael grinning at me. My eyes traced the movement of his to the floor, where there lay a crumpled ball of paper. Once Ava was done speaking and Señor Goldfarb's attention had shifted to the other side of the room, I leaned over and scooped it up.

Those earrings are hideous. You have terrible taste.

I balled the note back up and threw it at him. It bounced off his chest. He let out a muffled squawk that he managed to turn into a cough. He unrolled the paper, smoothed the crinkles out, and scribbled something else before brushing it back onto the floor. I leaned over to pick it up before he sat back up, and our fingers brushed each other's. Sparks danced up my arm and straight into my stomach, where they bloomed into something warm and soft. I glanced over at him; he had pressed his lips together hard, clearly trying not to laugh.

He reminded me so very much of my brother. Not the side of him that other people saw—the one that killed eleven people and made me wish I were dead—but the side of him that listened to me cry when I had a nightmare and told me I was beautiful after one of the drummers made fun of my hair. The side of him I missed.

I smoothed Michael's note, which was already beginning to fray at the creases, out onto my desk. *And you immediately turn to violence. Nice job.* The bloom in my stomach turned to ice. I couldn't breathe. I darted another glance over at him. He was still smiling. He wouldn't be smiling if he knew what violence really was.

I went back to the note. *You can't deny your terrible taste. Because you were talking to Ava about her earrings when you could have been talking to the handsome guy next to you.*

I started breathing again. It was just a joke. It was just a *joke,* stupid Lucy. I scribbled quickly, *Who? Señor Goldfarb?* and sent it sailing back. I couldn't hold back a snicker as his eyes widened and he clapped a hand to his chest, his head falling forward in mock pain.

"Señor Silverman." Goldfarb's beady eyes fixed on Michael. Michael sat up, adjusting himself in his chair. "Is there a problem?"

"I just thought I was having a heart attack," Michael said seriously. Someone behind us tittered. "False alarm, though."

Goldfarb pursed his lips. "Have your heart attack after class, *por favor,*" he said. "Now answer *número tres?*"

It wasn't long before I felt the sting of the paper ball, and I glanced over to see Michael grinning at me again. Heaving a heavy sigh, I picked apart the note. *Dinner again tonight? My house. We never got to eat that ice cream. Or finish our talk.*

I caught his eye and shook my head. Quickly, so he wouldn't see how hot my cheeks were getting. *Band practice,* I mouthed.

He shrugged with one shoulder, smooth and easy, like a big cat's loping stride. *I have swimming,* he mouthed back. *After practice.*

A few paper cuts later, we established that he'd be driving me and that he would not, under any circumstances, be making anything with fish or anything Asian. *But how could you not like sushi?* was his plaintive reply.

I turned away and raised my hand. It was only after Señor Goldfarb called on me that I realized I had no idea what question he'd even asked.

I found myself in band practice before I really had a chance to think about what I'd gotten myself into. With Michael, obviously. I didn't know whether I liked him because of him, or whether I liked him because he reminded me of my brother. And that was a problem.

When the Vanns became the Blacks, the elder Blacks were shocked when I told them Lucy wanted to do band. Julia had done band for years and played almost every instrument there was: she was best at anything with a reed, the clarinets and saxes and oboes, but she could buzz some scales out of the tricky brass instruments and their traitorously simple-looking valves, and even once or twice got a sound out of a flute. But Julia had also been in the band room, shaking behind a music stand, when everybody died. The Blacks assumed that being in any band room, no matter how different from the one she'd left behind, would be traumatizing.

Well, as usual, they were wrong. I couldn't be any more traumatized than I already was. If anything, the band room was a sanctuary. Sure, it had music stands identical to the one I'd hid behind. But it also had music, complicated music that took all my focus to stay on top of. It didn't give me time to think about anything else.

We finished with a resounding crescendo, and I shook my head vigorously, trying to shake off my music daze; whenever I finished a practice, I found afterward that I could barely remember what had happened during. So it wasn't until then that I noticed Michael propped against the wall, his head cocked and his eyes closed. I snuck up next to him and bumped him with my clarinet case. "Did we bore you that badly?"

His eyes flew open. "I was listening," he said indignantly. "Trying to hear your . . . um . . ."

I quirked an eyebrow. "This is a clarinet."

"Exactly. The clarinet is my favorite instrument," he said. The smell of chlorine came off him in nose-searing waves, and his hair stuck up in peaks. "I'm thinking of taking it up."

"No, you're not."

"No, I'm not," he agreed. "I would just mangle it anyway. Much wiser to leave it in your capable hands. Though I can carry it for you now, if you want."

"So gentlemanly," I said, handing it over. He took my case and held it against him like it was something precious. Which it was.

"Ready to head out?"

I could feel the other band girls' eyes scraping against my back. Guys like Michael generally stayed far away from our wing. Yes, I was ready to go. Before long, my back would be pink and raw. "I just have to run and tell Alane I don't need her to drive me home," I said. "She's finishing up show choir."

As Michael and I walked together to the chorus room, which was right next to the student parking lot, the fumes of chlorine clouded around me like fog. It, like everything else lately, made me think of my brother.

Like Michael, my brother had been a swimmer. He hadn't been the best swimmer on the team. He hadn't been the worst swimmer on the team. But he threw himself into it and he worked out and he practiced until he finned through the water, leaving nothing in his wake but a rush of bubbles.

Ryan got into swimming shortly after I got into band, when we were thirteen. He started out in band with me, lugging around a trumpet case to all our practices, setting up his stand next to me in my bedroom (never his) so that we could play together. But it never captured him the way it captured me. I could lose myself in the streams of notes and hear, instinctively, if one went wrong. He could squawk and blare and honk, and it all sounded the same to him.

Still, he kept at it, because we had band period together. One day after practice he lingered by my seat, tossing his case from hand to hand in a way that made my heart jump into my throat. "There's a meeting after school today. For anyone who's interested in doing swimming this winter," he said.

I blinked. "Okay?" I was about as interested in doing swimming as I was in committing seppuku.

My brother shifted on his feet. His trumpet made another dangerous journey up and down. "I really want to do it. Are you going to do it with me?"

Even though, as I'd said, I really didn't want to, my first instinct was to say yes. We did everything together.

But then Liv's words wormed their way back into my brain. *Talking about you. Laughing at you. Weird. Creepy. It's like you're in love.* "I would rather drown," I said. "But you should do it."

Ryan settled his trumpet case on the ground. "Really? You think I should?"

"I totally think you should," I said. My body strained to envelop him in a fast hug, but my brain, once again, rebelled. "It would be fun. I can go watch your meets."

"You would go to my meets?"

"Of course I would!" I said. "I'll be the loudest person in the stands."

He went to the meeting, and he joined the team, and he bought the regulation Speedos in red and black, our school colors, and the red-and-black swimming cap, and the goggles that made him look like an alien. He shaved his legs and his chest with a pink ladies' razor to reduce friction in the water, and he smiled sheepishly as girls—other girls! Who weren't me!—cheered for him from the stands and murmured admiring things about his butt and his abs in that bathing suit. It made me want to grab a towel and cloak him in it as soon as he escaped the pool.

And it turned out I wasn't the loudest person in the stands. Liv, who had been the one to tell me to stay away from him, to give him space, had been the biggest cheerer of all.

"So Alane is in show choir?" Michael asked.

I jumped, feeling almost as if I'd walked through a portal to the future. I hadn't, though; I'd just walked to the chorus room. "Yeah," I said. "She's lead soprano. She totally rocks."

"Ah," Michael said, cradling my clarinet case in his arms like a baby. "You're quite a musical pair, you two."

I was in the middle of rolling my eyes when Alane rushed out, her cheeks pink. Most of the choir kids had already packed up and left, their chatter a stream in the hallway. "Sorry, Lucy," she panted. "There was a . . . oh, hi, Michael."

"Hi, Alane."

"You don't need to drive me home today," I said. "I'm going to go home with Michael."

This stopped the flow of speech, but not for long. "Oh, okay," she said. "Oh, but Lucy. There was a guy in show choir asking questions about you. It was creepy. I finally threatened to call the cops, and he left."

"My dad's a cop," Michael said, already reaching for his phone. I automatically laid a hand on my clarinet case to keep it from falling. "Want me to call—"

"What did he look like?" I asked, my stomach lurching as I imagined what she'd say. *Smart glasses. Rumpled suit.*

"Tall and thin," she said. "Old. Like thirty, maybe. And he had these square glasses. He was kind of cute. Like, in a nerdy way."

My stomach clenched like a fist. "He was asking questions? He asked for me by name?" He'd probably been hoping to find me alone.

"Yeah," Alane said. "Your middle name, even. It's Julia, isn't it? Lucy Julia Black. I don't remember you ever telling . . ."

Whatever she was saying faded into a roar. My heart was thumping so hard I thought it might bust free and break through my chest in a shower of viscera. I'd flop around on the floor like a dying fish while Alane looked on, chattering about my middle name.

I grabbed her by the shoulders, my fingers digging into the soft muscle. I could tell from her sudden wince that I was hurting her, and I didn't care. "Where did he go?" I shook her a little bit, and Michael grabbed me by the arm.

"Hey, now," he said. My fingers loosened, and I realized that Alane's eyes were shiny, her breathing fast and shallow.

"Sorry," I said, and let her go. "But did you see where he went? It's important."

She rubbed her shoulder. I could see the indentations I'd left in her shirt; her efforts were doing nothing to smooth them out. "Out toward the student parking lot," she said. "Lucy, are you okay?"

I was already moving. "I need to find him," I called. Michael's footsteps sounded behind me, keeping pace, but Alane hung back, the noise of her breathing getting smaller and smaller and smaller until I couldn't hear her at all.

I burst into the sunshine and scanned the parking lot frantically, shading my eyes. I couldn't let him get away this time. I ducked and craned through the parking lot, through the rows of cars, through the clusters of kids, until finally, there he was, black suit and all, climbing into a car at the far side of the lot. There was no way I'd reach him before he pulled out, so I made a snap and potentially incredibly stupid decision.

"Michael, we need to get in your car now and follow that one," I said, pointing. His mouth opened, and I knew he was going to ask why. "I'll explain later," I said, vibrating with impatience. "We just need to go." I couldn't keep doing this. If Spence wanted me alone, he'd get me alone.

Michael could wait in the car and run Spence over if he got too threatening. Michael was, apparently, good at running people down.

If Michael's car hadn't been parked only two spots away, I don't know what I would have done. Probably sank to my knees and cried right there on the pavement. But he *was* parked only two spots away, and miraculously there wasn't anyone right behind us, so we were peeling out of the parking lot in thirty seconds flat, the back of Spence's car a respectable three vehicles ahead. I admittedly knew zero about cars, but even I could tell his was nice: black, shiny, and sleek, its make one of the *L*s: Lamborghini, Lexus, Lincoln.

Spence took a hard right. Two of the cars between us drifted straight, but Michael obediently carried us right. "Is that him?" he asked. "Your ex?"

"Yes," I said.

"He's old," he said, his voice as taut as a guitar string. "I should call my dad. Remember the license plate."

Idea noted. I typed the number in my phone: 3RTR779.

Spence's car made a left. We were now directly behind him. I could see his head bobbing above the seat.

"Seriously, I think we should pull over and call my dad," Michael said. "If he's stalking you, following him could be dangerous."

"We need to follow him." My heart rapped against my ribs. "I need to know where he's going. Where he's staying. He can't keep popping up like this."

"We can put an alert on the car." Decision seemingly made, Michael coasted toward the side of the road.

No. No. I couldn't lose Spence, not again. I couldn't let him go.

As soon as we stopped, I threw open the door and stepped out of the car, fully ready to follow Spence wherever he was going. I didn't even think about how slowly I would be going in comparison to Spence. Maybe my ankles would sprout wings. I was on the right side, after all. The good side. The hero always wins.

I only made it maybe twenty feet before I felt the fingers close around my arm. *Spence.* I jerked away before my mind could remind me that *Hello, Lucy, you just saw Spence drive off in front of you; there's no possible way he could be behind you now.*

It was Michael, of course. "Lucy, are you okay?" Michael said, and he touched me again on the arm. He wasn't grabbing me this time; his fingers were gentle, and his voice was deeper than I'd ever heard it before.

"He got away," I said flatly. I couldn't believe I'd let Spence escape. Again. It was almost a comedy of errors at this point. "Of course I'm not okay. Because he'll be back, and he might kill me." Or worse. I'd rather be dead than be Julia Vann, and all that it entailed, again.

"It'll be okay," Michael said. "We'll talk to my dad. I'll have him look up the plate number. He can pay a visit to your ex's house."

"No!" The word burst out of me before I could stop myself. My head twinged with what felt like the beginning of a stress headache. Or a brain tumor. "Don't send your dad. My ex is dangerous."

"You were willing to send me after him." I couldn't tell whether he sounded proud or hurt. "Either way, we should talk to my dad. Let's go to my house."

I trailed after him. I didn't have many other options.

Re: Ryan Vann, age 10

I spoke with Ryan's parents when his session let out. As soon as he saw his whole family in the waiting room, Ryan raced out to take the seat next to his sister. They bent their heads together and whispered. As I approached, beckoning the parents into my office, the twins looked my way and giggled.

"Mr. and Mrs. Vann," I said once I sat down, "Ryan feels he hasn't been making much progress with the MST. You know how important it is that the family and school take part in this treatment. A psychologist can only do so much without the involvement of the family in this type of therapy. I wanted to check in on your progress."

Both parents looked distinctly uncomfortable. "We've just been so busy," the mother began.

"I've been traveling every week on business," continued the father.

"And I've been so busy with class, with grading, it's all I can do to keep a clean house and get the children fed."

"We're trying, Doctor, we swear. It might just take a little more time."

"And the school?" I asked, struggling not to lose my temper. "Have you heard any news from the school?"

If possible, their expressions sank even deeper into discomfort. "We've received a few calls from the school therapist," the mother said. "Apparently Ryan's been skipping his sessions. I spoke to him about it, but with him, there's only so much you can do. . . ."

I couldn't stop a flare of rage from sparking in my throat. "You sound like you've already given up on him," I spat more than said. "He might improve on his own, but he might not."

"What about medication?" the father asked. "Isn't there something you can put him on?"

Medication. I couldn't help but scoff. Anybody can just *medicate* someone. The behavior analysis unit won't come knocking on the door of someone who gives up on fixing a sociopath and pumps him full of medication instead. Also, as a psychologist, I couldn't actually prescribe medication, but that was beside the point. "In my professional opinion, medication would not be the best option here." In my professional opinion, saying "in my professional opinion" is the best way to make people trust you. "The specific types of medication we would use aren't a permanent solution and might be dangerous. They could turn him into someone entirely different. We just want to calm these urges. In my professional opinion, therapy continues to be the best option, but it has to be regular and it has to be done."

"I know," the mother said. "I know, I know, we know. We'll try harder. We promise."

I didn't have high expectations when Ryan came in for his next session two weeks later. "How are you, Ryan?" I asked.

"Fine," he said.

"How were your last two weeks?"

"Fine."

"How are your talks with your parents and your school therapist going?"

"Fine." He peeked up a bit at this last word and, I swear, I saw pure anguish in his eyes, so hot it nearly burned me. "My parents said you wouldn't let them give me pills."

"That's right," I said.

He blinked. "Thank you. I didn't want to take pills."

"You're welcome," I said, and something softened in his eyes. I moved on to the therapy. "Have you been talking with your parents and your school therapist?"

"I heard my parents talking, and my mom said she was on some pills," Ryan said. "She said they made her feel like a zombie sometimes. I don't want to feel like a zombie."

"I don't want you to feel like a zombie, either," I said. "How have your sessions been going? You have been talking with your parents and your school therapist, right?"

He stared at the floor, or his feet. "They said I should tell you yes."

My heart sank to my feet. "So you haven't been talking with your parents and school therapist?"

"No," he muttered. He looked up, eagerly, I thought. "But I didn't kill anything these last few weeks." Eager. Like he was looking for approval. *My* approval. I'd made some kind of breakthrough. A tiny one.

Still, words stuck in my throat. What was someone supposed to say to that? "Well," I said finally, for lack of anything else to say. "I'm glad to hear it. It sounds like you're making progress."

A smile lit up his face, flashing like a lightning streak. But quick as lightning, it was gone. "It won't last, though." He sounded disturbingly matter-of-fact. "Even if I really want it to."

My stomach churned. "Anyone can change," I said. "Even you. No matter what anyone else tells you."

He gifted me another smile, though this one was sad, heavy. "No," he said. It was patient—that was the word. He was smiling patiently at me, like suddenly he was the teacher and I was the student. "But you're making a good effort. Really. And thank you again for the pills thing."

No matter what I asked, no matter what I said, he wouldn't say another word after that.

EIGHT

To be quite honest, I half expected Michael to dump me by the side of the road and speed off into the sunset, his car lightened of its burden of crazy. But he was too nice for that. I'd half expected that, too, so my two half expectations canceled each other out.

Instead, the ride back into town was quiet and uneventful aside from the throbbing of my head and the whiteness of Michael's knuckles on the steering wheel. The stress of letting Spence get away had manifested itself physically as a horned demon that stomped on my brain and clawed at the inside of my skull. I would have welcomed it, if only it could have stopped me from wondering why Spence had gone to all the trouble of hunting me down and following me, only to run away whenever I got close.

The first one to die in the band room had been Evan Wilde, my ex- and/or forever-boyfriend. At least, that was what the coroners told the reporters; I didn't remember anything from that day. Traumatic amnesia. It was fairly common, the doctors said, for someone who had suffered a trauma as big as the band room.

He'd been shot head-on, right between the eyes, standing against the back wall, his arms crossed over his chest. He wasn't in band, you might ask, so why was he there? To that I would say—and I did say to the police and the reporters—I don't know. I might have asked him to come, but I didn't remember. I remembered crawling out of bed to the sound of my brother's blaring alarm. I remembered dozing in the passenger seat of his car. I remembered walking into homeroom and taking my spot smack in the middle of the room beside Liv. I remembered going to the band room and carving my name into my music stand and my brother pulling the gun out of his—my—backpack. But that was all. Everything after the shine of the light off the metal of the gun was a total blank.

Speaking of Liv, though. Speaking of Liv. Once upon a time Liv was my best friend. Best friends don't break up the way boyfriends and girlfriends do. You can't dump a best friend, or cheat on them. So once upon a time Liv and I knitted friendship bracelets and exchanged best-friend charms, each of us the proud owner of half a heart. Then struck a dark and stormy afternoon, and by last period there was a cool distance between us, a frisson of tension not unlike the fizz in the air before a lightning storm. But even so, the words automatically popped out whenever someone asked me about her: "Oh, yeah, she's my best friend."

Liv was, the coroners said, the second to die. Just as Evan was dropping to the floor, his head cracking against the windowsill and his blood beginning to soak into the carpet, my brother was already bounding up the risers. Some kids were beginning to scramble, or to scream, but not Liv. She was seated in the middle of the top row and hadn't yet stood or thrown herself away—maybe she was frozen in fear. The bullet took her in the chest, and she tumbled backward, a music stand falling to cover the wound.

Or so the coroners had said.

Michael and I hadn't spoken a word by the time we pulled into his driveway. He turned off the ignition and just sat there for a moment, letting the sensor go *ding, ding, ding.* I didn't mind. I felt as if all my energy had slithered out the soles of my feet and melted into a lukewarm puddle on the floor, and that wasn't even counting the throbbing in my forehead.

"So," Michael said, "are we going to talk about what just happened?"

I rested my cheek against the taut strap of my seat belt. "My head hurts."

Michael's hands were still tapping the top of the steering wheel, and a vein was pulsing next to his eye. "Lucy," he said, "we could have died. You tried to confront someone you said was too dangerous for my dad to meet. And my dad carries a gun."

"I think you're being a little bit dramatic." Michael's house, a charmingly compact split-level with glaringly red shutters, swam before me. I shut my eyes and melted into the black.

"Lucy. Lucy, are you okay?"

My eyes popped back open. His house had obediently returned to its proper position, even if it was a little bit hazy around the edges. "No. I mean, yes. It's just a headache. I just need to sit down."

He tastefully neglected to remind me that I was, indeed, sitting down, and then led me up his front stoop and into his kitchen, which was patterned almost entirely in red, white, and blue. His parents must be very patriotic, I thought as I sat down at the kitchen table.

"Here. Drink some water," Michael said, handing me a glass.

I drank some water. "Thanks."

He sat down beside me with a thump. To avoid his eyes, I lowered my head to the table and pressed my cheek against its cool surface. I fully expected him to start asking questions again, at which point I planned to start banging my head against the table until it exploded, but he didn't say anything. I could hear him sipping water, the quiet glugging of it down his throat.

Finally, he spoke. "You remember the license plate, right?" he said. "You put it in your phone? I'll have my dad look it up. Maybe it'll help."

I pulled out my phone and recited the numbers. He

stepped into the other room to make the call. I propped my chin on my hands and listened hard. Words floated back through the entryway: *some creep following my friend; she's seen him behind her car every day for, like, a week; she just wants to make sure he's not a threat. No, Dad, I'm not going to go after him with a baseball bat; that was a onetime thing.* I cocked my head, and my interest grew. So he wasn't just some pretty boy with a nice smile and a nice tan. He could lie with the best of them, aka me. And he had a violent side.

Maybe we would be good together.

Michael walked back in, tucking his phone in his pocket. "My dad's going to look him up for us," he said. "Don't worry. In the meantime, you should eat something. I was going to teach you how to chop vegetables the right way, but you should probably just sit there. We can do that next time."

I smiled at him as he took up his spot by the stove. "You shouldn't even bother. I'd be terrible anyway," I said. "I'm not good with knives. I'd be terrified of serving you a salad with bits of Lucy finger in it."

"It's not so bad once you've got the hang of it." He grabbed an onion and mushrooms and reduced them to chunks in a blur.

"Now you're just showing off."

He flashed a cocky smile over his shoulder. "So what if I am?"

The vegetables hit the pan with garlic. The rich, earthy

scent of them filled the kitchen, and my mouth watered. "What are you making?"

"I make a mean lasagna. So mean it tortures puppies and steals lollipops from little kids."

"I love lasagna."

He stirred the pan, and just as the scent grew fuller somehow, he dumped in a can of diced tomatoes.

"*Canned* tomatoes? Surely you jest."

"Would you like to make the sauce?" Michael raised an eyebrow. "I didn't think so."

I rested my head again on the table. The pain seemed to be getting better. To distract myself from the weight of my eyelids, I asked, "So you said you have sisters?"

"Three. I'm the youngest," he said, giving the pan another stir. It smelled almost like pizza, and I had to lift my head to avoid drowning in a puddle of my own drool. "Alicia, Alianna, Aria, Michael. I'm the only one who didn't get an *A* name. Just one of the many things that make me special."

I rolled my eyes. "Are any of them at home?" Meaning would any of them want some of this lasagna? Because I was pretty sure I could eat the entire pan right now.

"No. Alianna and Aria are in college, Berkeley. Alicia lives in Manhattan and does something in advertising. Or fashion. Something like that."

"How could you not know what your own sister does?" I always knew what my brother was doing. *Always.* I knew when he was sleeping; what class he was in; how long he'd be at swim practice; what movie theater he went to on his one and only date, when I'd begrudgingly made him go out with Liv to stop her whining about how cute he was and how he would never, ever notice someone like her.

He shrugged and tasted the sauce, then lowered the heat and topped the pan with a lid. "She's thirty-two. By the time I was potty-trained, she'd pretty much moved out. She went to college at NYU and only came home for Christmas and a few weeks in the summer. She's more like an aunt than a sister, honestly."

My face felt stuffy with tears. "That's so sad."

As the cops escorted me out of my high school for the last time, I didn't cry. I held my mother as she sobbed over my brother's still form, and I didn't cry. I didn't cry when we left behind the only home I'd ever known.

And yet, right now, I felt as if I was going to cry.

Maybe my headache was giving me brain damage. Maybe it was a tumor after all.

I changed the subject. "So, swimming. How long have you been—"

Michael's head jerked, and he pulled his phone out of his pocket. I could hear it buzzing; he propped it between his shoulder and his ear as he filled a large pot with water and then flurried it with salt. "Hey, Dad."

I perked up. My teeth started to hurt, like I'd eaten too much sugar.

"Uh-huh. Uh-huh. Okay. No, not now. Okay. Wait one sec." He grabbed a pen and a scrap of paper from the counter and scribbled something down. "I'll let her know. Thanks. Bye." He hung up, and when he turned around, his face was grave. "That license plate belongs to a Joseph Goodman, address 477 Gates Avenue, phone number 707-555-1299. Does that sound familiar?"

"No," I said, my mind whirling. It could be an alias for Spence. If he was out here stalking me, he probably wouldn't do it under his own name. He was smart. He was a doctor. Or the car could be stolen. Joseph Goodman might be some feeble old man, doddering, milky-eyed, oblivious to the missing car he never drove.

There was only one way to find out.

"Thanks for talking to your dad," I said honestly.

"You're welcome," Michael said. "Do you want me to give this Goodman a call? Threaten him?"

I jerked my chin at the stove. "Your water's boiling."

He dropped sheets of pasta into the pot and turned back to me. "Do you?"

"No," I said, oddly touched. He might have taken a baseball bat to somebody at some point, but a baseball bat couldn't fix what was happening here. A baseball bat could shatter Lucy Black's precarious existence, though. "Listen, it might just be a coincidence. Maybe it wasn't even him and I freaked out over nothing."

He clamped his lips together and shook his head. "It didn't seem like nothing, Lucy."

"Can we just not talk about this for a little while?" My words were squeezed, as if I were forcing them through a clog in my throat. "I just need a few hours where I can not think about him." I didn't specify which "him" I meant: Spence or my brother. "Okay?"

He looked down into his boiling water, then at me, then at his pan of simmering tomatoes, then at me again, and then he did something entirely unexpected: he strode over to me, knelt before me like I was about to knight him or something, and wrapped his arms around me so that his face hit my shoulder. Not my chest, I noted. I wasn't surprised. He was a good person. He deserved better than me.

Still, I leaned my head forward, rested my nose in his hair, and drew in a deep, shuddering breath as his curls tickled my nose. He smelled like chlorine, with a hint of garlic and onion, or maybe that was just the sauce finally beginning to come together.

I didn't say anything, and neither did he—if we didn't speak, neither of us could ruin this moment. No, that role was left to his father, who closed the front door with a slam and announced his presence with a couple of very emphatic throat clears. Michael and I jumped apart; my chair skidded back a full foot, and Michael just barely escaped slamming his head against the counter. The shock startled away my own headache.

"Evening," his father said gruffly. He was still in his uniform, police hat firmly on his head, his chest shiny with multiple badges. "You're Lucy? The one being followed?"

"That's me." I pasted a smile on my face. "But it's okay. I'll be okay."

98

The look he gave me made me feel as if he could see through my skin, from the coils of my small intestine to the *glub-glub-glub* of my heart to the blood pumping toward my face. I felt worse than naked. "Well, you let me know if someone's bothering you," he said. "I'll take care of it."

I had a feeling his version of taking care of it was very different from mine. "Thank you, sir."

He shot Michael an appraising look. "Well, then," he said. Michael was staring into his sauce like there might be pirate treasure hidden in its depths. "What are we having?"

When Michael's dad thumped down at the table and his mother, a stout, pink-faced woman with iron-gray curls tight against her head, followed suit shortly thereafter, my head began running through all the excuses I could think of to get out of there: I wasn't feeling well. I just remembered I was deathly allergic to tomatoes. My dog got smashed by a bus and I needed to be there when my parents rushed it to the vet.

I kept delaying, though, and before I knew it, I was shoveling lasagna down my throat. I was content just to eat and watch them interact, almost as if I were watching animals in a zoo or subjects in a medical study. Look how the mother gently rubs her son on the upper arm when he accidentally lets a curse word slip, her grip firm but not hard enough to leave a bruise. Observe the father laughing at a joke his wife made, spraying little globules of tomato onto the table's clean surface. See the son's eyes glow as he looks at the researcher, and watch how the researcher reacts by suddenly becoming very intent upon her pasta. The way this family touched, the way they looked at each other, the way they poked fun—it was love, and I found love endlessly fascinating.

After the lasagna came ice cream, and after the ice cream came shocked exclamations of "Look how late it is!" from the mother. "You should get home, Lucy," she said. "I'm sure your parents are worried sick."

I didn't say, *Sure, if by worried sick you mean having no idea I'm even gone.* "Yeah," I said instead.

"Will you be okay driving home?" the mother asked.

"I don't drive," I said.

"Why not?"

I stood. "I just don't. I can call my dad."

"Don't call your dad," Michael said. He shot an annoyed look at his mom, and a wave of calm swept over me. So it wasn't all love all the time. "I drove you here; I can drive you home."

"Thanks."

His parents kissed me—actually kissed me—goodnight, and sent me on my way with a plastic container of lasagna. It sat in my lap, heavy and warm, and I knew I'd toss it as soon as I got home. It just wouldn't taste the same in my kitchen.

"Well," Michael said as we pulled up to my house. The ride had been quiet, again, but this one was a comfortable kind of quiet. Like the quiet after a thunderstorm, when the air is soft and everything still smells like rain. "I guess I'll see you tomorrow."

"I guess. Thanks for the ride." We stared at each other; the look in his eyes, soft as the air, made my stomach squirm.

"What do you think of the name Julia?" The words burst out of my mouth without any warning.

Michael cocked his head. "It's a nice name," he said. "Nowhere near as pretty as Lucy."

He looked at me and I looked at him, and before I could stop myself, I leaned over and pressed my lips against his cheek. He stilled; I could feel his heart beating under his skin. His skin was smooth. He swallowed hard, and the reverberations traveled through his bones and his muscle and his smooth, smooth skin and straight into my own head. "Lucy . . ."

My fake name broke the spell, and I pulled away, feeling like an idiot. I sprang out of the car, afraid my traitorous mouth would say—or do—something else. "Good night!" I called, and fairly sprinted into the house. I made sure not to look back, not even once, but I didn't hear him pull away until I'd stepped inside.

Tomorrow. I'd see him tomorrow. A happy glow spread outward from my stomach, but I squashed it before it could reach my heart. I had other things to think about.

Tomorrow, danger or not, I had to pay a visit to 477 Gates Avenue. And Mr. Joseph Goodman.

NINE

I spent the rest of the night on a hot date with my friend Google. It's amazing—and a little bit spooky—how much you can turn up with a name, an address, and a phone number.

Okay, the name alone—not so much. It turns out there are a whole lot of Joseph Goodmans in the world, a positive plague of them. When I Googled his name, most of what came up were profiles and reviews of a cosmetic dentist to the stars. When I dug a bit further, a plethora of others came sprouting from the earth like mushrooms after a storm: a minor-league baseball player, a middle school teacher who had won a number of community-service awards, a police officer who had thrown himself in front of a bullet intended for a past mayor—the bullet had embedded itself in his lower leg, leaving him with a prosthetic limb and several commendations for bravery—and a local theater star with his own website and a clearly overinflated ego. My Joseph Goodman could've been any one of them, or none of them.

The address brought me more luck. Google Earth brought it onto my laptop screen in high-def: it was a small, humble ranch with brown streaks on the siding and a dry, patchy lawn. Though the Google Street View car had clearly trundled by during the daytime, all the windows were shut tight, and the pile of newspapers on the front stoop showed that nobody had been there in at least a week. Or at least that nobody had gone outside. It was an unassuming building that could've been located anywhere. This particular one was located an approximate twenty-eight-minute car ride away, according to the handy directions Google Maps pulled up.

"Lucy?" I jumped. My eyes burned as I turned to look at my mother. She was hovering in the doorway, her nails tapping nervously on the frame. She probably wanted to varnish it or something. "Are you still up?"

"No, I'm very clearly asleep," I said.

"No need to be rude," she said mildly. "It's past midnight. You have school tomorrow."

Before the band room, my mother would have told me to get my butt in bed. Now she just kept tapping her nails.

I wanted her to tell me to go to bed. "So?" I dared. "So I'll be tired. I can stay up however late I want."

Click. Click. Click. "You're only seventeen," she said.

"And?"

The nails clattered harder, as if she were trying to poke holes in the wood. "Lucy . . ." She trailed off.

"Yeah?"

Footsteps thumped behind her, and I startled to my feet as my dad loomed in the hallway. "Lucy Black," he said. "You heard your mother."

"She talked, but she didn't say anything," I said. Tears jumped to my eyes, blurring my parents into an abstract painting.

He glared at me, then swung his arm around my mom's shoulders. "Go to bed, Lucy," he said, pulling her away. "We'll talk about this tomorrow."

I knew we wouldn't.

I woke a painful half hour early the next morning to steal my dad's gun. After I'd dragged myself out of bed, brushed my teeth, and rubbed the stickiness from the corners of my eyes, I remembered that we no longer had a gun. It was in the Elkton police station's evidence room, sealed inside a plastic bag, marked with an evidence number, and abandoned inside a cardboard box stacked among hundreds of other cardboard boxes.

Maybe it was for the best. I didn't have to rush in, guns blazing. Given what he knew of my brother, Spence probably wouldn't take that well. He might be dangerous, but I remembered him as tall and weedy, stringy in the arms and legs. I could take him. I could certainly outrun him. All I wanted to do was fix him with my cold stare and ask him why he was following me. Really, if he wanted to hurt me or kill me, he'd had plenty of chances to do it already. Clearly he wanted something else.

I'd go by the example of Eddie Meyer, the third to die according to the gripping, Pulitzer-nominated narrative of the attack, pieced together by ace reporter Jennifer Rosenthal, aka Jenny, from the police reports, coroners' reports, interviews with students, and one incredibly unhelpful talk with the sister of the shooter. Right after Evan and Liv were pierced by bullets and everybody else was either too shocked to move or scrambling to find an exit, Eddie grabbed his baseball bat (like Evan, he was not in band; if only I could remember what he'd been doing in that band room, I'd have the final piece for Jenny's puzzle) and rushed my brother. My brother shot him five times in the chest. Poor Eddie—he was brave, but he wasn't very smart.

When I said I'd go by Eddie's example, I didn't mean die. I meant I'd face the danger head-on.

So pepper spray it was. Just in case.

Alane picked me up promptly at seven-thirty-five, as she did every morning. She was so unfailingly punctual I sometimes wondered if she idled around the block, waiting for the perfect moment to pull in front of my house. "So?" she greeted me as I slid in. "How'd your date go?"

"It wasn't a date." I rummaged around in my purse, making absolutely sure the pepper spray was at the very bottom. It was, naturally, forbidden at school, but this wasn't Elkton, where, I heard, kids now had to walk through metal detectors and endure bag searches just to get to class. Like that would have stopped my brother. "Hey, I need a favor."

"Oh, come on," she said. "It was so a date. He cooked you dinner at his house. If that's not a date, I don't know what is."

"Fine. It was a date. It was fine," I said. "His parents were there, so it was a little weird."

Her mouth dropped open, and she blinked so many times, and in such rapid succession, I worried she couldn't see the road in front of her. "You've already met the parents?" she said. "Lucy, how could you not tell me this?"

I shifted uncomfortably in my seat. "It wasn't like he was, like, 'Hey, Lucy, meet my parents. We're having dinner with them.' It was more like they walked through the door and plopped themselves down at the table."

"Still." She sighed and fluttered a hand against her heart. "That's got to be a good sign. As long as they liked you."

People always liked me. "I think they did," I said.

"Oh, good." Her eyes fluttered this time, like she was dreaming. Seriously, was she watching the road? "It's important for your boyfriend's parents to like you."

"He's not my boyfriend," I said automatically. Okay, time to change the subject. "Soooo, I'll love you forever if you give me a ride somewhere after school today."

"You've already promised to love me forever," she said. "Are you going back on your word?"

I raised my eyebrows and pursed my lips. "I might have to have Michael's babies instead."

"Never!" she said, scandalized. "But I have a dentist appointment after school, babes. Can we take that ride tomorrow?"

I made my shoulders sag, ducked my head so that my hair fell around my face in a curtain. "It's really important," I said, my voice low. "I mean, like, life-changing important. And I have to go today. Maybe I could ask Ella for a ride. Or Michael."

"What kind of chauffeur would I be to make you do that?" she said, though she was frowning. "I guess I can make my mom cancel my appointment. I hate the dentist anyway. Where are we going?"

I wondered if she was going to see Joseph Goodman, self-proclaimed dentist to the stars. Maybe she'd get to see him after all. What an unpleasant surprise that would be. "I'll tell you later."

"A surprise!" she exclaimed, perking up. "How exciting!"

This was why I loved Alane. It wasn't the same kind of love I observed yesterday, the glowing looks and admonishing touches to the shoulder, but it was love regardless. I think, anyway. I've always found it hard to tell.

School was a shooting star; before I could even make a wish, it was gone, and I was meeting Alane outside the chorus room. Alane bounced into the hallway, hair twisted back off her shiny face. "So, where are we going?" she asked as she followed me out into the parking lot.

"To Gates Avenue," I said. "Outside Sunny Vale. On the border of Madison."

"All the way out there?" she said. "Why?"

I might as well stick to the same story I told Michael. Keep things consistent. That was one of the rules for lying well: don't confuse yourself unnecessarily. Always choose the easiest path, and the easiest path was usually the most consistent one. "Did I ever tell you about my ex-boyfriend?" I said. I picked a name, ripe for the plucking, from the air. "Andrew?"

"I don't think so," she said, climbing into the truck. I followed, doing my usual scan of the pavement under the hole. No change today. Too bad. I could've used a lucky penny just then. "Did I ever meet him?"

The truck roared to life. "No," I said. "He was from before I moved."

"Andrew, Andrew, Andrew," she said. The waves of kids passing by, their cheerful chatter, washed over us. "No, I don't think you ever did. But you might have. You know my memory."

"Like a sieve," I agreed. "In one ear and out the other."

"Well, you don't have to sound so damn cheerful about it." She flung an arm around the back of my seat and turned her head to back out. The waves of kids parted, scattering to the sides. "What about this Andrew?"

"He was . . ." Strategic pause. Lowered eyes. Pause held

long enough so that she'd glance over and take note of my lowered eyes. "Not a nice person. The total opposite of that, in fact. He . . ." I stopped. Another lesson in lying well: sometimes your silences can say more than words without actually saying anything at all.

"I understand," she said kindly. "You don't have to say any more. I'm sorry."

I shrugged and did that thing where I touched a phantom bruise, this time on my cheek. "It built character," I said. "It made me who I am today."

"That's a good way to look at it."

"Thanks," I said. "But . . ." I waited for her to look over again. I wanted to make sure she saw me touching my cheek. It was one of my best strategies. "I think he's here. I think he found me, and that he's following me."

She went rigid in her seat, nearly rear-ending the car in front of us. "That guy after show choir . . . the old one."

"That was him," I said. "And he's not *that* old. I'm almost positive it was him. And he was at Crazy Elliot's, too. That's why I freaked out."

"Oh my God," she said, and her lips moved again, saying the words silently. As if she were praying. "So . . ."

"I want to talk to him," I said. "I don't want to call the police. It could be nothing."

"Are we going to his house?" She slammed to a violent stop. I opened my mouth to protest before realizing we'd just hit a red light. "Lucy, that could be really dangerous. If he's following you . . ."

"You'll wait in the car and watch," I said. "I'm not going to go into his house. I just want to confront him and tell him to leave me alone. That I'm not the weak little girl I used to be."

"But still, Lucy . . ."

"You have my permission to dial nine-one-one if he tries anything," I said. "But he won't. I know he won't . . . hurt me." She looked skeptical. "Not in front of people, anyway."

A storm passed over her face, shadowing her eyes, but she sighed. "I don't approve, but you're going to do it anyway, aren't you?"

I nodded. She sighed again. "So it's safer if I'm there with you."

"Exactly," I said.

"Seriously, though—"

"I need to do this," I said.

She didn't say anything else.

I could tell when we left Sunny Vale and entered Madison—and not just by the big sign announcing just that; the land beside the road turned from charming homes with manicured lawns and cheery shopping complexes to dirt and trees. I could barely make out the small, shabby houses nestled far back from the road. Even the road got bumpier; though, really, everything was bumpy in Alane's truck.

We finally turned onto Gates Avenue, which was so rutted and rocky it might as well have been packed dirt rather than asphalt. It was lined by houses, but sparsely, so each resident could just barely see their neighbor; it would take real effort to ask to borrow a cup of sugar on this street. A mile or so up the road, we pulled over in front of number 477.

Alane regarded it uneasily. "It's not too late to turn around and call the cops."

I clapped her on the shoulder. "You wait here, okay? With your phone?" I asked. She nodded, her lips pressed so tightly together they turned pale around the edges, like a sore. "I'm going to talk with him on the stoop. If I go inside, call the cops."

"Okay." Her knuckles on the hand clutching the phone were pale, too. "I hope this . . . helps you."

My own hands balled into fists. "Me too."

As I got out of the car, my heart was hammering and my hands were shaking. I pushed my shoulders back, though, and lifted my chin high. *Spence wouldn't hurt me. If he wanted to hurt me, he could've done it already.* I repeated it like a mantra, a rap, against the pounding in my ears.

I gave three quick taps on the door. The front of the house was streaked with brownish-green mold; the blinds were drawn tight, and part of the gutter dangled off the roof over the stoop, loosing a steady drip of rusty water onto the concrete.

The door eased open a crack, and all my muscles tensed. "Julia Vann, it's about time. I've been waiting."

Not Joseph Goodman. It *was* Spence, the lenses of his glasses shining through the crack. I craned my neck to peer inside and noticed the chain lock was on. Almost like he was the one who was scared.

Of me.

The idea filled me with enough confidence to speak. "You've been following me," I said. "I'm here to tell you to stop. To leave me alone. Or I'll call the police."

Spence let out a dry laugh, though he didn't unlock the chain. "It's been surprisingly hard to get you alone, Julia—"

"And my name isn't Julia anymore." I talked over him. "It's Lucy. If you're going to talk to me, if you're going to come to my school and invade my space, my name is Lucy Black." My heart beat so fast I thought I might pass out, just give up, and crumple to the stoop. "And it doesn't seem like you've been waiting a long time to talk to me, considering every time I get near you, you run away like a coward. Even now you're hiding behind that door. What are you so afraid of?" My voice was heavy with sarcasm. "I'm a teenage girl and you're a grown man. Are you worried I might pull your hair? Scratch you?"

"No," Spence said. He sounded thoughtful. "That's not what I'm afraid of."

"Whatever it is, I don't care." I was on a roll, gathering words as I tumbled, a snowball rolling through newsprint. "Just stay the hell away from me or there'll be hell to pay. For you." In case that wasn't clear.

I turned to go, my chin held high, shaking in the breeze like the upper stories of a skyscraper.

"You sound just like your brother."

I froze. Being careful, very careful, I turned back around. One careless motion and I might shatter. "Excuse me?"

"I've been trying to get you alone for a reason, you know," Spence said. I could tell he was being careful, very careful, too. "You didn't wonder why?"

I didn't care. I didn't *care*. Spence was part of Julia Vann's life, like Ryan, and I was Lucy Black now. Lucy Black didn't have to wonder why. "I just want you to leave me alone," I hissed.

Alane was still far away in her car; she couldn't have heard Spence's comment. I couldn't let her hear any of Spence's comments. Maybe it had been a mistake to have her drive me here. "I don't want anything more to do with you or with Elkton." I turned again to go.

"He said to tell you he loved you."

I stopped and swiveled again. "Why are you doing this?" My voice broke. Somewhere distant I heard a car door bang shut, and the sound reverberated through me. "I've been through enough. Just leave me alone."

Spence's face was grim, his chin set. "He told me last week."

Everything came to a stop. "Excuse me?"

"You heard me, *Julia Vann*."

"Lucy?" Alane, jogging across the lawn, face flushed, held her phone before her like a shield. What had she heard? "What's he doing? Do I need to call nine-one-one?"

He slammed the door shut. Of course he did. I wasn't alone anymore.

"No," I said. "Go back to the car."

Alane stopped in her tracks. "Are you okay?"

It couldn't be. I would've known. Hell, the world would've known. It would've been in every newspaper, on every breaking-news alert, on everybody's social network. If Ryan Vann had woken from his coma, even Lucy Black would've known within minutes.

And if not Lucy . . . Julia would have known. Julia would have known in her bones, because she knew everything about her brother. She would've felt his awakening as her own, a heightened consciousness, a nagging feeling of "something isn't right."

I launched myself at the closed front door and pounded on it with my fists. "Open the door!" I screamed. Words scraped at the inside of my throat. "Get back out here, you coward!"

"Lucy! Lucy, stop." Hands grabbed at my back, but they couldn't pull me away from the door. I was a girl possessed, the Big Bad Wolf blowing, blowing, blowing in vain at the pig's brick house.

Alane's shriek brought me back to earth. I spun, panting, to see that I'd thrown her off me in my flailing. I'd pushed her right off the stoop. She was trying to lift herself up, though from the wincing as she tried to put weight on her left leg, it wasn't easy. Fury drained out of me into a puddle around my feet. "Oh my God," I said, and jumped down beside her. "I'm so sorry. Are you okay?"

"My ankle," she said through gritted teeth.

"I'm so sorry," I said again, my heart fluttering in panic.

She had to forgive me. "We'll go to the hospital. I'll take you to the hospital." I glanced behind me, fleetingly, at Spence's door. I wasn't done with him, but I wasn't going to learn any more today. And I wasn't going to play into his game; look what he'd done to me with a few carefully chosen sentences. He was probably lying anyway. My brother was never supposed to wake up.

Alane snorted. "*You're* going to drive me to the hospital?"

I leaned over so she could put her arm around my shoulders, so she could use me like a crutch. She couldn't be mad at someone who let her use her as a crutch. "I'm so sorry."

"It's my left ankle," she said. Again, no forgiveness. "I can still drive."

The drive to the hospital in Sunny Vale was a short and silent one. Alane tried to call her mom but got voice mail. I spent the ride staring out the window, Spence's words tumbling over and over through my mind. He had to be lying, I told myself. He had to be playing some kind of game with me. My brother couldn't really have woken up.

I sat with Alane as we waited in the emergency room; I figured it was the least I could do. I kept the conversation light, talking about Michael's legs and Ella's new haircut, but Alane stuck to one-word answers and head shakes and nods. Still, she let me go with her into the examination room, sit beside her, and hold her hand as the doctor poked and prodded at her ankle and she sucked in her breath.

"Looks like a sprain," the doctor said finally. "I'll wrap

it up for you. You should try to stay off it for a few weeks, but you won't need crutches or anything. How'd you do it?"

Alane opened her mouth, but I spoke over her. "She fell," I said loudly. "Tripped. On a root." I couldn't let her say anything that might expose what we'd been doing.

She let me talk for her but shrugged off my arm the second the door closed behind the doctor. "What the hell, Lucy?" she said. "Or is it Julia?"

"I don't know what you're talking about," I said slowly. I thought I might vomit.

"Your ex called you Julia Vann," Alane said. "Did you change your name when you moved here?"

My breath caught in my throat. I could bash her over the head with that IV stand so hard she'd lose her memory. I should. Because all she had to do was Google *Julia Vann* plus *California* and she'd see everything. I was results one through seventeen, where I was briefly interrupted by a Julia Vann who had died of cancer at age eleven in San Francisco and a high school–aged Julia Vann who was agonizing over whether to go to college at Stanford for no money or play volleyball at UCLA with a full scholarship, and then it was back to me. "No," I said.

"Yes," she said. "I heard him. Why did you change your name?"

My mouth opened and closed. I wanted to tell her. I wanted to tell her everything. But it was risking too much. I couldn't handle seeing her face dim as she looked at me.

Nobody in Elkton had wanted anything to do with us. I couldn't handle the same thing happening here. But I couldn't hide anymore, either. She already knew the truth, or would as soon as she Googled me.

"I have to go." I pushed the words out through tears, and turned and walked out.

I was really, really, really going to miss her.

Still, my mind was whirling with what Spence had said. It was a blessing, kind of, because it drove away the thought that I'd probably just lost the best friend I'd ever had. I had to call my parents and tell them we'd have to leave. Again. I knew for a fact that my mother couldn't take it, couldn't take the looks, couldn't take the reporters. She'd scrub her way straight through the downstairs carpet and into her own grave.

I couldn't call them now, though, not when I was still shaking. So I called Michael. "Hey," I said. My voice was shaking, too. "Are you done with swimming? I kind of need a ride."

He didn't ask questions. When his car rounded the curve of the visitors' lot, I felt as if I were going to burst into tears for the second time in only a few days. For the second time ever. "Thank you," I said as I climbed in. "Alane sprained her ankle. And . . ." If I was going to be leaving town anyway, why bother telling the truth? "Her mom is there with her, and she told me I could leave. I have a ton of homework."

"I hope she's okay," he said. "You want to go home?"

"Yes, home," I said. Home, for however long it would be mine.

We kept ourselves busy with inane small talk ("How was the swim meet?" "How was band?" The farthest from "How are you feeling as your life crumbles around you?" as we could get) the whole ride home. All talk, though, was immediately extinguished when we saw what was waiting for us in my driveway.

Both my parents' cars. And a black car, smooth and sleek, license plate 3RTR779.

Re: Ryan Vann, age 10

It hasn't been two weeks since my last session with Ryan, but his parents called in this morning to arrange an emergency session. Fortunately I had a cancellation this afternoon and was free. They practically dragged him into the waiting room, accompanied by his sister, Julia. There were black smudges around his hairline, like he'd been covered in tar or black paint and someone had tried to scrub it away.

"What happened?" I couldn't help but ask, right there in the waiting room. I should've known better. The parents did. They didn't speak until the five of us were safely in my office. I sat at my desk, the parents in the chairs across from me; the twins sat on the couch, their heads bowed together. The girl shook like a leaf, but Ryan was, as always, calm and still as stone, staring at the floor. His sister was whispering in his ear, her hand on his, like she was trying to calm him. "She should be trying to calm herself," I thought before turning back to the parents.

"Ryan decided it would be a good idea to light a little girl's tree house on fire," the father said, his teeth clenched. "The little girl was inside at the time. She barely escaped."

Ryan's cheeks were working unconsciously, like he was grinding his teeth. He was nervous, I was surprised to see. He'd never appeared nervous before. The sister seemed to have taken note, too; she was patting his hand now, and while I couldn't hear her, from the movement of her lips it seemed as if she was telling him everything was going to be okay.

"The girl's family isn't going to press charges," the mother said, her voice shaking. "The poor thing was traumatized enough. We need to—you need to make this stop, Doctor. Fix him."

I literally had to bite my tongue to keep from bursting out with *I've been trying to treat him, and you've been stymieing me at every turn!* "First of all, there's no fixing to be done, because he isn't broken," I lied. Even then, I knew I was lying. "Second, we all need to do our part. You. The school therapist. And Ryan. We can't help Ryan if he doesn't want to be helped."

The father slapped a hand onto Ryan's shoulder so hard it reverberated around the walls of my office. "Ryan does want to be helped," he said. "Ryan does want to change. Don't you, Ryan?"

Ryan wouldn't meet my eyes. He wouldn't meet anybody's eyes, unless the tips of his shoes had suddenly sprouted a pair. "Yes," he whispered.

"Good." The father stood, and the mother followed suit. The mother turned and gestured to the sister, who stood reluctantly, her eyes on her brother. "We'll leave him in your capable hands, Doctor."

That was the problem. "Wait," I said. "Can I speak with Julia for a moment? Alone?"

The father nodded, and the mother followed suit. They didn't even ask the girl. "We'll see you in a minute," the father said. "Come on, Ryan." Ryan followed his parents out the door, turning for one last over-the-shoulder glance at his sister. She didn't stop looking at him until the door had closed; then she turned and looked at me.

"Ryan said you wouldn't drug him," she told me, like she was a teacher telling me I'd passed a test. Now that her brother was gone, she'd stopped shaking. "He was really happy about that. Thanks."

So he told her what happened in my sessions. The girl sat back down, and I sat in order to better address her on her level. "Julia, your brother needs help," I said. "I'm sure you know that by now, right?"

She was kicking her feet in front of her—left, right, left, right—and watching her toes. "He kills things sometimes," she said. "But he said he'd never hurt me. Ever."

"He burned down a little girl's tree house," I said. Left, right, left, right. "He could've hurt her very badly. Could you please look at me, Julia?"

She met my eyes but didn't stop kicking. "He does bad things," she said.

"I know," I said. "But you can help me help him. May I ask you a favor, Julia?"

She blinked at me. "What?"

"If he's going to get better, he needs to do his therapy," I said. "I think that if you ask him to go to his therapy, he'll do it. Will you do that for me?"

She shrugged bony shoulders. "I guess. I really want him to get better."

I could've hugged her; I didn't, because that would have been unprofessional. "I promise I will not give up on your brother," I told her. "I will be patient, and I will talk to him, and I will help—"

Something hit me in the shin, and I flinched. She'd kicked me. The girl had kicked me. She was studying my leg, the way it jerked, with a look of mild surprise. "Oops," she said. "I didn't mean to kick you. Sorry."

I smiled reassuringly at her. "It's okay," I said. "And thank you for your help, Julia."

She hopped to her feet, a little smile on her face. "You're welcome," she said. "Are we done? I have to go to the bathroom."

"We're done," I said. "Would you send Ryan back in, please?"

She bounded out the door without a second glance. A moment later, Ryan shuffled in, his eyes on the floor. "Look at me, please," I said.

The *please* did it; as I was saying the first part of my sentence, I could see his jaw tighten, his fists clench, but everything loosened when I said that magic word. He brought his chin up to look me in the eye. He was small for his age, and thin, and the overall effect was that of an impoverished chimney sweep. If only that were his problem; I could toss a few dollars at him and send him on his way. "Listen to me, Ryan William Vann," I said, doing my best to sound strong and commanding. "I promise, I swear, I will help you, or my name isn't Dr. Atlas Spence."

"You won't give up?" His voice was tiny, afraid. "Never? You won't give up on me?"

122

"Never," I assured him. "We will talk and we will work and we will make things better."

He looked back down and muttered something.

I couldn't be sure, but it sounded like "That's what I was afraid of."

TEN

The sight of the black car in my driveway turned my insides to ice; I had to move slowly, carefully, or they'd shatter and break. "It's him," I said. My lips were numb. "He's here."

Michael reached for his pocket. "Don't get out of the car. I'll call my dad."

He couldn't call his dad. I stopped him with a touch to his arm; I hoped I wouldn't freeze him, too. "Don't," I said. "He could have my parents in there. I need to deal with this myself."

"No way," Michael said. His arm tensed under my grip. "He's dangerous."

"I can talk him down," I said. "If I don't come back out in fifteen minutes, then you can call your dad."

"Lucy—"

I didn't have time to reason with him. I hopped out of the car and did my best to form a reassuring smile. My lips felt like skin stretched over a skull. "I'll be right out," I said, and walked quickly toward the front door, rummaging for my pepper spray in the bottom of my bag. I didn't look back.

It was dark inside, and every shadow lurked in a suspicious manner: the armchair might well have been a crouched man lying in wait, gun tucked into his armpit, and the coatrack a killer poised beside the closet door. My heart tattooed a rhythm against my ribs—*Spence is here Spence is here Spence is here.*

"Hey!" I called, hoisting the pepper spray. "Show your face or I'll call the cops."

A glow was shining around the corner, in the living room. "Lucy," my mother called. Her voice was shaking. "Come in here, please."

My ears pricked. It was definitely her voice, but it might not have been her talking. Spence could be in there holding a gun to her head. "What's going on?" I called back, still clutching the pepper spray.

"Just get in here." That was my father. I considered backing away and running out the door, back into Michael's waiting arms. I actually thought I heard the front door creak open behind me, as if I'd pushed it open with my mind.

"What's going on?" I repeated.

"We need to talk to you." My father again. Usually he sounded angry, commanding, no matter what mood he was in. Now he only sounded numb. "Come in here. Please."

The pepper spray fell limply to my side. My father never said *please.*

I stepped into the glow of the living room and blinked in the sudden light. My parents sat side by side on the couch—though not touching, never touching—and across the coffee table, in chairs, sat two men in blue police uniforms. One was bald; the other had a head of bushy white hair.

"You must be Julia Vann." The cop with white hair stood and extended his hand. "Nice to meet you, Julia. I'm Officer West, Sunny Vale PD."

"My name is Lucy now," I said coldly. I didn't shake his hand. Eventually his smile faltered and he slowly lowered his arm.

"Lucy, then, whatever you prefer to be called," he said. "This is my partner, Officer Goodman."

The name zinged through my head. Officer Goodman. Joseph Goodman. It couldn't be a coincidence. But why was Spence driving a cop's car? Staying in a cop's house?

What I did know: I couldn't trust anything this Officer Goodman said.

"Good evening, Lucy," Goodman said. He was very studiously not looking at me. "Mr. and Mrs. Vann, did you want to speak to your daughter alone?"

"Mr. and Mrs. Black," my father corrected, his tone entirely void of emotion. A black hole. A Black hole. "I think it's best if she hears it from someone other than us."

My stomach squirmed. "Hears what?" Ryan had woken up. I waited for the words. I had to hear them in front of my parents. That would make them real, solid, something I could grab onto.

"Miss Black," West began, "there's no easy way to say this, but Ryan has gone missing."

That was unexpected. "Excuse me?"

My mother reached out and touched my father's knee. I couldn't remember the last time I'd seen them touch. "Last night, the night security shift got to . . . Ryan's room and realized he was gone," she said, her voice trembling. "They don't know where he is, or who took him, but he's gone."

"Wait," I said. My heart was pounding so hard I thought it might explode. I thought *I* might explode. "But he's still in a coma."

My father sighed. "I told you we should have told her."

I thought for a moment that he was talking to me, but then I realized he was looking at my mother, who in turn was staring hard at the floor. "We did the right thing," she said.

My father sighed again. "Yes, but now—"

"We did the right thing," my mother said loudly.

"What are you talking about?"

Now my father was looking at the floor, too. I snuck a glance, but there was nothing there. Maybe they were hoping the floor would split open and swallow them up. "Ryan was only in a coma for a week."

"You're lying."

My father didn't respond to my accusation, just kept talking, as if this was a speech he'd rehearsed. "Ryan woke up shortly after the police moved him to their facility. They brought us in to talk. They said it would be better if he underwent rehabilitation without the attention of the media. He wouldn't have to face trial until he could talk again."

"You don't understand, Julia," my mother said. I was still so stunned I didn't even bother to reprimand her for using my real name. "He wasn't himself. He was a mess. He could barely breathe on his own. We thought it would be best for you if you continued to think he was . . . gone. So you could make a fresh start."

My heart squeezed and wrung itself out, a piece of wet laundry. How could I not have known? How could Julia not have known? "What were you planning to do once it hit the media?" I said. My hands shook. "Once he recovered and had to face trial?"

My father looked at my mother. My mother continued to look at the floor. "We were going to tell you," he said helplessly. I knew that was a lie. They either hadn't planned that far ahead or, more likely, hadn't thought at all about how it might affect me.

It didn't matter now anyway. "I need to see him," I said. "Take me to him."

"We can't," my father said, and now he looked at me. I expected his eyes to be as distant as they usually were, but they had glossed over with what I had to assume were tears. "You heard what the officers said. He's missing."

"Don't worry," West said, his tone assured. "We're doing all we can to track him down. It's only a matter of time."

"How could you let him go missing?" My voice rose to

a pitch I figured only dogs could hear. "He was well enough to escape? To get away? Is that what you're saying? You let him go?"

West's plastic smile faltered. "We're doing all we can," he repeated.

That falter in his smile. "You need to find him," I said. My voice rose again, this time to a shout. "Don't you know how dangerous he is? Don't you know what he did?"

"Lucy . . . ," my mother murmured.

"How well was he? Could he talk? Did he kill anyone when he escaped?" I said. Or yelled. I might have yelled. "You're really here to see if we're hiding him, aren't you? To see if he's made it here? How did he go missing, exactly? Or did one of your own people help him? Was it—" Spence. Spence had to have something to do with this.

I sank onto the couch and bowed my head. "You might as well leave," I said. "He isn't here."

"Of course he isn't here," my father said. Overly loud, I thought. "We would have called you immediately if he was. And if he should happen to show his face, we'll call you immediately. Gentlemen . . ."

West and Goodman popped to their feet. "If you have any questions, of course, don't hesitate to give us a call," West said. "You have my card."

"Thank you," my mother said faintly.

"I'll see them out," I said, jumping up.

"There's really no need—" West began.

"Nonsense," I said, baring my teeth in what I hoped

looked like a grin. "Wouldn't want you to get lost, would we? It's only polite."

My parents let me go. They shouldn't have let me go.

I escorted the two cops to the front door, which I blocked. Not really blocked, of course. If they really wanted to move me, they could've easily pushed me out of the way. "You have one last chance to tell me what's really going on here." Before what? I didn't know. I just hoped it sounded sufficiently menacing.

Goodman leaned in. Onion breath washed over my face. "I don't know what you're talking about," he said softly.

And then they were gone, and I was shaking. Somewhere far away I could hear my parents' steps on the stairs. They were going to their bedroom, I assumed, to hide from me. They always seemed to be hiding. As I was growing up, it was my mom in her pills, my dad in his work; my dad still hid in his work, but my mom now hid in her cleaning. It was like they thought of Ryan and me as afterthoughts, as brief diversions in their real lives.

"Lucy?" I jumped in surprise.

"Michael?" He was lurking to the side, in the doorway of the kitchen. I hadn't even seen him in the dark. "What are you doing here?" It seemed like a million years ago that I'd turned into ice and left him outside. Now all the ice had melted.

"I got worried." In the dark, shadows took up residence in the hollows of his cheeks, in the pockets under his eyes.

He looked curiously vulnerable. "Why did they call you Julia?"

"I . . ." My voice broke, falling and shattering on the tile like the glass I'd thrown at my brother the time he told me he had a crush on a girl in his social studies class. We'd only been in fourth grade, but I'd never forget the fury that tore through me. "I'm the only girl you'll ever need," I'd told him, and I'd been right.

"I . . ." I sank to my knees; the broken shards of my voice sliced free the words I'd kept safe inside my head. "My real name is Julia Vann," I said flatly before Michael had the chance to say anything. I knew he'd ask. He might as well hear it from me. Alane already knew, after all. I stood, steadying myself against the wall. "My brother is Ryan Vann. You've heard of him. You've probably heard of me, too."

"Ryan Vann," Michael said slowly. I flinched to hear my brother's name. For over a year now, the only place I'd heard it had been inside my skull, where it echoed with loneliness. "It doesn't ring a bell."

"You know him," I said. "Ryan Vann. Elkton. Eleven dead."

I could see the moment it hit him; his eyes widened and he sucked in a sharp breath, which was followed by a lengthy exhale that made me think he was going to throw up. "You're the sister," he said. "The only one who came out alive."

He kept staring at me like he wanted me to confirm. I wasn't sure exactly what to say. "Yup, that's me!" I said finally in a far-too-perky sort of way.

"Oh my God," he said. I tensed. If he was going to lunge at me, I was going to have to move fast. "I'm so sorry."

I relaxed just a tiny bit. "You're not going to hit me?"

"God, Lucy! Sorry, Julia, Lucy, whoever you are. Why would I hit you?" Now he looked angry, and his fists were balled. I shrank back into the wall. He seemed to realize the effect he was having and hopped back, his fists opening like flowers bursting into bloom. "God, no, Lucy! Julia! I would never hit you. Why would you even think that? That's insane."

"It's not so insane," I said coldly. "After my brother . . . did what he did, nobody would talk to us. We had reporters outside on our street twenty-four hours a day. We had to disconnect our phone line because people kept calling to yell at us and tell us to get out of town. They blamed us."

His shoulders sank, and he suddenly looked six inches shorter. Not in a bad way, though. He became more approachable, somehow, like I could sink right into him. "That's crazy," he said, and then added, "Not on your part. On their part. How could they blame you? You didn't do anything."

A snort escaped, and then a laugh, and then suddenly I was on the floor again, hysterical, barking gasps shaking my whole body. I thought they were supposed to be laughs, but I wasn't entirely sure. "Thank you for that," I said once I'd calmed down enough to speak. "I appreciate it." And so, in that moment, I knew I'd fallen for Michael Silverman, both figuratively and literally.

And that meant he had to go. "You should leave, Michael," I said. "It's time for you to leave."

My brother was not kind to people who'd wronged me. I, of course, felt that Michael was doing the opposite of wronging me—he was righting me. But my brother wouldn't see it that way. He'd see Michael as keeping me away from him, of steering me away from my own blood, and so he'd have to do something about Michael. For my own good.

A little girl had wronged me, once. Her name was Gabriella, and her mother had a French accent, which made her mother the coolest person in the world. Most of us would get embarrassed and shuffle away whenever our parents came near, but all Gabriella's mother had to do was smile down at us and say *"Bonjour,"* and somehow Gabriella became even cooler. She compounded her coolness with a cool tree house, which became the cool hangout spot for all the neighborhood cool kids.

Naturally, we all wanted to be her friend. Even me and Liv. We'd follow her around at recess and crowd beneath her when she took her spot (the throne, we called it) atop one of the slides and tell her how beautiful she was, even though in truth she kind of looked like a rat.

One day Gabriella smiled down at me and told me to get lost. I blinked at her. She elaborated: "You and your brother are weird. I don't want you here." I had no choice but to go.

Liv waved at me as I went, then turned away guiltily. She didn't want to sentence herself to isolation by my side.

I didn't want to tell my brother. I really didn't. This was after Fluffy had met her untimely end, and so I knew exactly what he was capable of. But he caught me crying by the side of the playground. His brows knit together and his breath came in short, sharp blasts, and I thought that if I didn't tell him quickly he might hit the wall and hurt his hand, so I told.

He just listened silently, then sat down beside me and let me put my head on his shoulder. I thought I was safe. I thought Gabriella was safe.

Later that night, I heard the sirens.

Gabriella's father, who was almost as cool as her mother, had built Gabriella a tree house fit for a princess. From what I understand, Ryan had snuck over to her house, waited for Gabriella to climb the tree, and then set fire to it. She had to jump to escape, and she broke her arm. Her hysterical mother saw Ryan watching from the woods; he couldn't resist admiring his handiwork. My father, the lawyer, persuaded her to not call the police, told her that a court case and all the questioning would only traumatize their little girl more.

I couldn't let Michael become a Gabriella. I had to end this once and for all, and for that I had to find Spence. I shook my head firmly. "You have to go, right now."

He crouched beside me. From where I lay, sideways, his

concerned smile looked more like a grimace. "I can't leave you here like this."

I sat up so fast I nearly crushed his jaw with my skull. "Oh, don't worry. I'm not staying here," I said. "As soon as you leave, I'm calling a cab. I need to go to a house on the border between Sunny Vale and Madison."

He rubbed his chin, and I wondered if it was finally starting to sink in, all he'd mired himself in when he smiled at me that first time. "Why?" he asked.

"I need answers," I said. And Spence was the one who had those answers. Most likely he knew where my brother was and what happened to him. I had to find out what he wanted from me, once and for all. He'd clearly only tell me if I was alone. "It will be dangerous. I can't let you get hurt."

I was already thinking of everything I had stashed in my closet, deciding what I did and didn't need to bring. "My brother either escaped or was kidnapped from the hospital, and a man who knows the truth lives in that house."

He blinked at me once, twice, three times. "Those were police officers who were just here."

"Yes."

"Then shouldn't you let them handle it?"

"No," I said. It would take too long to explain why. "Please leave."

"Wait," he said. I could practically see the cogs in his head grinding against each other, turning everything he thought he knew about me into dust. "Your crazy ex-boyfriend."

"Doesn't exist," I said dully. "The man you saw, the man who was following me, was my brother's psychologist. The man I need to find now." I watched the gears turn. "I'm sorry I lied to you."

"You don't have to apologize. I get it. I get why you wouldn't want me to know who he was, who you really were. Given everything that's happened to you." He was silent for a moment. When his mouth opened again, I knew immediately what he was going to say. "Don't take a cab. I'll drive you."

I crossed my arms. I didn't have time to stand here and argue with him. I could bash him over the head with the vase on the table in the hall, quickly, before my parents heard him scream, and tie him up with the television cable. By the time he worked his way free, I'd be long gone.

And yet, I didn't move. "Why would you do that?"

"Because I like you and I want to help you," he said. My heart broke a little at his naïveté. Now I wanted to curl him up in sheets of Bubble Wrap and tuck him safely into a chest in the attic, where he'd never get dinged or scratched.

"You don't like me," I said. "I know your type. You think very highly of yourself. You think you can fix everything. So when you see someone who's broken, it's like a moth to the flame." He looked confused, so I added, "You're the moth. I'm the flame."

"That's not even true," Michael said.

"Because you can't fix me. I'm too far gone. Trust me on that," I said, and immediately knew I should have kept my mouth shut. I'd just stoked the flame, called the moth, and now I'd never lose him.

"No one's ever too far gone," he said sincerely.

I let out a dark laugh. I hadn't realized I had so many laughs in me before today. "Fine, then. I could use an extra pair of hands. Wait here for a second. There's some stuff I need to bring."

I'd enjoy watching him try to make me whole. It wouldn't work—I was a jigsaw puzzle with a piece long lost under the couch. There'd forever be that empty space in the stretch of blue that might have been a bird or a plane or a bomb.

He nodded, and my heart broke a little bit more. He was basically a golden retriever in human form: big, sweet, earnest, and a little bit dumb.

Upstairs, I scribbled a quick note for my parents in case they came looking for me: *Went for a ride with a friend. Don't worry about me. I'll be back soon. Love, Julia.* I paused and stuck the end of the pen in my mouth, considering whether I should scratch out Julia and write Lucy, who was, after all, who I'd been for over a year.

I left it as it was. Lucy had never really existed, and she certainly didn't exist anymore.

I grabbed a tote bag—not a backpack, never a backpack—and threw a bunch of stuff in there, turning each item over and over in my hands before stuffing it in with the rest. I left enough room for a few pairs of underwear in case things went wrong and I had to run. As I was in my drawer, scuffling around back for the laciest pair (Michael might be a golden retriever, but he had the legs of a Greek god, after all), my fingers brushed the edge of that one last picture. It sliced me right across a pad, bringing forth a thin line of red and a burst of a swear. Instinctively, I shoved the photo away, but once I'd sucked on my finger for a minute, I pulled it back out and considered.

This was my brother's cheek pressed against mine. This was my brother's hair in my eyes. This was my brother's slightly crooked front tooth, exposed in a beaming smile. This was my brother, before.

I tucked the photo into the pocket of my bag and slung it over my shoulder. "Michael," I called down the stairs, determination burning in my stomach, "I'm ready to go."

ELEVEN

After Evan, Liv, and Eddie, five kids died in quick succession. I didn't know them well then, but their names had since engraved themselves on my cerebral cortex. Elisabeth Wood. Irene Papadakis. Nina Smith. Danny Steinberg. Erick Thorson.

According to reports, those five had scattered toward the doors of the band room. There were three exits: one led outside to the athletic fields behind the school, another to the hallway that contained the instrument closets and the chorus room, and the last to the main school building. Ryan stood in front of the third, brandishing his gun. Elisabeth Wood, Nina Smith, and Erick Thorson had stampeded to the first. Irene Papadakis and Danny Steinberg—a couple, apparently—had raced hand in hand for the second. All five found their respective doors stuck. Superglue in the locks, the police later discovered.

My brother shot them all in the back. Elisabeth Wood, Irene Papadakis, Nina Smith, Danny Steinberg, and Erick Thorson bled out slowly. Nina Smith had been the last to die; she'd still been breathing, however shallowly, when the paramedics got to her. She died on the ride to the hospital, leaving any final words—or testimony—unsaid.

Our car ride was largely silent, a stark contrast to my memories of the screaming in the band room. I hadn't realized how late it had gotten, but when I thought back over this endless day, I couldn't believe how slowly it had gone. It was almost midnight. I hoped Goodman worked the night shift—it seemed he might, if he'd just left my house. I had to hope. I wished on stars shining white against the bruise-colored sky.

When we turned onto Spence's street, I took a deep breath. "Park down that way." I directed him past the house. He parked along the curb, and I hopped out, hoisting my bag over my shoulder, before he pulled to a stop. "We're going to go in through the back," I said. I squinted at the driveway. The black car wasn't there. Good.

"Won't it be locked?" Michael asked. We crept through someone's backyard, then slowed as we approached Spence's. Or Goodman's. I didn't care whose house it was, as long as Spence was in there. "Do you have a key?"

"No. I have something better." I pulled a lock pick from the front pocket of my bag and brandished it like a sword.

As it was only the size of a bobby pin, it wasn't very effective in inspiring anything but a roll of his eyes.

"A bobby pin?" It was sharp, though. It could totally poke out one of those eyes, if that was what I wanted to do.

"It's a lock pick. I'm going to pick the lock."

Lock picking isn't one of those skills they teach you in school. I'd had to teach myself. I wish I had a good reason for learning, something exciting and daring and romantic, like that my parents would lock me in a dark, dank basement cell and make me work my way out, or that I was the apprentice to a famous magician who trained me to undo locks with my teeth and my toes while under six feet of water. But really it had always been something that had fascinated me; I liked the thought that I could access anything anyone tried to hide from me.

And I'd always worried one day my brother would try to hide me.

It was too dark to see much, but I imagined Michael's face blanching. "That's illegal."

"You're not going to be taking part," I said. "You're going to stand guard while I'm inside."

"No way! What if he goes after you?"

"I can handle it," I said. "I really need you out here. You have to tell me if someone else comes home. Whistle."

"No," he said. "You can't go in there by yourself."

"Trust me," I said. "I can handle it. It's not like he's going to hurt me. I just need to talk to him, and I know if I knock on the door he won't answer." He probably would

141

answer, but that would involve giving up the element of surprise. I never liked to give up the element of surprise, not if I could help it.

"I don't like it."

"But you have to do it if you want to help me," I said impatiently. "Whistle if you see someone coming. Don't come inside no matter what. Promise."

"I can't promise that," he said. "If I hear you yell or anything, I'm running in there after you."

"Fine," I said. I wouldn't be the one yelling.

With that decided, Michael loped around the side of the house, his hands in his pockets. I quickly picked the lock on the back door—it wasn't even a dead bolt—and slipped inside.

The inside was just as shabby as the outside, with furniture probably bought off Craigslist scattered throughout: a couch with decorative blotches of something brown surrounding a rip in the cushion; a coffee table that leaned heavily to one side. The snores made it immediately apparent where Spence was, but I took the long way around just in case Goodman had parked his car in the garage or he had a lady friend over. The whole place smelled like old beer and dirty socks, and the kitchen was cluttered with dishes and pizza boxes. Gross.

But Spence was right where I wanted him. Alone. And I was ready.

I stopped to dig through my bag. As soon as I found what I needed, I placed the bag quietly behind an armchair.

I might need to move quickly, and I couldn't afford to have it slowing me down.

I tiptoed out of the living room and through the hallway. Just a few seconds later, I was blinking down at Spence's sleeping form. He was sprawled diagonally across the bed, sheets and blankets half covering him, his pillow hanging off the side. Everything smelled like BO. I wrinkled my nose, but I didn't have a hand free to hold it. I leaned over and pressed what I held in one hand against the side of his head.

His eyes popped open.

"Morning, sunshine," I said. His Adam's apple bobbed. "I've got a gun to your head. You can feel it, right?"

"You wouldn't dare shoot me," he said, but without much conviction.

I let out a cold, dry laugh. "Try me." Sure enough, he stayed frozen aside from his throat, which bobbed and worked as if he were trying to vomit a cue ball. "I've got these zip ties." I dangled them over him with my other hand. "You're going to take them, fasten your ankles together, and then fasten your arm to the bedpost. No sudden movements, now." I took a step toward the headboard, holding my hand firm, and let him grab the zip ties. I tensed, ready to fly into motion should he try to move, but he did exactly as I'd asked.

I took a big step back, out of range of his arms, and tossed aside what I'd been holding: a soda bottle I'd modified by weighing it down and bending metal around the lip.

When held to the head, it felt exactly like a gun. At least, it felt exactly like a gun to people who had never had an actual gun held to their head. Those lucky people.

"Now, let's get comfortable," I said. I leaned against the wall and crossed my arms. Without his glasses, he was squinting at me, bunching his face up into an ugly expression. He was wearing an old white T-shirt and what looked like plaid boxers. "Interesting. I thought you might sleep in those suits of yours. That would explain why they're always so wrinkled."

"I'm not telling you where Ryan is," he said immediately.

"I didn't ask you where Ryan was," I said. "It's interesting that you would jump to such a conclusion, though, isn't it?"

He only stared at me, his eyes lasers of fury.

I sighed. "Your friend Joseph Goodman paid a visit to my parents today. Or at least I'm assuming he's your friend, considering you were driving his car and are sleeping in his house. He's a cop, so I'm guessing you used him to help you break my brother out of the state facility. How'd you do it? Are you paying him?"

Spence's silence might have meant yes, might have meant no. To be honest, I didn't care either way. I just wanted to rattle him enough to make him crack. "You're *so* paying him," I decided. "You don't have the social skills to persuade him otherwise."

He just continued to glare. This wasn't going to get me anywhere. I changed tactics. "So your buddy—employee—

said my brother was missing. Apparently he woke up from his coma a long time ago. Apparently he's been talking. You wouldn't know anything about that, would you?"

A muscle ticked in his jaw. "I was your brother's psychologist. I was helping him."

"Ah. I see. Did they bring you in to talk to him after he woke up? Did you kidnap him? What did he say to you? Did he convince you he didn't do it or that he was out of his mind at the time? He's charming, my brother. Sociopaths usually are."

The muscle ticked harder, like it might spring free from his face and run away.

"You've been following me for several days," I said. "You've been trying to get me alone. To talk to me. Well, now you have me alone. Go ahead. *Talk to me.*"

He was silent. He'd been trying to obtain the element of surprise, following me everywhere. Maybe now that I had the advantage, he wasn't sure what he should say.

"Do you know where my brother is?" I asked. "Did you help him escape? Did you and your buddy kidnap him? Are you holding him somewhere?"

Still nothing. If anything, his eyes narrowed, burning more intensely into my skin.

"I don't have time for this. You're just trying to stall until your buddy gets home. Sorry, Doc." I bounced myself upright, took a scan of him to make sure he was tightly secured, and strolled out of the room. I could hear him spring into action as soon as I left, but any struggling would only tighten the ties, and unless he had a knife lying around in his bed—I was pretty sure he didn't or he would have pulled it on me already—the ties would hold fast.

As I'd expected, someone who couldn't be bothered to wash his dishes or pick up his clothes also couldn't be bothered to properly secure his guns. There was Goodman's stash, two guns lying right there on the table. I was almost disappointed. I'd practiced so much on picking safes and locks, and I wouldn't even get the chance to put my skills to use. I was even more disappointed by the feel of the gun I lifted from the table. I'd never held one before, and it didn't make me feel as powerful as I thought it would. It was just cold. And heavy.

I wondered if my brother had felt the same way.

Sure enough, Spence was still properly secured when I made my return, his eyes slits of molten lava. "Untie me right now," he said. "We're doing this for his own good."

"Then why is everything so secret? What did he tell you? What did he say?" I paused. "What did you do with him?"

Spence licked his lips. They were dry and flaky, like a shedding snake. "He's safe," he croaked. "He's safe now. Just let it be."

"If he's so safe, why were you out here following me around?" I clenched all my muscles. "Tell me where he is. Tell me what you want from me."

He said something under his breath. I leaned in. "I didn't hear you."

He spoke up. "Your brother talked to me," he said, his voice curiously flat. "He told me to find you. I'm here because of him."

I stiffened. "You're lying. Ryan would never talk to you."

"But he did." Now his voice was calm, curiously calm for someone tied to a bed. You'd think he was telling me there was too much mayo on his sandwich, or that it was supposed to rain later this week. "So you know why I've been so eager to get you alone. Talk to me, Julia. I can help."

He was lying. He had to be lying, or he'd be more specific.

But I'd thought he was lying last time, too.

I had to talk to my brother. "Tell me what you did with him."

"All you need to know right now is that he's safe. And you can be safe, too. Talk to me, Julia."

I ignored him and leaned in closer, so close he could smell my breath. I hoped it smelled like anger. "You have one more chance," I hissed. "Tell me what you did with him."

He said nothing. My fingers tightened around the gun. He was doing this on purpose. He was trying to *hurt* me on purpose. He deserved to be scared. He deserved to wonder whether he was going to die, the way I'd wondered whether I was going to die behind that music stand, because Spence hadn't fixed my brother the way he'd said he would.

I had to threaten Spence with the gun. It made me feel like I had a belly full of grave dirt, worms squirming and all, but I had no choice. I couldn't walk meekly back into the night and let him keep coming after me. If anything, his reticence made him more menacing. He only wanted to talk to me when he had the upper hand.

And he had done something with my brother.

In the end, I got the words I needed: 5464 Harmony Lane. I sliced through the zip ties, stuck them in my bag, and left him alone in the silence.

When I emerged from the back door and made my way around front, Michael was standing in front of the house with his arms crossed, his jaw working with worry. He nearly threw himself at me as I came into view. "Thank God, Lucy—Julia," he panted. "I was about to bust in there. You were in there so long I was starting to panic."

My heart was finally starting to slow down. "I'm done. He told me what I needed. Thanks for standing guard. Everything's okay." I sighed. "We're going to have to part ways now, though."

He looked like an explosion had gone off inside him; he clutched his stomach, holding himself together, and his shoulders hunched forward. "What do you mean?"

"I need to go back to Elkton," I said. "My brother's been talking about the shooting. The police called in Spence to talk to him. Spence was his old psychologist. Something my brother did or said or whatever persuaded Spence to help break him free, and he's now being held in one of Spence's buddies' houses in Elkton awaiting further instruction."

Michael laughed. It wasn't a funny laugh, or a happy laugh. "That's insane," he said. "That's just . . . insane."

"Well, it's what's happening, so if it's insane, then so be it," I said.

"And what are *you* planning to do in Elkton?" He grabbed me by the wrist. Not hard—if I'd pulled, my arm would have slipped free. I didn't pull, though. "Let's call my dad and let the police take care of it."

Words stuck in my throat. "No police. Not yet. I just need to talk to him," I said. "Because he's awake, and he's alive, and he's . . ." I didn't even know what to say. Once I would've said *my other half.* Now I wasn't sure. "You and your"—I made swirls in the air—"sister-aunt in New York City who you never see wouldn't understand."

He shook his head. "I don't think I can do this. Your brother is . . ." Notorious. Infamous. Dangerous. ". . . a murderer. And he's probably being held under armed guard. What makes you think you can just waltz in there and talk to him? I'm telling you, let me call my dad. He's good at what he does. He'll keep it under the radar."

"No cops," I said firmly. "A cop helped kidnap him in the first place. If you call the cops, I swear to God"— I'll kill you—"I'll never speak to you again." Saying those words almost made me gasp with the hurt, but I held firm. Showed no weakness.

He shook his head. "Then you're going to have to do it alone. This is too much for me. I'm going home. I'm sorry, Lucy . . . Julia." He released my wrist, and my arm swung free. "I'll drive you home, if you want." He leaned in and hugged me.

Standing there, my cheek nestled against his chest, felt right. Suddenly the thought of going at this alone froze me so quickly I thought my ankles might shatter. I pulled back, stood up on my tiptoes, and before he could back away, pressed my lips to his.

Judging from the way he lowered his hands to my waist and pulled me in close, he wasn't that intent on leaving me behind. He smelled salty and still a little garlicky (let's be real: garlic is a beautiful smell), and the stubble coating his jaw scraped my chin. I pressed myself more firmly against him, parting my lips and letting his tongue slip inside my mouth, making me warm and golden and tingly from my throat to my belly.

I pulled away first, meeting his eyes with mine. He blinked a few times, looking dazed; he still gripped me by the waist, as if I were the only thing keeping him standing.

"I need you with me. Please come," I said. I blinked hard, trying to keep my eyes from glistening. I was pretty sure it didn't work. "Please don't leave me. Everybody always leaves me."

He sighed, cleared his throat, and ran a hand through his hair, leaving it sticking up in all sorts of weird directions.

Then he sighed again and pulled me back to him. "I'm here with you, Julia," he said. "I'm here."

We walked hand in hand to the car. I smiled a small, secret smile.

The ninth to be shot was the band director, Mr. Watson. At this point, only Mr. Watson, two other kids—Penelope Wong and Sophie Grant—me, and my brother were left standing. We called Mr. Watson "Mr. Walrus"—he had a belly big enough to swallow the room, perpetually red cheeks, and a mustache that drooped past the corners of his mouth. We only called him Mr. Walrus behind his back, of course. Walruses (walri?) had tusks.

Those tusks had been on full display the day of the incident. With no exits available and my brother bearing down, Mr. Walrus had decided to take those last two students' safety into his own hands; they had hunkered down on the floor, halfway under one of the risers, as if that would save them. Mr. Walrus flattened himself on top, covering both of them with his bulk. He might have begged and pleaded, or he might have gone to his death stoic and resolute. All I know is that my brother stood over him, fired down, and shot him in the back of the head. He died quickly, which was more than I could say for the two kids under him.

My brother had never been one to let something suffer unnecessarily, at least not on purpose. He was practical.

Spiders he took outside. Mice he trapped in release cages and let them run free in the woods or, one very memorable time, in Liv's bedroom. Even when our school had cockroaches and they were running around in the hallway bumping into walls, poison eating away at their rudimentary nervous systems, he went around crunching them all beneath his boots, giving them the small gift of quick deaths, if not painless ones. Even with the animals he killed, Fluffy and the others, he always killed them quickly before he cut them open to look at their insides.

That merciful trait was in full evidence in the band room that day. Sure, a lot of kids died. For some reason, known only to him, they had to die. But with the exception of poor Nina Smith (and that was unintentional), they all died within a few minutes. They might have had to die, but nobody had to suffer. Nobody except for me.

I took the gun with me, having stuck it in my bag with my zip ties and pepper spray and the photo of my brother.

I didn't know which item was the most dangerous.

As we got in the car, I crammed my bag back under my legs and snuck a glance at Michael. He still looked hesitant. I shifted in my seat so that our sides touched. Heat radiated through me. I touched his upper arm. "Thank you again."

"For the ride?"

I gave a little laugh. Ha-*ha*. "Not just the ride," I said. "For everything." I ran my hand down his arm and stroked the side of his thumb, curving my fingers so that my nails trailed over his skin. I felt the muscles in his wrist shiver. "For coming to Elkton with me. I don't know if I'd have the strength . . . to do it alone."

He smiled at me. Sunshine washed over my face. "Of course," he said. "I'm happy to be here. I want to be here. For you."

I smiled back. My cheeks felt cold.

"What's the address?" he asked, his finger poised over the GPS. I told him, and we set off. I kept sneaking glances at him, afraid he'd come to his senses at some point and turn this car back around, but he kept staring straight ahead, his fingers clenched around the steering wheel. The only sign he was still nervous was the twitching in his jaw.

I meant to think over strategies for getting inside the next house, for getting to my brother without alerting the guys who were sure to be in there with him. Instead, I fell asleep.

"Julia. Julia, wake up. We're in Elkton. I think."

I startled awake. The familiarity of the scene outside my window sucked all the breath from my lungs. The south of the state was beautiful, but it had been so white, so clean, so new.

Elkton was different. Elkton was home.

Here, there was actual weather, winters where I had to wear a coat and summers where we went to the beach. Here, the fog descended so low and so thick, walking through it was like walking through clouds, or a dream. Here, there

153

were endless vineyards stretching off into the rugged mountains where I'd gone hiking with my brother as a kid.

"We're almost there, I think," Michael said. He was tapping his fingers on the steering wheel again. He was nervous, probably because of what he thought I'd do next. I wished he'd just quit thinking. "Twenty minutes away."

I rustled in my seat, my nerves suddenly exploding. I was glad I had that gun. I hoped I wouldn't need it, but it made me feel safe.

"Are you okay?" Michael said. He reached over and squeezed my knee. I grabbed his hand before he could pull it away, and squeezed back.

"No," I said. It felt good to be honest, for once. "But I will be."

TWELVE

The house where my brother waited was past my old house. I debated whether I should look, or whether I should spend the time studying my increasingly fascinating shoes. Something rusty and brown crusted one of the toes; I sighed and rubbed it off, grinding it into the carpet of the car.

By the time we approached, I felt like I had no choice but to look. I was too curious; I wondered if reporters still thronged the street out front, if there were still eggs drying on the siding, if the new owners had repaired the front window through which some well-wisher had thrown a brick. Or if there were new owners at all. Maybe the city had just leveled the place altogether, pushing my entire childhood underground, as if my brother and I had never stood against the kitchen door and let our mother mark our heights on the wood. As if we'd never existed.

But it *was* still there, still squat and white, still

impeccably manicured. The red slashes down the front of the garage (more well-wishes) had been painted over, and the shutters had been repainted a dark green. An unfamiliar car sat in the driveway. It was a good thing I wasn't driving, because I probably would have smashed that intruder right through the garage door.

A million years ago, I had driven through that garage door. Like I said, I could drive; I just didn't. Maybe the third time I'd ever driven, my mom had come to pick me up from band practice, and I'd driven us home. I'd coasted down the road, through a number of lights and intersections, and had so proudly pulled us right into the center of the driveway. Then I'd hit the brake, only instead of hitting the brake I'd hit the gas. Oops. There went all my bat mitzvah money.

"Everything okay?" Michael asked, snapping me back to the present.

I startled in my seat. "That was my old house," I said. I blinked furiously. "It's hard to see it."

"It must be hard," Michael said. He licked his lips. "Do you mind if I ask . . . why . . ."

"Why he did it?"

"Do you know?" He chewed on the inside of his cheek. "Of course, if you don't want to talk about it, I completely—"

"No. It's okay." I sighed and rolled my shoulders. "He didn't leave a note or anything. We never knew why. But I know. It was my fault."

Electricity charged the air. "What? You didn't—"

"I didn't do it, obviously," I said, and leaned forward, hunching into myself as if I were a snail and could curl inside my shell. "But it was my fault. I failed him. I was supposed to help him, and I clearly didn't do it very well."

"Julia. You can't blame yourself." Michael's hand, warm and heavy, fell onto my shoulder. "This is in no way your—"

"He was in therapy for a while. Because of the things he did. We should have known." My hands, resting on my knees, curled into fists. "I should have known."

"It's okay. It's going to be okay." He rubbed my shoulder up and down, up and down, his fingers sliding over the bunched muscle beneath. "You're going to talk to him. That's why we're here, right? So we can find him."

I let the muscle ease just a bit, just so he could feel me relax. "Right."

"It's not your fault."

"Say it again."

"It's not your fault."

I let myself relax fully, and he took his hand off my shoulder, apparently confident he'd saved the day, yet again. "Ten minutes away," he said. "Do we have a plan?"

"I have a plan. You just need to follow me and try not to make any sudden movements or talk too loudly." I'd tucked the gun I'd taken from Spence's place in my pants, where it pressed right up against my spine. I knew later I'd have bruises like an abstract painting. You'd be able to hang me in a museum right next to the Picassos.

"I still don't like this."

"I know." I just didn't care. I couldn't afford to care right now.

My dead best friend had once lived on Harmony Lane. Fortunately she'd lived near the end, so we didn't have to pass her old house. Seeing my old house had been enough for one day; I didn't know if I could take Liv's, too. Just thinking of her sent a stab of pain through my chest.

Liv's distinguishing characteristic had been her niceness. If she'd been in Harry Potter, she most definitely would have been a Hufflepuff. I told her this once, and she got mad at me. Like, legitimately mad, not fake mad. She didn't speak to me for three hours before I finally rolled my eyes and told her I'd totally made a mistake. She should have been in Slytherin with me.

Maybe she wasn't that nice, come to think of it. But still, I'd never once seen a food drive to which she didn't donate or a volunteer shift at the elementary school for which she didn't sign her name, and she was known for feeding and petting the stray cats that lived in her backyard, even though she was allergic. That was what I'd planned to say at her funeral, except, of course, I hadn't been allowed to go.

"Here we are." Michael slowed in front of the house, but I waved him on, craning my neck as we passed. It was almost disturbingly ordinary: neat black shutters, two floors, patchy green grass. A tricycle lay on its side on the front lawn, and I stifled a flash of fear that Spence had given me the wrong address.

Too late to worry about that now.

Michael pulled to a stop a few doors down, and I hopped out. "Thanks," I said. "You can keep watch again."

He shook his head. "I'm not keeping watch again," he said. "Anything could happen to you in there. I'm coming in with you."

I didn't have time to argue. My brother was in there; people could be hurting him as we spoke.

Or worse, my brother could be hurting other people.

I clutched my lock picks tightly in one hand. "Fine," I said, and took off. I slipped my flats off so I wouldn't stumble as I ran, and prayed I wouldn't hit a nail. Grass flew beneath my soles, moist and scratchy. I hoped Michael would have enough sense not to yell after me—not my real name, at least—and wasn't disappointed. I heard him grunt and scramble for the lock on his door, but by then I was already in the backyard. He didn't stand a chance.

Still, my hand was shaking as I picked the lock on the back door. This situation was a lot more volatile than the one at Spence's house—I hoped it would just be the two guys Spence specified plus Ryan inside, but for all I knew the entire Elkton police force could be hosting their annual pizza party in the living room.

The door cracked open easily, and I slipped inside. There *was* a dead bolt, only it had been left unlocked, which was odd. The air had the feel of a museum: the house smelled kind of musty, and there was a stillness to it, like no one had moved through it in a long time. I held my breath and listened hard.

I didn't hear anyone talking or moving. Maybe Spence had given me the wrong address after all.

Wait. I couldn't hear anything, but I could smell something. Something distinct. I closed my eyes and inhaled deeply. I knew this smell, and just its presence sent me hurtling back to the band room. I had to clench my fists and bite hard on the inside of my lip not to scream.

It was blood. The house hung heavy with the smell of blood.

The door pushed me from behind; I grabbed for the gun without thinking. Before I had the chance to aim it, I saw the intruder was Michael; relief swept through me like a cool breeze.

His eyes were practically popping with annoyance, and then he caught a whiff and shrank back. "Is that blood?" he whispered. His eyes flickered to the gun in my hand, but then right back up to my face. He trusted me. He trusted me with a gun.

I gave a curt nod. My heart was hammering sickly in my throat. I could hardly breathe. "Wait here," I whispered back. I almost dropped the gun, my hand was so sweaty.

He shook his head and grabbed my other hand. I didn't bother arguing. I knew this time I wouldn't win.

Together, we crept through the hallway and into what appeared to be the living room. The house had an open layout, the rooms flowing into and out of each other without doors or walls in the way, and everything was modern and chrome and white.

Except the couch. The couch *had* been white. Now it was a canvas of red and brown and a shade of purple I'd never seen before. It could hang on the museum wall right next to my back.

I took a few steps forward, holding my breath again. Someone—or something that had once been a someone—was sprawled over the cushions, his head propped on the armrest as if he were taking a nap. I squinted.

Someone had shot the figure straight in the mouth; small, jagged bits of his teeth were scattered on the cushions around the remains of his face and all over the floor. Even Joseph Goodman, dentist to the stars, couldn't help him now.

"His teeth," Michael whispered. Then he leaned over and threw up on the dead guy's feet.

Pride was hot in my chest. I wouldn't throw up. I hadn't even thrown up in the band room. "There should be one more. Where is he?" I whispered back, ignoring the smell of sick.

Michael shook his head and wiped his lips with the back of his hand. I looked over the room. Aside from the scene on the couch, everything was white.

Except . . .

Spatters of red led toward the staircase. I didn't think they were from the dead guy; there was no way he could have moved anywhere after that wound. I jerked my head at the blood spatters, and Michael nodded slowly, heavily, glancing at the gun in my hand from the corner of his eye. I knew he didn't like it, but it wasn't as if he had a better idea.

And he trusted me.

Together, we set off after the spatters. We had to move quietly—those spatters suggested injury, but not necessarily a mortal one.

I was glad for the warmth of Michael's palm in mine.

Upstairs was just as white as the downstairs. I'd thought it was modern at first, but now the endless expanse of nothing was beginning to unnerve me. The bloody trail continued. I felt like Hansel and Gretel must have felt, following some especially macabre bread crumbs.

The spatters took us to a closed door at the end of a hallway—a bedroom, I assumed. I squeezed Michael's hand. He squeezed back, shooting a jag of strength up my arm, through my shoulder, and straight into my heart. I squared my shoulders, clutched the gun in my other hand, and kicked open the door.

The second guy waited inside. I lowered the gun. He'd be no threat in his current state. He stretched half on, half off the bed, his legs—one mangled, one whole—resting on the floor, his head and arm resting on the blankets, the bloody hole of his chest propped up against the bedside. My best guess was that he'd been shot with something heavy in the shoulder downstairs—probably someone aiming for the chest and missing—and then shot in the knee later. The shooter had finished with an accurate shot to the chest.

Michael released my hand; I glanced over to see him retching again. The air was cold against my palm. I listened hard, but there was no sign of the shooter.

The shooter. Who was I kidding? My brother. There was no sign of my brother.

I took another step into the room. I was looking for something. I wasn't sure what, but there was something here.

I found it on the other side of the bed. A photo. The same one I had in my bag.

I wondered how he'd gotten a copy. It wouldn't have been hard for someone to find it. Julia Vann had had it as her profile picture a while back. It was a good picture.

I wondered why he'd left it behind. Saliva lodged in my throat. I folded the photo into tiny fourths and stuffed it in my pocket.

Footsteps sounded behind me. Michael. "What was that?" he asked, his voice strangled.

I swallowed. "Nothing," I said. "I thought I saw something, but it was nothing."

The rest of our time in that house passed in a blur. Somehow Michael and I found our way out of that room and back down those stairs and back through the living room and out the front door, which we left hanging open behind us like a missing tooth.

Michael had his phone out by the time we reached the car, but he looked too petrified to speak. I laid a hand on his arm to stop him anyway.

"What are you doing?" he asked. Guess I was wrong.

"Don't call the police."

He looked at me like I was crazy. Ha. I was getting there. "Of course we have to call the police," he said, speaking slowly and moving his lips in big, exaggerated shapes that served to annoy me more than anything else. "Those men in there were dead. They were . . . murdered. And there's a dangerous—" He caught my eye. "Sorry."

"Don't be sorry," I said. "My brother is dangerous. But if we call the police right now, they'll suck us up into questioning. They'll want to know what we were doing here. How we knew to come here. How we knew those men. And even if we tell them we had nothing to do with it, who's to say they'll believe us?"

"My dad is one of them," Michael said. His Adam's apple bobbed up and down, up and down. It was hypnotizing. "The police are good. They wouldn't—"

I found his hand and squeezed, which stopped the words clean in his throat. "Once your parents find out who I am, where I brought you today, do you really think they'll let us be together?" I said softly. "Especially with your dad being a cop."

Up and down. Up and down. "My dad would never . . ." I didn't even have to squeeze his hand; he trailed off on his own.

"Exactly," I said. "So we say nothing. Someone will realize what happened eventually." Like the good doctor and his friend. I couldn't imagine they wouldn't be checking in with these guys every day or two. "If a few days go by and we don't see it in the news, we can make an anonymous call from a pay phone."

"Okay," Michael said. "I trust you."

I squeezed his hand again. "Don't worry." And then, to myself as much as to him, "Everything will be okay."

That might have been what the two kids trapped under Mr. Walrus had thought. They couldn't move. They couldn't run. They had to lie there—reports say for three full minutes—as Mr. Walrus soaked them in blood and agonize as my brother grunted and strained, trying to roll Mr. Walrus over. He finally managed. Their names were Sophie Grant and Penelope Wong. They were freshmen and I had only spoken to them once before that period.

And then, with everybody dead or dying around us, my brother and I had twelve minutes alone.

Re: Ryan Vann, age 10

Ryan Vann is no longer a client. This will be my last entry on the subject.

After the fire, we—Ryan's parents and I—bumped up his sessions here to once a week. I met with him twice. Both times, I noted that he appeared to have regressed. He barely spoke; when I pressed him to speak, he gave me only one-word answers.

I was frustrated, to say the least. But I certainly wasn't prepared for what happened this afternoon.

Which is to say, simply, that he didn't show up. His mother came instead.

"Dr. Spence," she said, "I'm sorry this is so last-minute, but I need to cancel Ryan's appointment."

"I'm sorry to hear that," I said. "When shall we reschedule?"

The corner of her mouth twisted. "We're actually going to switch to a different psychologist," she said. "Ryan told us he feels uncomfortable with you after his last session."

I thought back to his last session. Nothing out of the ordinary had happened: I'd asked him how he was, how things were going, how he was doing in spelling, had he killed any small animals lately. Ryan had responded *fine, fine, fine, no,* and stared at the floor. We'd spent the last fifteen minutes in silence, me waiting for him to talk, him daring me to.

"How so?" I said.

She looked distinctly unsettled. "Look, Doctor," she said. "I know he's a liar, and what he said probably isn't true, but he's still my child, and I can't—"

"What did he say I did?" I interrupted. "Lying is a hallmark of conduct disorder. If he said I behaved in an inappropriate manner, I can assure you it isn't true."

"I know it probably isn't true," she said miserably. "But I still can't . . . He couldn't even tell me. He was too embarrassed. He told his sister, and Julia had to come to me." She shook her head. "When your child tells you that, you can't put them back in a room with that person. As a mother, I just can't." She was already moving toward the door.

"We can have supervised sessions," I bargained, following. "An aide can sit in with us if Ryan is willing."

She didn't stop. "Goodbye, Dr. Spence."

I stood and watched her go. She grew smaller in my view, her shoulders slumping and her hair hanging forward, as if she were crumpling in on herself. "Mrs. Vann!" I called after her. "He's going to grow up and do something terrible if we don't continue these sessions. Kids like this don't just spontaneously recover."

And still she didn't stop.

As I file this in Ryan Vann's folder, all I can say is that, for the first time, I hope I'm wrong.

THIRTEEN

My brother was looking for me. He was going to find me. Two weeks after Michael and I drove away from the dead men as quickly as we could, that was one of the things I knew for sure.

The dead men in the house popped up on the news the day after we returned to Sunny Vale. I spent the first week back in a state of paralyzing panic, freezing every time the school loudspeaker crackled to life or the doorbell at home rang, afraid the police had found a footprint or a trace of DNA that they'd pinned to me and Michael. But they never came. I had remembered to wipe doorknobs, and it seemed our car hadn't been spotted by any neighbors. True, Michael had left some congealed stomach contents behind, but the police didn't have the technology they had on TV. They couldn't trace it back to him without something to compare it to. We were safe, or so I hoped.

That second day back after Elkton, I distracted myself from my constant state of anxiety by going to apologize to Alane. She didn't show up to school on Monday, so my mom was kind enough to drop me off at Alane's house the next morning. "I am the worst friend in the world," I said through tears as soon as she opened the door. "I can't believe I just left you there at the hospital. If you close the door in my face right now, I totally won't blame you."

I stood and waited for her to close the door in my face. Not because she was so angry at me, but because she now knew who I really was.

She didn't close the door in my face. Instead, she burst into tears, too. Now we made a matching pair. Collectibles. "I Googled you," she said. "I can't believe what you've been through."

We might have stood out there all day, except that her neighbors were beginning to leave for work, and so there were some stares. "Come in," she said, and turned her back to limp inside.

Turning her back to me so blithely? Trusting me not to stab her or shoot her or strangle her or whatever everybody back home thought I'd do?

That meant more to me than the open door.

I cried on her shoulder. She cried on mine. Tears got everywhere. It was soggy. "I feel like such a jerk," I said. "I mean, I was a jerk. You were in the hospital, and I was acting like such a jerk, and I just ran off, and—"

She shook her head. "I can't believe I didn't know,"

she said. "Did that guy have something to do with your brother?"

I closed my eyes. I knew I could tell her the truth. "He's missing," I said. "My brother. And he's awake. We don't know where he is."

She rubbed circles into my back the way a mother would do. Not *my* mother, of course, but maybe a different mother, to a different child. "It'll be okay," she said. "It'll be okay."

The second week brought the police. I nearly choked on my own lungs when I woke up one morning and opened the window to see a black car idling out front, two androgynous figures in suits reclining in the front seats. Not Goodman and West, I saw when I squinted. Two other people I could only assume were cops.

They didn't come for me, though. Or for Michael. We were still safe.

No, they were clearly looking for my brother. The word was out, and suddenly there were men and women in black suits everywhere I looked. They must have thought my brother would make a beeline for me. I hadn't seen him. I wished them luck.

Fortunately, the police were keeping quiet about my brother's escape. The police clearly knew he was on the loose, but the news and the papers and the Internet hadn't picked it up. Slowly I let myself breathe.

At the end of that second week, early on Saturday morning, my mom knocked on my door and, without waiting for an answer, stepped into my room. From the way she was wringing her hands, I could tell she had bad news. "Bring it on," I said. Whatever she had to say couldn't be worse than what I was thinking.

My mother perched on the end of my bed. She stared at me, but her eyes kept flickering away to take in the crumbs on my desk and the dirty clothes scattered over my floor. She sighed. "Lucy, I have some bad news. Do you remember your and . . . and . . . your old psychologist, in Elkton?"

My stomach turned to ice. "Dr. Spence?" Oh no. He'd talked. He was back. He was coming for me.

"Yes." My mom scooted closer and laid a hand on a lump in the blankets she probably assumed was my knee. It was actually a bag of chips, but close enough. "He was found dead in his home. Out here, actually, near Sunny Vale. He must have moved. Didn't you say you saw him once?"

The ice moved up my chest, turning my skin cold and clammy. I didn't answer her question. "Do they know what happened?"

My mom sighed, and the corner of her mouth twitched. "The police say it looks like . . . that it looks like . . ." She sighed again, and she looked down at her lap. "Like it was murder. Like it was . . . like it was . . ."

She didn't finish. She didn't have to. We both knew what she was trying to say.

"That sucks," I said. My voice trembled. "Does it look like he's . . ."

"They're going to be watching our house," my mom said. "In case Ry—" She changed course abruptly. "It does suck. It sucks hard."

I cocked my head. I'd never heard her speak like that before. She'd probably leave the room and go wash her mouth out with soap. "Thanks for telling me," I said.

She moved away. I kind of hoped she'd try to pat my knee again, but no luck. "You're welcome," she said. Or even pat the bag of chips. She could've tried to pat the bag of chips again, and that would have been just fine.

I had two pictures left of my brother now. I kept them behind my underwear drawer, and I kept my brother in my mind. I was ready for him.

Monday morning I climbed into Alane's car, books cradled in my arms. "How's Michael?" she asked.

"Fine," I said. "I think." I hadn't seen him since our trip to Elkton. Well, I'd seen him, of course, at school. That was unavoidable. But every time he'd tried to talk to me, or to kiss me, I'd turned away. He'd even shown up at my house a few days ago, ingredients for chicken noodle soup in hand. I'd had my mom tell him I wasn't home, but he'd looked up before he got into his car and seen me watching him from my bedroom window.

She looked at me sadly. "He really likes you, you know."

"I know. Even though he knows who I really am."

She gasped. "He does?"

"Yeah." But he still liked me. He really shouldn't. I'd had two boyfriends back in Elkton: Evan, whose blood probably still soaked the band room floor (they would have changed the carpet, of course, but blood doesn't come out of concrete; I knew that from experience), and before him, Aiden Williams. Aiden had met his end in a tragic car accident. Totally unavoidable. Or so the police said. "But my brother is out there. And my boyfriends don't fare so well when my brother is around. I can't put Michael at risk."

"Ah. Right." A spasm of fear contorted her face for a moment, and I remembered: my best friends didn't fare so well when my brother was around, either. "Do you think . . . what do you think is going to happen?" Her knuckles were white on the steering wheel.

I knew what would happen, or at least what my brother hoped would happen, because I knew the inside of my brother's head as well as I knew mine. Better, maybe.

Right now he was searching for me. I would literally be willing to stake my life and Alane's life on that. He'd probably hide out, lie low for a while, after Spence's murder, but then he'd come for me. I didn't think he'd be so bold as to steal a car, because he'd want to take as few chances as possible to avoid ending up back in police custody. That would be fine with him. He was patient. Maybe he'd steal some kid's bike, or buy a bus ticket. I could even picture him walking, his curls matted with dust from the side of the road. Slowly but surely, he'd make his way to me once again.

Assuming he could. Goodman and West had talked

about Ryan being in rehab. I didn't know what that meant. He might not be anything like he had been. Which could be a good thing.

Once he was here, though (assuming he made it), there were a few more possibilities. Like I said, he was patient; he wouldn't storm into homeroom, shouting drunkenly and waving his arms around. He would sit, and he would watch, and he would figure out the best time to strike. And by strike, I mean make himself known. He might want to start over, maybe disguise himself, move in with us as a cousin or a family friend or a tragic, pathetic orphan. No, not that. Ryan was many things, but he was not pathetic, or at least he'd never, ever see himself that way. No matter what, I knew he'd want me. It was just the matter of what he wanted from me. If what he wanted from me was something I could give. If he was angry I'd moved on without him.

There was another possibility, but I couldn't even think about that.

And then it struck me: it had been too long. He wasn't quite so predictable anymore. He might have changed wherever he'd been the past year, or, more importantly, his feelings for me might have changed. I couldn't wait for him to find me. I'd have to find him first. I had to find him and be absolutely sure he wasn't planning on doing anything stupid. I had to keep Alane and Michael safe. And I had to keep Ryan safe from the police. No matter what he'd done, he was still my brother, and I still had to talk to him. I still loved him. I couldn't let them kill him. Not now that he'd sprung back to life.

"I think everything is going to be okay," I said. I'd find another ride home today.

She didn't respond, only turned back to the road, her face expressionless. Without her customary smile and enthusiasm, her cheeks were ashy and her lips thick. I turned my attention to the black car trailing us and waved in the rearview mirror. The black suit didn't wave back.

As soon as we parted ways after homeroom, Alane's smile back but a little shaky, I saw Michael waiting for me in the hallway. Well, he was talking to a few of his friends, swaggering high fives all around, and very deliberately not looking at me, but I could see he noticed me from the way his eyes flickered and the way his chest pointed in my direction. Body language—he should learn how to mask his.

His friends retreated as I approached, leaving Michael alone. He turned away, showing me his back, and rummaged in his locker. When I'd been standing there for a full five seconds, he glanced over his shoulder. "Oh, hey," he said dispassionately. "Didn't see you there."

I had to keep him safe, but I couldn't bear to let him continue thinking I hated him. I rolled my eyes, then grabbed him by the shoulders, spun him around so fast his shoes squeaked, and kissed him hard on the mouth. It was almost like kissing a cat; his muscles were stiff under his skin, bunched like coiled springs. He gasped as I pulled away, and in the corner of my eye I could see people staring. I didn't care.

"Well, hello to you, too," he said.

"I don't like playing games," I said. "I like you. You like me. And I appreciate all you've done for me and the way you've kept my secret. But we have to keep our distance for a little while." I looked from side to side, then spun quickly to look behind me. I turned back with a pointed look. Sure, I'd been dramatic, but I had to make sure he got—really got—what I was saying. "My brother could be anywhere."

"Julia—"

"Call me Lucy."

"Lucy, come on. I'm not scared. If he—"

"I have to go." I turned my back and walked away, nearly running down Ella, who'd been hovering nearby. She wrinkled her nose at me and I was sure she was going to say something, but I just kept walking.

That was my attitude for the rest of the day: I just kept clear. When Ava of the hideous feathery earrings turned around to model her newest creation (a necklace made of pinecones and birdseed), I smiled tightly and turned my attention to Señor Goldfarb, who was talking about some verb tense or other. When Michael threw notes at me, I let them bounce off my chest and land with crisp thuds on the floor. When I saw Alane waiting for me after show choir to give me a ride, her knee jiggling nervously, I backed away, texted her that my mom was going to pick me up, and used another exit. I lived about a forty-minute walk from the school. That was acceptable. That was okay. For now. Maybe one of the black suits would give me a ride.

My parents weren't home when I got there, but our new security system was blinking a reassuring green. I didn't think Ryan would hurt me.

Still, it never hurt to be careful.

I had never gone inside this house's garage, and it took ten minutes of deep-breathing and relaxation exercises to calm myself enough to do so. Even then, my hands shook and my throat went dry as I opened the door. A blast of musty air hit me, and as I flipped on the light, spots I hoped were spiders skittered in the corners of my vision.

I hadn't driven since the car accident that killed Aiden. I hadn't been driving then, either, actually, but after that I'd never wanted to put my foot on a gas pedal again. It had taken lots and lots of relaxation exercises even to make myself get into the passenger seat of a vehicle.

Aiden was my very first kiss and my very first boyfriend and the very first boy (besides my brother, of course, which was a very different case) to whom I said "I love you," even if I hadn't really meant it. I'd loved his eyes that flashed from brown to gold in the sun, sure, and the pale stubble that graced his glass-cut jaw. I'd loved the way he'd hold me to him as if otherwise I'd float away, and the way my knees would literally wobble when he touched me. I loved the way my throat would go raw from cheering every time he scored a goal on the soccer field, and the envious glances

I'd get from the other girls every time Aiden would stop at the sidelines to scoop me into his arms for a good-luck kiss. But I hadn't loved him.

My sophomore year. Aiden's senior year. An old car that was always failing: the brakes were frayed, the air conditioning was the breeze from an open window (and the windows were always open because the levers were broken), and the radio was stuck on a country-music station, which I thought was the worst part of all. It really wasn't much of a surprise when the brakes stopped working altogether and we'd sailed through the fog, shrieking and screaming, into one of Elkton's monumental ivy-covered trees.

I tumbled out of the car with some scrapes, some bruises, and a broken wrist. Aiden was pierced through the chest with a tree branch as thick as his leg. He'd barely had the chance to wheeze out one final cry before his eyes fluttered shut forever.

The tree didn't make it, either; it was shattered into mulch that now carpeted some stranger's garden.

Without my brother, I might have died, too. Somehow he was there, pulling me from the wreckage. He'd cradled me by the side of the road, whispering into my hair, as Aiden blinked his last blink and my wrist dissolved into symphonies of pain.

Just the thought made me shudder. This car, in this garage, wasn't the same car as then, but it looked too close for my taste: four wheels, a windshield, a steering wheel I really, really didn't want to sit behind. I brushed hair out of my eyes; strands stuck to the sweat beading on my forehead. I couldn't depend on my brother anymore, obviously. I couldn't depend on Michael or Alane. I had to depend on myself, and in order to depend on myself, I had to be able to drive a car.

I got as far as touching the door handle before my heart seized and my throat swelled shut. I gasped for breath. Funnily enough, as soon as I backed away I could breathe just fine, though my heart still hammered. Maybe the problem was that I was allergic to my car.

Well, forty minutes wasn't so long to walk to school.

As I went back inside, I consoled myself with the thought that I'd be getting a ton of exercise. I'd be so healthy I'd squeak. My legs would be super toned and I would maybe even get my first-ever tan and—

Something creaked. I froze.

My parents hadn't gotten home yet; they would've pulled into the garage, or I would've heard them in the driveway. "Hello?" I called. "Ryan? Is that you?" A footstep, then the yawn of a door. I froze. A black suit? "Ryan William Vann, you have thirty seconds to show yourself or I'm going to scream."

"Whoa. Whoa, Lucy, whoa." It was Michael's voice; I relaxed a tiny bit but remained alert. Ryan could be holding a gun to his head for all I knew.

"What am I, a horse?" I called. "How did you get in my house?"

"Dude, I was worried about you!" This was Alane. I crept

179

through the hallway until they came into view—Michael and Alane stood in the entryway, their foreheads creased in concern, and then there was also . . . Ella. Ella of the black pixie cut and the crush on Michael. Worry wormed through me. Had she heard me call for Ryan? Of course she'd heard me call for Ryan. I had practically been screaming. "Your text felt weird, and someone told me they'd seen you walking into the woods after school. I was afraid you were mad at me or something." She paused for a moment. "Also, your door is open. You shouldn't just leave it open like that."

Had I left the door open? I didn't think I'd left the door open. But I might have. I hoped I had.

I stole a glance at Ella. She was smiling a small, secretive smile. That was bad. Did she recognize my brother's name? "Ella, why are you here?"

She stole my glance back and directed it at Michael. "Michael's giving me a lift home," she said. "I'm just along for the ride."

That was right. Ella was a swimmer, too. My breathing came a little bit easier. "You guys shouldn't be here," I said. "You should go."

Alane and Michael stood like statues, their legs spread and arms crossed. Ella looked back and forth between them and shrugged, then pierced me with her eyes. "I'm not getting in the middle of this," she said. "I'll be waiting in the car, Mike."

Mike? Really? "Why'd she call you Mike?"

"Because it's my name," Michael said. "Listen. We need to talk."

That kiss in the hall had clearly been a mistake. I just hadn't wanted him to think I really didn't like him. He was clearly too dumb to understand the intricacies that came with kissing Lucy Black *or* Julia Vann. "No, *you* listen," I said. "You know all my secrets. You know what happened to my last boyfriend and my last best friend. I can't take the chance my brother will go after you." Alane opened her mouth, but I steamrollered right over her. "Don't try to convince me otherwise."

"I talked to my dad," Michael said. I remembered the warmth around that family table. "The state police are out searching. His department is helping them. They're all looking for him, and they're going to find him."

"He will stop at nothing," I said flatly, "to get to me."

"You've said that," Alane said. There was something different about her I couldn't quite put my finger on; it was as if she'd rechanneled her nervous energy and cheer into a fierce sort of determination. That was it—she wasn't fluttering her hands or patting me on the shoulder. She stood still, erect, her chin high, her eyes flashing. "Which is why we can't let you do this alone."

"You trusted us with your secret," Michael said. "Now trust us with this."

I felt like I was going to choke on the tears rising in my throat. "You guys . . ."

Alane stepped forward and slung an arm around my shoulders. "Michael's going to go take Ella home, and we are going to do something suitably girly and frivolous," she said. "I could go for painting my nails. Do you want to paint your nails?"

I smiled through the blur of tears. "Yes. Yes, I do."

She tightened her arm, nearly choking me again. "Only you'll have to do both of us, because I can't paint my nails without getting the polish all over. I'm pretty sure my cuticles are still tinted orange from the last time."

"Are you kidding me? Your *fingers* are still orange from the last time." I forced a fake laugh and let her hug me so hard I could barely breathe.

Everything would be okay. I had to believe that, or else I'd drown for real.

Re: Ryan Vann, age 17

I was right.

Generally being right doesn't make one this unhappy.

Nine months ago, Ryan William Vann shot and killed eleven people in his high school band room. His sister, Julia, traumatized, shaking, covered in blood, was the only one to come out alive. Well, Ryan—the client, now—came out alive: in an attempt to shoot himself in the head, he put himself into a coma for a few days. Or the doctors had put him into a medical coma. I'm still not entirely sure. There's a reason medical doctors call us fake doctors.

A week or so after the shooting the client opened his eyes, blinked, and asked, "Where am I?"

This is all according to the state police, who are on the case. They hadn't leaked any of this to the media. They'd taken the client to one of their secure facilities, ostensibly for rehab before the stress of a trial. Off the record, one mentioned Ryan had said a few very interesting things as he was coming out of his coma, things that merited observation before throwing him to the lions of the public and the justice system.

Officer Ali Noor is the one who came to find me. "You're Dr. Atlas Spence, correct?" he said, glancing down at his fancy, slick phone.

"Yes," I said.

"Good," he said. "And you had Ryan Vann as a client when he was a child, correct?"

I tensed. "I'm not speaking about this to the press," I said, already retreating into the safety of my office. "Have a nice—"

He put out his hand and stopped my door from closing. It was that one gesture, that expression of authority, that made me listen.

"Let me speak with you inside," he said.

He explained that he was from the state police, and then let me examine his ID and phone two of his superiors. He explained that Ryan Vann had awoken from his coma almost nine months ago. "But I haven't seen that in the papers," I said.

"You wouldn't have," Noor said. His manner was crisp, efficient. "We're keeping it quiet. We want him to have the chance to complete his rehab, to finish relearning how to talk, and then we want to talk to him before the lynch mob comes out. Find out why he did it." He chewed on the inside of his cheek. "He said a few . . . things when he was half-conscious and coming out of the coma, but once he woke up for real, he clammed up. He's finally well enough to be interrogated."

"Interesting," I said cautiously. "So what does this have to do with me?"

Noor sat back in his chair, folding his hands on his lap. "He says he'll only talk to you, Doctor," he said. "So what do you say?"

What do you say to something like that? Obviously I said yes. This was the career opportunity of a lifetime. I wouldn't just be Atlas Spence, PhD, psychologist. I would be Atlas Spence, PhD, criminal psychologist brought in to consult with the state police. Who knows? This could be the first of many cases.

I hadn't seen the client in many years and had braced myself for how he was sure to look, but I still had to hold in a gasp after Noor and another officer escorted me to Ryan's room at the secure state facility. I walked into the tiny, spare white room, outfitted with a cot and a sink and a toilet like a jail cell, to see Ryan sitting on his bed, facing the wall. Or maybe the window. There was a small window, high up on the wall. Barred, obviously. I couldn't imagine he could see out of it, but maybe he just liked facing it. Pretending he could feel the air on his face. "Good afternoon, Ryan," I said.

He turned. "Is it afternoon?" he said. His words were slow and slurred and looked painful as they came out; only the right half of his mouth opened all the way. "It's hard to keep track sometimes."

He seemed sane; that's what surprised me most. He was painfully skinny, and his chin was covered in a patchy coating of stubble. He moved one arm, his right, restlessly, tapping out a beat on his knee. The other, the left, hung by his side. Paralyzed, maybe, or partially paralyzed.

"It's three o'clock in the afternoon," I said. "I heard you wanted to talk to me."

"I do," he said, quite agreeably, quite different from the belligerent boy I remembered from so many years ago.

I moved closer, smiling in what I hoped was an approachable way. "Then let's talk," I said. "How are you today?"

And he didn't say another word.

That's the Ryan Vann I remember.

FOURTEEN

Alane stayed over that night; she'd already brought a bag with a change of clothes and a toothbrush, so she was pretty serious about this whole staying-by-my-side thing. "It's Michael's shift tomorrow," she said, and then wagged her finger in my face. "But no sleeping over for him, missy!"

I rolled my eyes. Alane hadn't so much as kissed a boy before, and as far as I knew, she had no plans to kiss anyone in the near future. It was as much a lack of access as it was a lack of desire; there were no straight boys in show choir, which was where she spent most of her time outside of school. There, or voice lessons. I'd heard her sing several times, and her voice always raised goose bumps on my arms.

Alane fell asleep quickly on the air mattress I'd pulled out of storage, her breaths dissolving into gaspy snores and the occasional squeak. I stretched out on my bed and watched her. Her eye kept twitching and the corners of her mouth kept going up and down, like she was trying to smile—or scream.

When I couldn't bear to lie there and stare at Alane or at my ceiling any longer, I climbed out of bed and tiptoed down the hallway. I could hear the TV murmuring behind my parents' door. I'd never knocked to ask, but I had a feeling they hadn't slept much this past year, either. Not like they would tell me even if I had knocked. That would mean they'd actually have to talk to me.

I paused at the end of the hallway, which overlooked the great picture window opening out on our backyard. I couldn't see much in the dark, but so many things were croaking and chirping and sawing there might as well have been an orchestra out there. Something was moving, though, a shadow, a man-shaped shadow, maybe a man in a black suit. . . .

I squinted, and the shadow was gone.

Sometimes I felt like that was the story of my life: I'd try too hard to think about something, or to figure something out, and even if the answer was right there, in front of my face, I'd just keep staring blindly through it. That feeling applied especially to those twelve minutes—the twelve minutes that elapsed between my brother shooting Penelope Wong in the head and putting a bullet in his own.

I wondered if I'd begged for my life; maybe I'd thrown myself on the floor before him, touched my forehead to his toes, sprinkled the carpet with tears. Or maybe I was stoic and resolute, facing death with my chin held high.

Or maybe he hadn't meant to kill me at all. Maybe that was when he told me why he'd done it. Information my old pal Jenny wouldn't hesitate to suck out of me the way the ancient Egyptians would suck a soon-to-be mummy's brain out through his or her nose.

The answer was in there somewhere, swimming through my cerebral fluid like an electric eel; sometimes I felt the twitch or shock of it peeking through, but it always whooshed away before I could grab it. I didn't know whether I wanted to find it or not. Maybe I was better off if it stayed gone.

Wait. I squinted and scoured the darkness outside. There *was* a shadow beneath one of our trees. The eel twitched.

Alane opened her eyes blearily as I slipped back inside my room. "I thought I heard you," she said, rubbing them with the back of her hand. "Where were you?"

"Bathroom," I said, and climbed back into bed. A few clippings of grass scattered on my sheets, and I brushed them into the slot between my bed and the wall.

She sat up. Her jaw cracked with a yawn. "Everything okay? You were in there an awfully long time."

I flopped back and said a silent hello to my old friend the ceiling. "I'm fine. Everything is fine." My eyes burned. "Go back to sleep."

* * *

Alane was back to her old self the following morning, as perky and cheerful with five hours of sleep as I'd never been in my entire life. She didn't even drink coffee.

I, on the other hand, dragged with every step, even after I'd downed an entire mug of coffee (black). I felt as if the earth were trying to suck me under. I wished I could bottle some sort of essence of Alane, reduce her to a liquid in a perfume bottle and spritz myself every time I was down. I bet it would be pink. Neon pink.

"Lucy, Alane, good morning!" Michael met us at the school gates, his smile too wide and too bright, or maybe that was just my tired eyes whining. "How was your night?"

"So fun!" Alane chirped back. She splayed out her fingers. Her nails were pink. Neon pink. "We had so much fun!"

I wouldn't have minded dying so much at that moment. The prospect of eternal sleep was just too tempting.

"Your nails look great," Michael said with vigor. "Lucy, let me see yours!"

I displayed mine, which were also pink, and Michael clucked and cooed over them as well. Michael and Alane were so bright, so cheerful, that it took me a moment to realize Ella was also there, lurking in Michael's orbit like an asteroid that was about to crash. "Oh, hi, Ella," I said. I looked up at Michael. "Did you guys carpool again?"

"We live right down the street from each other," Ella said.

"Oh, you do, Mike?" I said.

Alane linked her arm through mine. "Lucy, we should get to homeroom. I still haven't done my history homework."

"Fine," I said, giving Michael and Ella the side eye. I didn't think Michael would cheat on me. Nobody cheats on me. But I did think Ella had a thing for him, and I didn't like that. Whether I wanted him or not, Michael was mine.

I turned to go with Alane, and then I saw Ella's smile. It was so big it warped her face, making her cheeks huge and her eyes disproportionately tiny. Anger ripped through my chest, and I wrenched my arm free from Alane, who let out a worried squawk.

"See you in Spanish, Mike," I said, and pulled his face down to meet mine. He kissed me back hungrily, with no hesitation whatsoever. I pulled back and met Ella's eyes. I was sure mine were shining in triumph. Hers were unmistakably shining with something else. "See you later, Ella."

I had homework to do first period—an essay on motifs in *Jane Eyre,* which I'd never read and had no desire whatsoever to read—so I was worn out by second-period Spanish. Not too worn out, however, to notice the flurry of whispers that met me when I stepped through the doorway. They increased with every step I took toward my desk, crescendoing as I sat down. I blinked once, twice. No. It couldn't be.

Ava was already seated in front of me. Her new earrings brushed her shoulders, a hideous mix of dried flowers that shed wispy petals every time she shook her head. I tapped her on the shoulder. She didn't move. I tapped again, harder, more of a drumbeat. She finally turned her head, but only a fraction of an inch. "What?" she whispered.

I didn't know why she was whispering. People were still filing in. We hadn't even started class yet. "I love your earrings," I said as enthusiastically as I could manage. "Even more than the ones with the feathers. They're so . . . fragrant. Like potpourri. How did you make them?"

All the color drained out of her face, puddled on the floor, and soaked my feet through my shoes, cold and sticky. "I have to pay attention," she said, pointing feebly in Señor Goldfarb's direction. He was currently flicking through his phone, probably on RateMyTeachers, trying to figure out why he was the only Spanish teacher without any stars next to his name. "Sorry. Don't be mad. Please don't be mad!"

I turned away from Ava, trying hard not to care. I didn't care about Ava, really. She could think whatever she wanted, really. I had more important people to care about. Really.

Speaking of people I cared about, Michael ran in at the last minute, just as Señor Goldfarb was taking attendance, so despite all my attempts to catch his eye, we didn't have a chance to talk before class began. Unless he was intentionally avoiding all my attempts to catch his eye. Unless . . . no. He already knew about my brother. He'd seen firsthand what my brother had wrought. I had to stop being so paranoid.

"All right, then, let's go through the homework," Señor Goldfarb said in Spanish. "We'll go down the rows. Ava, why don't you start with number one?"

Ava babbled something I could only assume was correct, as Goldfarb moved on to me for number two. "Er . . . Lucy?"

I met his eyes, but only for a second, since his quickly skittered away like so many roaches in a burst of light. "I don't have it," I said in English. I did have the homework. It was right in front of me. Goldfarb could probably read it from where he was standing.

"That's fine," he said, still looking at the floor. "Eliza, why don't you continue with number two?" The whispers started again, swelling from the corners of the room to the center; even Ava leaned over to whisper something in her neighbor's ear.

They knew. Everybody knew.

I had to get out of here.

I jumped to my feet, bumping into my desk, which lurched forward and slammed into Ava's chair. Ava leapt to her feet, too, letting out a shriek and stumbling toward the front of the room, covering her head with her hands, like I was going to pull a gun on her. I wouldn't. I would never. Even if her earrings were a crime against fashion so dire she deserved the death penalty.

"I'm going to the bathroom," I blurted, and ran for the door. Nobody tried to stop me. I didn't think anyone would.

Everyone was in class, so the hallways were largely empty. As usual, though, there were a few people walking around: bathroom trips, things forgotten in a locker, teachers patrolling for kids cutting class. Every single one of them glanced at my face and then moved out of my way, some going so far as to flatten themselves against the rows of lockers. They weren't doing that lightly; those combination locks hurt when you jammed into them.

When one literally threw herself into the lockers, making a bang so loud I nearly dove into the lockers myself from surprise, I spun around to block her way. She was so tiny she had to be a freshman, with braided pigtails and eyeliner so thick it looked like she'd drawn it on with a crayon. I almost felt sorry for her. "How did you find out?" I demanded.

Her eyes had gone so wide I could see all the white around her pupils. "I don't know what you're talking about."

I fought the urge to grab her by her pigtails and throw her across the hall. Instead, I leaned in close; she cringed like she wanted to pull away, but she had nowhere to go besides through the metal of the lockers. "I know you know," I said. "I know everybody knows. You almost smashed yourself trying to get away from me. Tell me how you know, and I'll leave you alone."

Her face was slowly turning a pale shade of violet, as if she had forgotten to breathe. "My friend told me," she squeaked. "She said some girl stood up and told everyone in her homeroom this morning."

A horrible feeling roiled in the pit of my stomach. "Do you know who it was?"

She vigorously shook her head, striking me with the ends of her pigtails. "I don't! I don't know! Some junior, I think, but I don't know!"

Some junior. Some junior. I was willing to bet this

freshman's pigtails on the fact that *some junior* had a black pixie cut and a crush on Michael. "Okay." I stepped back and watched the freshman flee.

I took a few deep breaths and closed my eyes, just for a moment. I would go to the bathroom, not to actually go to the bathroom, but to sit in a stall for a few minutes and regroup. To get some quiet so I could figure out what my next move should be.

When I opened my eyes, though, ready to head to the handicapped bathroom on the second floor, an old friend was waiting in front of me. Her smile was plastic, and she held a notepad and pen under her arm. Not under her armpit, I noticed. She'd learned. "Jenny," I said. "I see you're not in jail."

"Julie Vann," said my reporter nemesis. And there it was: the lightning bolt of *wrong* the nickname produced in me. Exactly what I'd wanted when I'd told her, so long ago, to call me Julie instead of Julia. "How have you been?"

"There's no way you could have made it here from Elkton this fast. Ella just told everyone this morning. Like, two hours ago," I said. I blinked a few times, hoping I had a brain tumor or something and she was just one of the resulting hallucinations. Alas, no luck.

Jenny clapped her hands together and smiled even wider. She had traces of red lipstick on her teeth, unless it was blood—it was entirely possible she'd just finished eating some babies. "I'm no longer with the *Sun,*" she said. "My story on the shooting raised my profile so much that I'm now with the *Los Angeles Times*. When we got this morning's tip you were here, I volunteered to check it out. How lucky is this?"

I tried to get around her, but she moved to block me. I balled my fists. The only reason I didn't haul off and punch her was because I knew she'd spin a story around it. *Sister of Shooter Goes on School Rampage, Attacks Innocent Reporter Recently Nominated for a Pulitzer Prize.* "Please get out of my way," I said icily. "I need to get to class."

"You're going the wrong way, then, aren't you?" Her smile didn't budge. It was as if she'd painted it on with her lipstick. "You're supposed to be in Spanish class right now with Mr. Goldfarb. You share that class with your boyfriend, don't you? Michael Silverman?"

I ground my teeth and made a mental note to text Michael and Alane as soon as I was out of this hallway: *Don't talk to any strangers about me. Don't talk to anyone about me.* "I'm on my way to the bathroom," I said. "You're making me miss our review."

"Well, I would hate to have you angry at me," Jenny said. "You've been through enough, you poor dear." Her fingers disappeared into her notebook and came out waving a business card, which she proceeded to shove into my front pocket. "Here's my new contact info, Julie. Give me a call anytime."

I plucked her card from my pocket and dropped it; it went whirling onto the floor like a downed helicopter. "I'd rather you go take a long walk off a short cliff."

The smile still didn't move as I turned to walk away. I could feel it beaming against my back as I continued down the hallway. Forget the second-floor bathroom—I ducked into a first-floor stall just so I could use my phone without some overeager teacher hauling me off to the office. Actually, today I could probably sit in the middle of the hallway and text and chat away, and nobody would dare approach me.

I texted Alane—telling her not to talk to any reporters or anyone she thought might be a reporter or, really, anyone at all about me—and then Michael. I slipped my phone back into my pocket and strolled right out the back doors of the school.

I knew the black suits would be lurking out front, but I doubted they'd be hanging around in back, where the athletic yards and assorted field houses stretched to the woods. I strode in what I hoped was a purposeful manner past a gym class circling the track (who, running in a pack, nearly stampeded each other in an effort to get away from me). I kept an eye out for more reporters, but I couldn't see anything besides trees and grass. If I did find reporters, the way I was feeling, I'd probably kill them. With my bare hands. I could if I really wanted to. That was what they wanted, wasn't it, masked behind all their probing questions and fake-sympathetic smiles? To prove Ryan and I weren't so different after all?

Beyond all the fields and field houses and the football stadium, which, thanks to kids hanging out under the bleachers, was always surrounded by clouds of smoke, there was a dense forest. It wasn't like it was endless, or haunted, or anything; it stretched for a few miles and then turned into a highway and a development of blandly identical split-level houses. There was a hidden path—weaving around a surprisingly deep patch of mud that bubbled with the shoes of unwary freshmen and over a log spanning a creek—that took students right behind Crazy Elliot's on the other side. Otherwise, nobody really came out here. There were plenty of other places to smoke or to get high or to make out, and it was an awfully long way to walk for anything else.

Which meant it was the perfect place for me to meet him. I didn't waste any time speaking; as soon as I saw him leaning against a tree, I collapsed into his arms and rested my head against his chest. "Everybody knows," I said. "Ella told. Now everybody hates me. I don't like being hated. I want everyone to like me again. I can't have people laughing at me or talking about me behind my back."

He breathed in, then out; his chest pushed into my cheek, then back. He rubbed my lower back with one hand and pressed my head against him with the other. With his fingers tangled in my hair, tracing lines of warmth onto my scalp, I could breathe again. "I'm so sorry," he said, his voice slow. "It's kind of my fault. Is there anything I can do?"

"Yes," I said. "Yes, there is something we can do."

Re: Ryan Vann, age 17

I've now had four sessions with Ryan Vann, if you can really call them that. By four sessions, I mean that I've entered the state facility, had Officer Noor and his partner escort me to Ryan's cell, and then, after a brief exchange of greetings, sat silently under the blinking red eyes of the room's cameras. I've tried everything in my arsenal to get him to talk: asking questions, talking about myself, making assumptions about Ryan and his life, matching his silence with silence of my own.

Today, I'm ashamed to admit, I might have gone too far in my attempts. Today was a talking day; I had planned to talk about Ryan and hoped he would chime in with additions of his own. "Eleven people died in that band room," I said. "Did you know that?"

His eyes didn't even flicker in acknowledgment; he just continued staring at the floor. "The world wants to know why," I said. "Your sister wants to know why."

His head jerked up. "Julia?" he said. Though he still had that slow, slurred way of speaking, I could hear the passion in his voice. "What about Julia?"

His sister. That was it. I'd tried talking about the parents, but I'd never once mentioned the sister. I should've thought of it sooner. "Julia moved south and is living under a false name," I said. "She had to flee Elkton altogether. She was being harassed because of what you did."

He'd moved from staring at the floor to staring at the wall, his breaths coming in short bursts like a bull's. "Is she happy?" he asked.

"She wants to know why," I said. "She wants to know why you did it."

He jumped to his feet and balled his right fist, his eyes still trained on the wall. The fingers on his left hand twitched, but they didn't close all the way. "She knows," he said, his voice smoldering. "She knows why I did it."

"Tell me, Ryan," I urged. "Tell me."

He sat back down. Folded his hands in his lap, tenderly closing the left one in his right.

Didn't say another word.

This is where—I'm ashamed to say—I lost it. I leaned forward and yelled in his face. "Why did you even ask me here? Why did you ask for me if you weren't going to talk?"

My fists had balled, too, and I was pretty sure my eyes were popping from a red face. I flinched when I felt Noor's hand on my shoulder. "Doctor," he said, "let's take a break."

Ryan didn't even look up as I left.

FIFTEEN

I didn't make it back to Spanish. Or history. But I swaggered into lunch with my chin held high and Michael on my arm. I didn't feel at all like swaggering, but I knew I'd need some swagger today. Okay, maybe the plan we'd formulated in the woods made me feel a tiny bit like swaggering. Mostly I felt like shriveling under all the stares I knew I'd get when I walked into the cafeteria.

I wasn't disappointed. People's eyes slid off me like oil off water as I swept through to our usual table, which was completely empty. I sat down in the middle; Michael sat beside me, and Alane sat across. I was the queen of my own kingdom. Queendom. "Well, this is fun," I said. "Anyone want to crawl under the table with me?"

"It's not so bad," Alane said, but her eyes darted about, and her cheer seemed as plastic as Jenny's smile. I followed her eyes to Ella, who sat in the far corner with our other usual tablemates. She had been staring as us, but ducked down when she saw us looking, as if it were even possible for her to hide.

"You can go sit with them if you want to," I said. "It's okay."

Alane recoiled like I'd hit her, then slid her sandwich out of her lunch bag and plunked it on the table. "How could you even say that?" she said, opening her ziplock bag as ferociously as it was possible to open a ziplock bag. "Be real, Lucy. Eat your freaking lunch."

"You might as well call me Julia now," I said. "Everyone knows anyway."

She cocked her head and considered as she chewed. "Do you want us to call you Julia?"

I considered, too. Julia had a brother who did horrible things. Everybody hated Julia. But Lucy hadn't exactly been a nice person. Lucy had pushed her friends away because she was so terrified of getting close to somebody again and then having them collapse in a pool of blood. Which wasn't exactly an irrational fear for someone who had once been Julia. "Yes," I said. "I want you to call me Julia."

The afternoon went about as well as I'd expected: more stares, more whispers, more people jumping away from me as I walked down the hall. I felt almost like Moses parting the Red Sea. So I was more relieved than anything when the intercom crackled to life in the middle of chemistry and summoned me to the principal's office. I didn't even have to wait; her secretary waved me right in. I assumed that had something to do with Jenny, who did seem to be waiting; she pursed her lips and crossed her legs when she saw me, probably biting back questions about Elkton or my brother or the sounds Michael made when I kissed him. I didn't say hello, and entertained thoughts of her getting detention as I walked by.

"Lucy, good afternoon," the principal said, removing her glasses and rubbing her eyes. She was pretty for an old person, with a mane of tawny golden curls and skin that looked so soft I wanted to touch it. It was smooth, but she had a neck wattle—the sure sign of a face-lift. "Or is it Julia Vann?"

"Yes, it's Julia Vann," I said. "The documents my parents gave you at the beginning of the year were forged. So if you want to kick me out of school, just get on with it. I won't blame you, and I definitely won't shoot you."

The principal flinched, then sighed. "Nobody wants to kick you out," she said. "And I certainly don't think you're going to shoot me or anyone else. You're not to blame for what your brother did, and I hope everyone here will eventually be mature enough to understand that. I wanted to call you down to prepare you for what's waiting for you on the front lawn."

Dread filled my stomach, sick and heavy. "I saw Jenny in your office."

She creased her brow. "Who?"

I gestured toward the door. "Jenny. Jennifer Rosenthal. She's with the *Sun*. Well, now she's with the *LA Times*."

"A reporter? One snuck in?" She sighed and rubbed

her forehead, then picked up her phone. "Nancy? Is there a woman sitting in the waiting area?"

I could hear the secretary's voice faintly through the receiver. "Yes, ma'am. She's the mother of a concerned student."

The principal looked questioningly at me. I shook my head as vigorously as I could without it sailing off and out the window. Concerned, my ass. "Red lipstick, blue pantsuit, that's Jenny."

"Did you hear that, Nancy?" the principal said. "She's a reporter. Get her the hell out of here." She hung up with a decisive click. Some of the dread drained out of me. A bunch of it still weighed me down, don't get me wrong, but the burden had eased a bit. Someone was on my side. "Now, Lucy. Julia. What would you prefer I call you?"

"Call me Julia." It came out easier the second time. I had never really been Lucy. I'd wanted so badly for Lucy to be real, but I'd only ever been Julia.

"Julia." She sighed. "I can't believe a reporter snuck in. Irv's been so vigilant about posting people at the doors."

So it had gotten to the point where people were trying to sneak in, then. "Are there more reporters outside?" I said wearily. "I hate the ones who yell. They're my least favorite."

The principal stared at her desk, as if she just couldn't bear to look me in the eye. "None other than the one in my office," she said. "Not yet."

"Well, that's a positive thing!" I said.

"Well . . . ," she said.

"Well!" I said. "That doesn't sound good."

"Well," she said again, frowning faintly. I could hear a bang in the outer office, like Jenny had kicked over a chair on her way out, or thumped on the secretary's desk. Or the ceiling had fallen in and crushed her. "There aren't reporters outside yet. But people have been posting about you online already, and I've received a number of calls from parents demanding your expulsion. A number of students, too, have stopped by to tell me they no longer feel safe."

I shifted in my seat. "I am not my brother," I said. "I didn't do it."

"I know that." The principal's smile was warm and unexpected. "That's exactly what I told them. We're a public school, Julia, so we don't have to worry about frightened donors. I just wanted you to be prepared for everything, and know that I stand behind you."

I took a deep breath, then another, then another. "I don't think I have to worry," I said. "I'm confident people will see the truth. They'll see that I'm not my brother. That I'm the opposite of my brother."

She gave her desk a comforting rap. "I hope so, Julia." The corner of her mouth twisted. "You don't take the bus, do you? If you can, you should call your parents and have them pick you up."

I imagined what would await me on the bus: more whispers, more stares, a sudden hard push to the back that would send me hurtling out the emergency door and into a long pink splotch on the highway. But then I imagined what would await me if I had to call my mother: the trembling would begin as soon as she saw the people clustered outside. The hard shaking would ensue once the reporters and potential angry parents swarmed the car, thumping on the hood and the windows. She'd shrink in her seat, trying to hide, but there wouldn't be anywhere to escape the noses flattened against the glass. "I'm okay. My friend is going to drive me home."

"Your friend. Alane, right?"

I nodded. "Alane. Or Michael. Silverman. He might take me today."

She steepled her fingers together, and her eyes turned flinty behind her glasses. "Alane and Michael are good kids. I hope they're right to trust you."

The dread seeped back into my stomach. She might profess to trust me, but she didn't, not really. In the end, behind everybody's smiles and reassuring words, all they saw was my brother. "They're right," I said coldly, and stood. "Am I done here?"

Her gaze didn't waver. "We're done, Julia. Like I said, do let me know if you need anything, or you're having any trouble with anything." She stood, too, and stuck out her hand. I shook it. Her skin was clammy even in the room's heat. "Please take care."

"I'll take plenty of care." I gathered my things and showed her my back, walking quickly and deliberately. I was glad to see she'd at least rid us of Jenny.

At this point, chemistry was almost over, so I headed straight to band. I lurked in the hallway outside the band room to wait for the class to empty out, then went in, took my seat, and took my time screwing together my clarinet, greasing each piece of cork. My old reed had chipped, so I let it die and stuck a new one in my mouth to moisten.

By the time I deemed the reed sufficiently soft and screwed it onto my mouthpiece, I realized I was the only person in the band room. If I stood up and yelled, my voice probably would have echoed. I laid my clarinet gently across the music stand and knocked on the door of the band director's office. The door cracked open. "Hello?" I called hesitantly inside.

"Oh. Lucy." The band director peered back out at me. She was rolling something between her fingers. I squinted. Was that pepper spray? Seriously? "You didn't hear the announcement? I canceled practice today."

I squinted further, narrowing my eyes into slits of suspicion. "I didn't hear any announcement."

"Yes, well," the band director blustered, "it was a bit last-minute. I sent around an email this morning."

So was it an email or an announcement? I opened my mouth to clarify, then felt myself deflate like a leaky balloon. "So what's next?" I asked. "Are you going to decide to have tryouts again, then decide another clarinet is more suited to second chair? Let me guess: I'll be cut."

The band director stared at her desk. Whatever she was

holding knocked against it. Her hand was shaking. Yes, that was definitely pepper spray. "I don't know what you're talking about."

Tears rose in my eyes, but I pushed them back. Or tried to, anyway. "Yes, you do. I know you do." But there was nothing to discuss; she only continued to stare intently at her desk.

I returned to my seat, picked up my clarinet, and blew into it as hard as I could, making a sound between a honk and a squawk that might have come from an angry moose. I could practically hear the band director cringe, so I did it again, and then again, and after the third time I realized my cheeks were wet. I pulled my clarinet away from my mouth, gently swiveled it apart, packed it carefully into its case, and took it to the hallway outside the chorus room, where I settled to a seat on the tile and waited for Alane, my head resting on my knees, so that anyone walking by would see me as nothing more than a head of hair and an anonymous pair of legs.

That was how Michael found me an hour and a half later. He nudged my hair with his sculpted calf. I looked up. "Hey there," I said. "How was swimming?" The chlorine drifted off him in waves.

"Good. Exhausting." He extended a hand; I grabbed it, and he pulled me to my feet. I staggered a few feet into him and rested there for a moment. "How was band?"

I pulled away. "I'm not welcome in band anymore," I said.

"What? No way," he said. "I don't think that's even legal. You should sue or something."

I shrugged. "I'm not welcome anywhere anymore," I said. It was becoming easier to accept, a dull thud rather than a sharp pain.

He gave my hand a squeeze. "We'll fix that," he said.

I let my eyes close and my head fall against his shoulder. "We will."

Alane came bustling out a few minutes later, cheeks red and eyes blazing. "I just told off half the choir," she said. "Lucy—Julia—we'd better literally be best friends forever, because I don't think I have any other friends left."

"You have me," Michael offered.

Alane punched him in the shoulder. It wasn't a play punch, either; the thud reverberated through the hallway. "You're a guy," she said. "Guys can never really be friends with girls."

Michael winced and rubbed his arm. "Okay, ouch," he said. "On that note, I'll take Julia home. I owe her a bowl of chicken noodle soup. It's my specialty and it makes all your problems float away in a stream of deliciousness."

"Unless there's heroin in it, I doubt it'll float away my problems," I said drily.

It was Alane's turn to thump me. "Don't even joke. Heroin would taste terrible in soup, anyway."

"You've tasted heroin?" Michael sounded totally serious,

but he jumped back before Alane could punch him again. "I don't think that's how you're supposed to do it."

"Anyway." Alane shifted her backpack. "You drive Julia. I'll go run interference."

"Run interference?" I echoed. "What does that even mean?"

"I thought I'd go talk to the people waiting and distract them so they wouldn't see you leave," Alane chirped. "It could be fun. I could give them fake interviews."

"Please don't do that," I said. "I feel that might turn into rats chewing on my toes really fast. Anyway, the principal said there weren't reporters out there yet."

Alane's smile faltered. "The parental brigade's shown up," she said. "Maybe a couple reporters, too. Not a ton of people, but I peeked out the window after practice."

I sucked air through my teeth. "How many?"

"Fifteen people, maybe twenty?"

My laugh was dry. "That's nothing," I said. "I've seen way worse."

"Yeah, I don't think we need any interference run," Michael said. "Julia, put on my hoodie and slump a little. We'll be fine."

Michael's hoodie was warm and a little damp on the inside and smelled like the pool's locker room—sharp chlorine and mildew and sweat—but I hunched inside it anyway and pulled the hood over my head. I held my books against my chest and ducked my head. "I'm ready. Let's go."

The wind met me in a roar, and I hung back for a

moment, afraid it was a wind made of voices, but sometimes the wind is just the wind. I could only see a small crowd: just as Alane had said, there were fifteen people, maybe twenty, clustered out in front of the school. Still, I didn't want them to catch sight of me, so I ducked my head and rushed.

"Go," Alane said, dancing a few steps backward. "I'll stay here to run interference if I have to."

I gave up. If I had to read about rats chewing on my toes throughout my childhood tomorrow, then so be it. It would be worth it. I drew Alane into a quick, hard hug. "Thank you," I said.

She wrinkled her nose. "You smell like a men's bathroom."

Somehow we made it to the car without interference. I slouched in my seat as Michael peeled away, leaving the rats behind.

SIXTEEN

My mom's car was in the driveway. My stomach tied itself in a knot. "Hang out here for a second, okay?" I said to Michael, and climbed out of the car.

The house smelled like bleach and disinfectant. "Mom?" I called. My voice echoed off the high ceiling of the entryway. "Are you here?" I had a sudden vision of Ryan holding a knife to our mother's throat, a thread of red peeking through, and then banished it. My brother would never hurt our mom, because she'd never done anything to hurt me. Not actively, anyway. "Mom?"

The squeak of a rag against an already clean floor announced her presence in the upstairs bathroom. She was scrubbing on her hands and knees; her hair was tied back in a low bun, but sweaty tendrils had escaped and stuck to her flushed face. "Mom?" I said cautiously, pausing in the doorway. The floor had turned into a mirror. I could apply liquid eyeliner looking in it and have it come out completely even. "Is everything okay?"

My mom sank back onto her toes and dropped the rag to the floor with a sodden thud. "Everybody knows," she said. "How did this happen?" Lines had etched themselves into her face over the course of the day. She looked as if she might be made of glass and shatter with the slightest movement. "Julia, Lucy, Julia, I can't do it again. I can't move again and start over again and become a new person *again*."

A crack ran down me, too. I crouched on the floor beside her. "We are not going to have to move," I said firmly. "I've got it under control." Still, thoughts of the crowd of people outside the school tingled at the back of my mind. Would my plan be enough? Yes, I told myself. It would have to be. Because if it wasn't, I would have to watch my glass mother shatter into shards all over the floor, and there was no way I'd be able to escape getting cut. "My friend Michael is here, and he's going to make us soup. You like soup."

Her eyes had turned into pits. "Michael, that boy? Your boyfriend?"

"Soup, Mom, soup," I said. "You love soup. Isn't soup your favorite food?"

A tremulous smile crept onto her face. "I'm glad you're together," she said. "I'm glad you have someone who loves you."

I gave a short laugh. "Love? I don't know about that," I

said, but the second the words left my mouth, I did. Know, I mean. Michael had held me and believed me after what happened in Elkton, and he'd stuck to my side like lichen even after all his friends wouldn't come anywhere near. When he looked at me, I saw the same glow I'd seen in the faces of his family as they'd sat around their kitchen table eating his lasagna. That was love, I was pretty sure. Love. He was in love. And it tasted like chicken soup.

My mom was watching me with a funny, tentative little smile. "I can see it dawning on your face right now, my dear," she said. "It's a beautiful thing."

"My face?" I asked.

"No," my mom said. "I mean, yes, of course you have a beautiful face. I meant the realization that somebody loves you. That's beautiful, too."

I reached over and picked up the rag. Soapy water and something that smelled astringent dripped through my fingers. "Come downstairs and eat. Michael is going to make us soup."

"Ooh la la, he's cooking for you? Sounds like a keeper." My mom grabbed the rag from my hand and wrung it out, sending water spattering over the clean floor. "No, I'll let you two have the kitchen to yourselves. Just no going in your bedroom with the door closed."

"Really, Mom." The thought of her staying in here, on her knees, scrubbing the spotless floor, was too heavy for me to bear right now. "I want you there."

She gazed at me for a moment, misty-eyed. "I'm happy you have him," she said. "Go eat your soup."

"Please . . ."

She looked back down at the floor. "Go eat your soup," she said. "It's probably getting cold."

I left my mom on the bathroom floor. She'd talked to me, and she'd put the rag down for a few minutes. That was progress. Right?

Michael was waiting for me at the foot of the stairs. "Sorry," he said. "When you didn't come out for five minutes, I was afraid something horrible had happened."

"And you thought you would save me with a carton of broth and a bag of vegetables?" I raised an eyebrow.

He waggled his. "My soup is deadly delicious."

This time he let me help him cook. Though my father had taught me how to chop an onion when I was young (you cut it in half first and then rest it on the flat sides, so it doesn't go slipping and sliding all over the place and you don't lose any fingers), I let him instruct me anyway. I waited until we had three perfect piles of diced carrots, onions, and celery, all ready to be dumped into our pot with some olive oil and garlic, before I broached what I'd been thinking about all day. "So, Ella," I said.

"Ella." He gathered each pile neatly between his hand and knife and dropped it into the pot, where the vegetables sizzled and released a cloud of savory aroma. "I'm sorry she told. I told her how angry I am."

I bit the inside of my cheek and leaned over the pot and inhaled deeply, more so he wouldn't see my distress than anything else. "That smells amazing," I said. "How long does it have to cook?"

"Just five minutes or so," he said. "Just long enough to release all the tasty odors."

"Tasty odors does not sound very attractive," I said. "I need to talk to Ella, but I don't think she or her friends will come anywhere near me. Everyone's afraid of me. Can you help?"

I moved out of the way so Michael could give our mirepoix a stir. "She has no reason to be afraid of you, right?"

The pain came back, dull and throbbing. He loves you, I told myself. He trusts you. He doesn't mean what he's saying. "Of course she has no reason to be afraid of me." I must have sounded wounded, because he dropped the spoon and leaned over to take me in his arms. "I understand where she's coming from. I just want to talk to her."

"That came out wrong," he said. His words vibrated against my hair. "I mean, you're mad at her, and you have every right to be."

"I'm not going to kill her," I said. "I shouldn't even have to say that. Jesus. I just want to talk to her and show her I'm not my brother."

He pulled back, then touched his forehead to mine. I closed my eyes and felt his breath, hot and damp, against my lips. "That sounds reasonable. I could do that."

"Have her bring some of her friends," I said. "I want them to see everything, too. And you, of course. You come. And don't tell her I'll be there. Obviously."

"That can be arranged."

"And I don't want the black suits there, either."

"Black suits?"

"The undercover police, whoever's been following me around," I said. "There's one outside right now. You didn't see him as you were coming in?"

His silence was answer enough.

"You should be more observant," I said. "Otherwise you might get yourself killed."

He barked a half laugh, which cut off abruptly as he realized I was completely serious. "Maybe it's good they're following you," he said. "At least they're keeping you safe. Wouldn't your brother go for you first, if he showed up?"

My entire body went stiff; bones locked in their joints, and my muscles turned to stone. I stepped back slowly, carefully, worried I'd shatter myself into a million pieces. "My brother would never, ever hurt me," I said. My words sounded strange—warped, almost—like I was listening to them from the other side of a long tunnel. "Never, ever, ever."

"Okay," Michael said uneasily. "Okay, I'm sorry. Sorry. Ah!" There was a sharper tinge to the smell from the pot. "The mirepoix is burning." He gave it a few quick stirs, then poured in the carton of chicken broth. "It's home-made," he said. I suspected he just wanted to fill the silence, as I couldn't possibly have cared less whether the broth was homemade from the bones of chickens he'd decapitated himself or whether it was straight off the shelf at Safeway.

The warm, salty, savory scent of roasting chicken filled the air. "Is there going to be chicken in that soup?" I asked.

"Um, there's supposed to be," he said. "But I forgot about it. It should still be good. If you really want chicken in it I can go pick up a rotisserie. Do you want me to?"

"Do you love me?"

I blinked. He blinked back. My question had stunned both of us into silence. "It's pretty soon for that, isn't it?" he said finally, stirring the soup.

"I guess," I said. "I just wondered."

He stirred the soup again, then added a sprinkling of salt and black pepper. Some crinkly green leaves followed. "I don't know," he said.

"That's fair."

"Yes."

"What?"

He'd turned back to the soup; steam puffed over his face, dampening his curls and reddening his cheeks. "I love you," he said, his words tumbling out as quickly as the bubbles roiled over the surface of the pot. "Yes. I love you, Julia."

A shower of warmth flurried from my chest to my knees, and my insides exploded into a shower of glitter, sparkling and flashing and making everything purr. But.

"How do you know?" I asked.

"What?"

"How do you know you love me?" I was watching him intently—the soft look in his eyes, the way his forehead furrowed even as the corners of his eyes crinkled.

"You're supposed to say 'I love you, too.'"

"But how would I know if I loved you?" I asked.

"You just know," he said.

"But *how*? How do you know you love me?"

He tapped the corner of his mouth with his finger. "Because I just want to be around you all the time," he said. "Because I lied to my dad for you." His voice grew thick. "Because I've never felt more at peace than when I have you in my arms and I know you're safe." Before things got *too* serious, he waggled his eyebrows. "And it doesn't hurt that you're smoking hot."

I laughed and obligingly let him fold me back into his arms. It felt nice—he was warm and strong around me. And I did feel safe, sheltered from guns, knives, and anything else that might try to hurt me—the bulk of his body would stop anything dangerous, or at least slow it down. I still didn't get it, though. How did he know he wanted to spend all his time with me? And what made him think I was worth dying for?

I pulled away and pasted a smile on my lips. "I love you, too," I said. I hoped it was true.

*   *   *

Over our soup, which we spooned into each other's mouths (a messy process), we decided we'd gather Ella and her friends tomorrow. Or, rather, I decided we'd gather Ella and her friends tomorrow and he nodded okay. He'd ask Ella and several of her closest friends to meet him in the woods at the end of the day. Ella would, naturally, say yes, because she was half in love with Michael and knew he was mad at her for what she'd done to me. I'd emerge from the trees and make my case. They'd fall to their knees in apology and beg my forgiveness. I wouldn't say no if they wanted to kiss my feet. I'd no longer be a pariah. The end.

My brother had other plans.

Re: Ryan Vann, age 17

I was given one more chance. "He still asks for you," Noor said, shrugging in the door to my office. "I don't know if it's a game, but if you're willing, and you promise not to lash out again . . ."

Of course I promised. What else could I do?

This was, after all, the career opportunity of a lifetime.

He wasn't sitting this time, or staring at the floor. "Good afternoon, Doctor," Ryan said.

"It's not afternoon," I replied. "It's ten in the morning."

He shrugged with one shoulder and smiled boyishly. Even with his smile so crooked, he was quite charming when he wanted to be. It wasn't a natural charm, though; it was something he could switch on and off like a light.

"I tried," he said. "You came back. I'm glad you came back."

"You asked for me," I said. "And I brought you something." I pulled a photo out of my pocket. It was a photo of him and his sister, one I'd found on a social-media profile of Julia's. It was a good picture. I was hoping it would get him to talk, that the sight of his sister would pull him over that edge.

He took it and brought it up to his face, searching it with his eyes, then lowered it. Whatever he was looking for, it wasn't there. "You said you would never give up," he said. "And you haven't. You're back."

This had all been some kind of test, I realized, or had it? It could just be a game, as Noor had warned. "Are you ready to talk now?" I asked.

"Come over here," he said. He glanced back down at the picture, as if he was bolstering himself.

I stepped forward, then hesitated, glancing back at Noor. Noor stood in the open doorway, arms crossed over his chest. He shrugged. *Your funeral,* he seemed to be saying.

Internally, I shrugged as well. There were cameras everywhere, and Noor was right there. Ryan had killed eleven people, but somehow I felt he wouldn't kill me.

I walked over and stood before him. "Closer," he said. "I have to whisper."

I leaned in, my heart pounding in my throat. He could reach out and strangle me. He could have a shiv hidden up his sleeve and stab me in the gut before I could blink.

And yet I leaned in anyway.

"I don't want the cameras to hear," he whispered. "I need to tell you something. About the band room. But you might not believe me."

"Tell me," I whispered back.

He told me. I wasn't sure I'd heard correctly—his voice was slurred, after all—but before I could lean in again, Noor cleared his throat. "Please step back," he said.

I obeyed. I couldn't not obey. I looked at Ryan. Ryan nodded.

I had some research to do.

As Noor and I left, me promising Ryan I'd be back the next day, I glanced over at Noor. "We've become friends, kind of, haven't we?"

He gave me what I thought was a dubious look. "Kind of," he said, though after a pause.

"I need your help with something," I said. "I want to look at the police records of the shooting."

He surveyed me, top to bottom. I was left feeling, absurdly, like a teenage girl being checked out by a boy she was pursuing. "I can do that," he said.

SEVENTEEN

"You're *what*?" Alane's eyes and lips were matching circles. "Were you just not going to tell me?"

"Of course I was going to tell you. I'm telling you right now." I'd met up with Alane after show choir, as usual, and told her about my plans for Ella. I hadn't worried about being overheard; every student who had to get through the hallway to the student parking lot had magically found an alternate route. It was like they thought I had a gun clamped against my side. "Do you want to be there?"

"Um, I think I should be. Don't you?" she said. "So that they don't all run away when you show your face?"

"They won't be able to run," I said. "I'll be blocking the path."

Alane slung her arm around me. "This sounds like you're aiming to give them heart attacks before you can even tell them why you're there," she said in an overly patient way, as if she were a wise old woman explaining something to a child.

Her tone raised my hackles. "Well, if one of them were by chance to drop dead of a heart attack, I can't say I'd be devastated."

She clapped me on the back. "That settles it. I'm coming. You need me."

I grabbed her hand as we walked back through the school. She squeezed. Was that love? "Do you love me?" I asked.

A surprised sort of laugh burst from Alane's throat. "Do I love you?" she said. "Did you really just ask me that?"

"I'm serious," I said. Her laugh died on her lips.

"Sorry," she said. "I thought you were kidding. Of course I love you. You're my best friend. You rescued me from a life sitting alone at the corner lunch table."

"Would you steal for me?" I asked.

Her whole face scrunched. "I don't know," she said. "It depends on the circumstances."

"Would you die for me?" I asked.

"Now you're being creepy," she said.

I forced a laugh as we walked into the woods. "I was joking! Obviously."

Alane rolled her eyes. "You weirdo," she said. "Come on. We have reputations to save."

She hadn't answered my question.

Alane and I found a place for ourselves between two trees and settled down onto the carpet of moss to wait. If

I ignored the potential bugs crawling all over me, it was almost like sitting on an especially velvety carpet. "So when are they supposed to be coming?" Alane whispered.

"Any minute," I whispered back. "Michael said they'd come right after swim."

"Do you know what you're going to say?" she asked.

I had an idea. "Kind of," I said. "I've rehearsed a few things—is that them now?"

I hadn't heard anything, but Alane nodded enthusiastically and gestured before us. Now that I listened hard, I realized there were twigs snapping, the swoosh of branches being pushed aside. Maybe I was psychic.

But the crunching and swooshing faded away like it had never been, bringing no Ella or Michael or hangers-on. Alane looked back at me and shrugged. Before she could say anything, though, it started back up again, from the other direction. As the sounds drew closer, words and exclamations drifted toward us on the breeze.

"Oh my God, Mike. I think a bug just flew in my eye."

"Just a little farther—I swear."

They crunched to a halt in a small clearing just off the path. Through curtains of branches and leaves, I could see six of them standing in a circle: Michael, Ella, and four of her friends, two of whom I recognized vaguely as having names that ended with -*issa*.

"So where is it?" Ella asked.

I wondered what Michael had told them to get them here. It didn't matter. Time to make my grand entrance. I grabbed Alane's hand again, and together we stepped into view.

"Hey," I said.

You would have thought my greeting had been a gunshot. It made Michael tense and Ella shriek; she tried to back away, but Michael grabbed her by the shoulder, sending a flame of jealousy through me. The Issas bleated like goats.

"Don't run," I said, holding my hands up, palms out. "I promise I just want to talk."

Ella yanked her arm free from Michael and shot him a withering look. "So this is what you wanted to tell me?"

"I had to lie to get you here," Michael said. "Sorry. Just hear her out."

She took another step back, a violent one, and clung, panting and trembling, to the trunk of a tree. "She's going to kill me," she said. "Just like her brother killed her old friends."

"I'm not my brother." My voice wavered a bit, but I struggled to keep it as even as I could.

"You had something to do with it!" Her face was round, red, vicious. "You were in that room, too. You could've stopped him. You're just as bad as he is." One of the Issas stroked Ella's hair. Ella jerked at first, but then stood there, glaring at me, letting the Issa soothe her. "I'm getting out of here."

"Wait!" This was getting out of hand. I had to get things moving. I raised my voice. "I'm not my brother!"

Dried leaves crunched, there was a collective gasp, seven people surfacing for air, and there he was.

My brother.

The first thing I noticed when I looked at him was, as always, how handsome he was. The stubble glittering over his jaw. The dark curls spilling over his forehead. His silhouette, sharp and defined, against the sun behind him. Even with the new frailties wrought by his injuries—the way his left eye drooped a little and his left arm hung by his side—he was still my brother.

The second thing I noticed was that he had a gun. For just a moment I was sent hurtling back to the band room, where I'd crumpled on the floor like a dying flower, crushed by the heavy metallic smell of blood.

"It's over, Julia." Words from the past. They echoed in my ears. *"We're safe now. They can't tell."*

I heaved and shuddered, rocked back and forth, then grabbed his outstretched hand and let him pull me to my feet.

I blinked, hard, and shook my head. I couldn't afford to go back there now. "Ryan," I said firmly. "Put down the gun."

Words sputtered on Ella's lips, but nothing came out. Her eyes were wide, and she was shaking so hard I could hear her body buzz like a hummingbird's wings. The Issas were bleating again. Alane, standing beside me, had frozen solid; chill emanated from her in waves. Michael . . .

Where was Michael?

"Don't move, and I won't shoot," Ryan said. A thrill ran

through me at the sound of his voice—I'd almost forgotten how deep and rich it was, like dark chocolate, with the way it melted all around me. Even more so now that his words slurred together. It actually made him sound more danger-ous. "Where's the bitch who ruined my sister's life?"

Water splashed to the ground. Ella had peed herself.

"Put the gun down," I said. I caught his eye, and his smile, at least on half of his mouth, was hard and blinding. I frowned a little and gave a shake of my head; he dropped the smile and etched a frown deep into his cheeks. "It's not Ella's fault. Nobody else needs to get hurt."

"Ella." The name rumbled deep in his chest. "Ella! Which one of you is Ella?"

One of the Issas squealed. "Her! That's her! She's Ella! It's all her fault!"

I snuck a glance at Ella. She'd gone white as a corpse; every freckle dotting her cheeks stood out in stark relief, as if they were holes poked in her face. "I didn't mean any-thing," she said. Each breath caught in her throat, and her words ran into each other like they, too, were trying to get away. "I'm sorry. I'm so sorry. I'll take it all back. Just don't hurt me, please."

I sidled toward her, my hands raised. Ella was staring so intently at my brother that she jumped in surprise, slam-ming into the tree beside her, when I inserted myself neatly between them. "This can't happen again," I said. "If you want to hurt someone, you'll have to go through me."

My brother squinted. For a moment I lost myself in the

barrel of the gun, in its endless dark eye. "Really?" he said. "After all she's done to you, you would . . ." He furrowed his brow.

Sacrifice, I mouthed.

His eyebrows jumped to his hairline. "Sacrifice," he proclaimed. "After all she's done to you, you would sacrifice yourself for her?"

"Yes. Because I'm not you. I'm better than you. And I won't let you hurt anyone else ever again," I said. My shoulders relaxed. He'd said all his lines. Now all he had to do was turn and melt back into the trees, where he'd be long vanished by the time any black suits made it to the area.

He bowed his head. "You've vanquished me," he said. I gave a minuscule shake of my head again. *Too dramatic.*

He winked, and I clenched my teeth, but he backed away, already lowering the gun.

And then hit the ground with a crash and a thud.

"Drop the gun!" Michael thundered. "The police are on their way!"

The dust cleared to show Michael straddling my brother, who had fallen on his stomach. His cheek was down against the dirt, his eyes half closed, like he had decided now would be a good time for a nap. The gun had flown a few feet away; one of the braver Issas ran forward and kicked it so that it skittered off harmlessly into the trees.

My heart stopped, and my stomach filled with lead. No. This wasn't how it was supposed to go. I lurched forward, my feet stumbling on the uneven ground. "Get off him," I cried. "He's got a gun."

Michael gave me an odd look. My brother wasn't moving; he was still as a corpse, his limbs heavy and sprawled out around him. His eyes were still half lidded, though I could see them beginning to flicker. He had to get out of here.

"Get off," I said, kneeling next to the pair. Ella, Alane, and the Issas had backed off, forming a ring of judgmental faces. Of judgment. They might as well have been barbed wire. I couldn't get too close to them. "You're hurting him."

"He's out cold," Michael said. "I think he hit his head or something." He gave my arm a somber pat. "Don't worry. I called my dad. They're sending the guys who have been following us around. He can't hurt you anymore."

My brother was beginning to blink. I had to do something fast. I couldn't let them get him, not when he was only here because of me. "Get off him," I said roughly. I was going blind from panic. "Or I'll never speak to you again."

Michael's expression didn't change, but his voice came out low, concerned. "Julia, are you—"

My brother bucked, and Michael, distracted, went flying. Ella screamed, and birds took flight from the surrounding trees, their wings flapping with the sound of a collapsing circus tent. Michael rocked, trying to stand back up, but my brother made it first, kicking Michael in the side. Michael groaned.

"No!" I shouted. The world was unraveling around me. "Stop it! Don't hurt him!"

My brother's eyes met mine, and everything around me stilled. The wind rushed to a halt, and the birds huddled above the clouds. Even Ella's scream cut off. In the midst of all the silence, his words were extra loud and clear. "I can't do it anymore," he said. "I'm going to end this."

My blood turned to sludge in my veins, my muscles all froze, and I couldn't seem to swallow the spit welling up in the back of my throat. "Don't you dare," I finally managed to say. "You *promised* me."

His arms were shaking. They'd changed, I noticed, grown weak. "You've shown me today. This isn't going to work. Ever," he said. "I'll give you until tomorrow. You have until tomorrow night."

My eyes swelled in their sockets, pushing against the bone of my skull and making my brain throb. "Don't you dare. Don't you dare. Don't you *dare.*"

He smiled at me like he knew when the world was going to end.

He did.

"I love you, Julia," he said, and then he went down again, Michael piling on top of him.

A sob burst from my throat. I was on the ground, pine needles pricking at my skin like a thousand shots, and everything went black.

EIGHTEEN

I woke to a buzz of activity: footsteps, authoritative voices yelling commands, somebody sniffling. Somebody's hand squeezing mine. I blinked; the trickle of sunlight through the trees was turning my world white.

The sniffling continued until I realized it was me. I squeezed the hand, seeking comfort in its presence, and it squeezed back. "Julia, are you awake?" someone said. Alane. The hand twitched as she spoke. Her hand. It was her hand. "Don't worry. They've got your brother. He's gone." She squeezed in rhythm with her words, but any chance of me finding comfort in it had blinked away. I sat bolt upright.

"How long was I on the ground?" I pushed myself up on shaky knees, but the trees and the ground and the sky whirled around me as if I'd hopped on a roller coaster. I closed my eyes to center myself, and when I opened them again I was back on the dirt. I propped myself up on an elbow and braced myself for nausea, but after a few tentative whoops, my stomach decided to stay put.

"Maybe five, six minutes?" Alane said. "You went down when the police got here. I was starting to get worried."

I took a deep breath, held it, and pushed myself to a sitting position. I felt for a moment like I was underwater—the air was thick, and everything shimmered—but it stopped. I released the air, almost expecting to see bubbles. "And they took my brother." They. I was betting "they" were Goodman and West.

"They took your brother."

I thought I should feel something, but there was nothing. I was empty. Hollow. I'd been pumped full of nothing, full of air, a macabre skin balloon. "Where's Michael?"

Alane jerked her head. "He's over there talking to the people in black suits. They're undercover state police, I think. They're going to want to talk to you, too."

"And the others? Ella?"

"She and Marissa had panic attacks. I think. The police took them all back to the school. I guess they'll talk to them there."

"Miss Vann? Julia Vann?" One of the black suits hovered over us, a woman for a change. She looked vaguely similar to me, actually: curly dark hair that she'd scraped into a tight bun; a pale, narrow face; a slight frame with disproportionately long legs. She had a black suit on, too, though hers was tailored and tucked around her waist and hips. "Are you feeling up to some questions?"

For a second there were two of her, then the images merged back into one. I blinked hard, scrunching up my whole face in the process. "I like your suit," I said.

She brushed nonexistent dust from her hips. "Thank you," she said. "Now, how did you find yourself out here in the woods this fine afternoon?"

"Well, you know who I am," I said. I licked my scaly lips. "What's your name? Don't you have to introduce yourself? I think you're violating my rights. My Miranda rights."

"I can assure you I'm not violating any of your rights, Miss Vann," she said. She was young, probably not yet out of her twenties, and she kept glancing at the officers around her, as if for approval. "Now, will you tell me—"

"Where did you take my brother?" I asked. "Why didn't anyone alert the media that he'd woken up? Or escaped? He's dangerous, you know."

She smoothed her hair back, though I hadn't seen one out of place. "I can assure you that he's safe and secure."

She must have been new to the force. Any seasoned vet wouldn't let someone they were questioning interrupt them. I knew that from all the time I'd spent with both seasoned vets and shaking newbies after the incident in the band room.

"Ella—the dark-haired girl who had the panic attack— told everyone at school about Julia's brother," Alane said. She ran her fingers up and down my arm, up and down, in what I could only guess was an attempt to soothe me. It didn't work. "Nobody would talk to her. Julia, I mean. So Julia asked Michael to get Ella out here so she could talk to her. Make her case."

235

"I really need to speak with Julia herself," the cop said. "Alane—Miss Howard—why don't you go wait over there? We'll want to speak with you, too."

Alane hesitated. "I don't want to leave Julia," she said. "She's hurt."

"You're a good friend." The cop didn't sound like she thought Alane was a good friend at all. She sounded like she'd be perfectly happy to stuff Alane in the trunk of her car and leave her there for a few hours. "But this is a police matter, and you're interfering. I wouldn't want to have to arrest you."

Alane's eyes went wide as fists. Still, she didn't retreat, which made a sort of warmth blossom in my belly, like I'd just chugged half a jar of honey. Was this love?

"Are you okay, Julia?" Alane asked.

A smile twitched at my lips. "I'm okay. You can go."

She glanced at me, then at the cop, then back at me again, then scuttled away, backward, not unlike a crab. I turned back to the cop to see a smile twitching on her own lips. "I couldn't have arrested your friend," she confided. "And even if I could have, I wouldn't have. I know she was just trying to protect you."

"You're totally new," I said. "None of the veterans are this nice to me."

"If you must know, I am new. They just called me in to help out this morning," she said. "And my colleagues are wrong if they're not nice to you. You're a victim here, not a criminal."

Tears stung at my eyes, and I was seized by the urge to hug her, hard. Was that love? "You're just saying that to get me to talk," I said.

"I promise I'm not," she said. The promises of cops mean nothing. "Now, tell me why you were here."

Lying or not, I loved this cop. I wanted to be around her every time I had to do a police-related thing, which sounded like Michael's definition of love. A little, anyway. Then again, I thought back to the glowing looks on his and his family's faces around that lasagna. I didn't think my face was glowing as I looked at the cop. Maybe this wasn't love. Probably it wasn't love.

"Like Alane said," I said. "Nobody at school wanted anything to do with me. Even my teachers. I just wanted to talk to Ella and make things right."

"Totally understandable," she said. "And what happened next?"

"Can you tell me your name?" I asked. "I'd feel better talking to you if I knew your name."

Her face, dappled with sunlight, flickered with surprise. "Of course. I thought I'd introduced myself already," she said. Definitely new. Or else she was right, and she'd introduced herself while I'd been on the ground, my head in Alane's lap and my mind drifting along with the clouds above. "I'm Officer Weiler. You can call me Miranda."

"Miranda. That's funny," I said. "Like the rights."

"Yes, like the Miranda rights," she said. "They were named after me."

I was all set to exclaim politely when she chuckled. "I'm just kidding," she said. "They were actually named after Ernesto Miranda in a Supreme Court case in 1966. *Miranda versus Arizona*. We learned all about it in the academy."

Last year, when she graduated? "Anyway," she said. "So you were in the woods, trying to prove that you weren't your brother." She shook her head. "From what I heard from the others, you did a damn good job of it."

Imaginary feathers puffed all over my back, and I had to fight the urge to preen them because, well, they didn't actually exist, and I would have looked like a total idiot. "Thanks," I said.

"Anyway, in the woods," she said. "What happened next?"

I walked her through the whole deal—the appearance of my brother, all the yelling, my heroic defusing, Michael mucking everything up. Though I didn't quite put it like that. "And now my head hurts and I want to go home," I finished. I had planning to do. Tomorrow evening, my brother had said. I pegged that, conservatively, as four o'clock. That left me less than twenty-four hours to fix everything that was wrong. Everything.

"And you had no idea Ryan was going to be there?" she asked.

I instinctively winced at the sound of his name. "No, of course not," I said. "If I had, I would have called the police immediately like a good citizen." I sighed and scratched my temple. "But I don't have any way of reaching you. So if I remember anything else . . ."

"Say no more." Miranda pulled a business card from her pocket. "You can call me, day or night. I'd prefer night. I'm not so much a morning person."

The card was on heavy, creamy stock, with the words CALIFORNIA STATE POLICE in letters that pushed back as I brushed my finger over them, as if they'd been written in a primitive form of Braille. I guess I'd never really thought about the police having business cards.

"Thank you," I said.

"Of course," Miranda said. "I live to serve the good citizens of the state of California." Her eyes strayed over my shoulder. "It looks like my colleagues are finished with your friends," she said. "You should get going before it gets dark. Go have some hot cocoa or something."

When I mentioned her goodbye to Michael, he reacted exactly the way I thought he would. "You're in luck," he said. "Because guess who makes the best cup of hot chocolate in all of California?"

I paused and stared up at the sky. The sun was beginning to set, tie-dyeing the sky with streaks of pinks and purples and blues. "I was going to say something snarky, like Irv the security guard, but I'm too tired to think of anything good," I said. "So I'll go with you, Michael, *you* make the best cup of hot chocolate in all of California, if not all of America, if not all of the world, if not all of the galaxy."

"You forgot the universe," Michael said. "But yes, otherwise all true."

Alane was still shaking when I pulled her in for a hug,

and she decided she just wanted to go home. "I don't mind if I have to settle for the powdered stuff in the microwave," she said. "As long as I get to be in my own bed."

"Are you okay driving?" I asked.

"I'll be fine," Alane said. "I'll see you tomorrow." She didn't look at me when I said goodbye, and she scuttled off into the dark, empty parking lot without so much as a glance back over her shoulder. I was left with the lingering feeling she just wanted to get away from me.

I was getting no such feelings from Michael, who buried his face in my neck the second Alane disappeared into her car. Not unlike a vampire, actually. "You promised me hot chocolate," I said. "I'm not kissing you until I get it."

He heaved a gusty sigh into my neck, shivering every nerve from my collarbone to the underside of my chin. "Think about how that sounded," he said.

"I'm basically a chocolate prostitute," I said. "And I'm okay with it."

We spent the ride in silence. Michael, I figured, was thinking over ways to make his ultrafamous hot chocolate even better (chili powder, maybe, or fresh vanilla?). I was thinking about my deadline. It was currently five o'clock. I had twenty-three hours.

And then the solution struck me. Duh. Of course. I spent the rest of the ride fervently planning.

"Are your parents around?" I asked Michael as we pulled into his driveway. Darkness yawned through his front windows.

"Nah," he said. "They're off helping Aria move into her new place, and then they're going out to dinner. When I called my dad back there in the woods, he said they wouldn't be home till late, maybe not till tomorrow."

"Aria's new place in Berkeley," I said.

"You remembered!" Michael said. We stepped through his front door, and his smile brightened up the inside more than any of the lights he'd flipped on. "Yeah, she had some kind of fight with her roommate, so she's moving to a different dorm room. With a new roommate she'll probably hate, too. But c'est la vie."

"I wish I could meet her," I said. Aria was the one closest to Michael's age, I thought; he'd told me she was a freshman in college. I wondered at their relationship. If he'd ever crawled into her bed to hold her as she cried.

"Someday you will," he said. "She'll be home in a month or two for summer break. I'll have you over for dinner."

Summer. I figured there was maybe, if I was lucky, a 50 to 60 percent chance I'd still be alive in summer.

"Sounds great," I said.

The rich, sweet, heavy scent of melting chocolate filled the kitchen, spiked with a nose-tingling dose of chili powder (I'd been correct). As he waited for the milk and the chocolate and the chili powder to bubble, Michael pulled me to my feet and into him. "Would you grant me an advance?"

I let him kiss me. He tasted salty, and that was when I realized I was crying.

NINETEEN

I lay awake for what felt like hours and hours before I got up to call Miranda. I glanced at the time on my phone before I started dialing. Somehow it was only ten o'clock.

Miranda picked up on the second ring. "Officer Miranda Weiler." She sounded brusque, businesslike. Quite respectable for 10:00 p.m.

"Hi, Officer Weiler?" I said hesitantly. "This is Julia Vann. You gave me your card earlier?"

"Yes, Julia." Her voice warmed. "Glad to hear from you."

I wasn't sure what to say after that. It had been a long time since any cop had been glad to hear from Julia Vann. "Yeah," I said. Tears pricked at the corners of my eyes. I wasn't sure exactly why. "Before you said I could call you. If I remembered anything."

I half expected her to hang up right there, but instead she said, "Of course, Julia. What did you want to talk about?"

On the phone she was just a faraway voice. Remote. She could be anyone. "Could we talk in person?"

"Sure," she said. I could picture her all dressed to go: crisp black suit, tight bun. "I'm happy to come by your house?"

I couldn't stop a laugh from exploding against the mouthpiece.

"Bless you," she said.

"Thanks," I said. I could just imagine how my parents would react should another cop show up at the door. My mom might have a nervous breakdown. "Can I meet you somewhere? There's this twenty-four-hour coffee place, kind of a diner, near my school. I can walk there. It's called Crazy Elliot's?"

"I know Crazy Elliot's," she said. "Nice place. Meet you there in half an hour?"

It took me longer than I thought it would to walk to Crazy's. Ten minutes in, I was wishing I'd worn a sweatshirt. Twenty minutes in, there were more goose bumps on my arms than there was skin. Thirty minutes in, I was cursing the glowing headlights of the cars that whizzed by for the sure warmth of their interiors.

So I was relieved to see, finally, the neon CRAZY ELLIOT'S sign. I went inside and stomped my feet like I was stomping away the cold. "Julia!" I heard, and looked up. Miranda was already there, sitting in a back booth, hands wrapped around a steaming mug. I sighed internally. I'd kind of wanted to beat her there.

Still, I waved and joined her on the cracked red vinyl. To my surprise, I didn't smell coffee. "You got hot chocolate," I said, raising an eyebrow.

Miranda smiled and took a sip. When she lowered her mug a trace of whipped cream decorated her upper lip, like she was a kid or something. "I sense judgment."

"Not at all," I said. I felt the tears again, pushing on the backs of my eyeballs, but I managed to hold them in this time. "I'll have one, too."

Crazy Elliot's made the second-best hot chocolate in town (after Michael's, naturally). I told Miranda all about it. "A little bit of vanilla is the secret, I think," I confided. "But Michael is convinced there's nutmeg in there, too."

Miranda shook her head and took another sip. "I think Michael wins this one," she said. "There's definitely a hint of nutmeg in here."

I shrugged. "I've never been much of a cook. That was my brother."

"I see," Miranda said. I expected her to punctuate her words with another sip, but she left her mug on the table. "You wanted to talk about your brother tonight, right?"

"Ryan," I said. It felt weird to hear her refer to him as my brother. That was how *I* thought of him. "Yeah. I . . . I know he did horrible things, and he deserves to be locked away, but still . . . I . . ."

"You care about him," Miranda said.

I stared at the table. My mug had left a sticky brown ring on the surface. "Yeah."

"And you feel guilty for it." Her voice was gentle. "You shouldn't. He's still your brother."

I shook my head. "It's so weird," I said. "I feel relieved because he's scary, and I'm happy that he can't hurt me or the people I love anymore, but I also miss him, and I feel guilty about missing him. I'm so confused."

She laid her hand on the table, like she wanted to reach out and grab mine. I almost wished she would. "That's normal," she said.

"There are enough people in my situation for you to say what normal is?"

"I didn't mean it that way," she said. "I just meant that . . . you know . . ." She took a slurp of her hot chocolate in what I could only guess was a stalling tactic, draining her mug down to the bottom. "That was so good."

I leapt up. "Let me get you another one."

"No, no." Miranda went to stand, but I grabbed her mug. "Julia, I—"

"You came out here at ten at night to listen to me talk about my feelings," I said. I was already walking backward toward the counter, moving much more deftly than I had the last time I was in this room. "The least I can do is buy you a hot chocolate."

I paid for her refill, then walked slowly back to our table, cupping my hand over the top to keep it as warm as possible. I set it down in front of her, and she peered down into it like she was gazing into a mirror. "Ooh, did you ask for powdered sugar on top this time?"

I smiled. "It's a Crazy Elliot's secret."

She stirred. "Thanks. That was so nice of you." She took a sip and smacked her lips. "Extra sweet."

"So my brother," I said. "He *is* securely locked away, right?"

"He is," Miranda said. "You don't have to worry. And I mean it: don't feel guilty."

"How securely?" I asked. "He escaped once already and came for me and my friends." All the moisture fled from my mouth and took shelter in my eyes. "He could escape again."

She reached out and, this time, patted my arm. Her fingers were warm. "He won't. Julia, Ryan is locked away in the basement of the Sunny Vale police station, behind two locked doors. There's only one exit from that basement, and it goes through the main office, where there are always officers present. You don't have to worry about him getting away again."

"Two locked doors?" My voice wavered. "My brother is smart. He could get the keys."

"He can't," Miranda said soothingly. She patted my arm again, and I jerked away. "The key is in a locked box. Don't worry—they keep a close eye on everything."

I breathed out, but it sounded like a sob. "What if he has someone helping him? He's charming, my brother, and he got someone to break him out of the hospital that first time. He could . . ." I paused and licked my lips.

"He can't," Miranda said. Her words had a blurry sort

of edge to them, like she was having trouble moving her tongue. "You can't even get into the police station without a valid police ID. They have security at the entrance. I'm telling you, Julia." Her hand shook, and she sloshed a few drops of hot chocolate onto the table. "You are safe."

"Thank you," I said sincerely. "Thank you for telling me that."

"I'll check on him tomorrow morning and let you know he's still there, if that would make you feel better. My shift starts at nine. Now," she said, and her hand trembled again, "was there something else you wanted to tell me about your brother?"

That was right. I'd gotten her here by telling her I had something to tell her. I looked down at the table. The drops she'd spilled made a shape almost like a dog. That made me think of Fluffy. Poor little inside-out Fluffy. "I wanted to tell you I was worried he might escape," I said. "But it sounds like you guys have it under control."

I walked Miranda to her car, and when I told her I had a forty-minute walk in the dark ahead of me, she insisted on driving me home. "If it bothers you, I'll drop you off down the block so your parents won't see you getting out of a cop's car," she said through thick lips. "Come on. Get in."

I smiled at her, and this time it was genuine. "Thank you. Thank you so much."

I didn't get in the car.

* * *

I awoke at 7:35 a.m. to the cry of my alarm. Miranda's shift began at nine. I had set my alarm for 7:50. Why was it going off now?

It wasn't my alarm, I realized. It was my phone. Alane. I peeked out my window to see her car idling in the driveway. Shoot. I'd forgotten to tell her not to pick me up.

The shrill of my phone stopped. She was getting out of the car. She was striding up the walk, her hands on her hips. She was ringing the doorbell.

I hurried down the steps, realizing how terrible I looked only after I'd swung open the front door. "I'm sick," I said as my heart lurched in my chest like a dying fish. "Sorry. I forgot to text you."

Her eyes raked me from top to bottom, and for a moment I imagined myself through her eyes. Still wearing the same clothes I'd worn yesterday, though now they were crusty with dirt and sweat; even I could smell them. Sallow cheeks and haunted eyes. "Are you okay?" she asked cautiously.

I let out a laugh that sounded more like a scream. "Just peachy," I said.

"You look like death warmed over," she said. "Actually, not even warmed over. You look like ice-cold death that's just clawed itself out of the grave using only its fingernails."

I couldn't muster up the energy to joke back. "I'm sick," I said. "I'm not going to school today. See you tomorrow." Hopefully.

I went to close the door, but she blocked it with her foot.

I tried to close it anyway, and she flinched, but she didn't budge. "You're hurting me," she said.

"I don't want to get you sick."

She shouldered her way into the crack, yawning it open a bit more. I leaned forward, but I was completely drained. Even standing required burning too much energy. I needed to down, like, eight espressos, and then I might be able to hold fast. That, or one perfume bottle full of neon-pink essence of Alane. I was willing to bet Alane never got sick.

"You're not sick," she said. "Something's wrong. Tell me."

I grunted as I pushed back against the door. "You're going to be late to school." And she was going to make me late for my shift. Well, for Miranda's shift. I had to make sure to get there before her and before she discovered her stuff was missing. The dying fish in my chest flopped and jolted my stomach, making me feel seasick, making me feel like I wanted to throw up. I could feel it beginning, a burning in my nose, a tingling in my cheeks.

This was my own fault. I'd wanted the loyalest of loyal friends, and when I'd pulled Alane away from her lonely lunch table and installed her on the social ladder, I'd gotten that. She owed everything to me. If I was going to push her away, I'd have to be cruel. I didn't want to be cruel to Alane. I loved her, I think.

Alane leaned in further, slowly but surely pushing me back into the foyer. I finally gave up, stumbling back into the wall and sliding downward. The tile floor was cool through my jeans, and I leaned my cheek against the wall, breathing deeply, staring intently at the ceiling and the floor and the wall and anything else that wasn't Alane. Which was difficult, as she was hovering over me, dipping and ducking her head, desperately trying to catch my eye.

"Something's wrong, Julia," she said. "Tell me. I can help you. Does it have to do with your brother?"

"It's over, Julia. We're safe now. They can't tell." The smell of blood was heavy, metallic, sticky against the inside of my nose. It rose in clouds toward my brain, choking it and suffocating me.

I let my brother pull me to my feet. "But eleven people are dead," I said. "It's not like we can just walk out of here. Like we can disappear."

"Of course not," my brother said, holding me tight against him. I breathed in deeply and let the smell of him—smoky, spicy, sweaty—block the smell of blood. "I have a plan for that. You'll just have to trust me."

The sob that escaped my throat surprised even me. "Everything has to do with my brother," I said. "Everything. And I'll never get away. I can never get away."

She settled to my side with a thump. Distantly, I could hear her truck rumbling. She'd left it on. "I can help you," she said. "I'm your friend." She linked her elbow with mine. "I love you, remember?"

Cruel. Whether I wanted to or not, I had to be cruel now. For Alane's own safety.

I stood up so quickly I knocked her aside; she went reeling and cried out as her elbow smacked into the wall with a thud. "You don't love me," I said coldly. "I don't know what love is, but I know I don't love you. I had a best friend, and she's dead."

She popped to her feet, her lower lip trembling, and stuck her chin out at me like a shield. "You're stressed out and you're hurt and you're sick and you probably feel like you're drowning," she said. "It's okay. I forgive you."

I didn't say, *Goddammit, Alane. I don't want you to forgive me. I want you to go and hopefully not hate me tomorrow.* "Please go," I said instead.

Her hands fluttered to her shoulders, then back down to her sides, then up again. I took a step away in case she was thinking of hugging me or something. I could already see the seams running through the world, slight, nearly invisible lines of air and dust that held reality together. If she were to touch me, I was sure they'd just split down the middle and tear the world apart. Tear *me* apart.

"Call me, Julia," she said. "Or come by. I'll be waiting."

I watched her go. She sat in my driveway for way too long, her phone to her ear; I bet my phone was shrieking upstairs. I knew she wanted me to race out and tell her I'd had a momentary lapse and of course we were best friends. Of course I loved her. That was the last thing I could do, though. Liv had died because she'd gotten too involved with me and my brother. I could never, ever let that happen to Alane.

I waited ten minutes or so after she pulled out to make sure she didn't come back, pacing circles through the quiet house. My parents, asleep upstairs, had no idea I was wearing a path into the carpet. I didn't know if they even knew their only son was being held minutes away; they certainly hadn't let anything slip to me. I never knew what they knew or didn't know. The only thing that mattered was that they'd think I'd have left for school with Alane. If I didn't make it back, their memories of me would hopefully remain pure, undiluted, clean as our bathroom floors.

Upstairs, I unpacked my bag and pulled out all the things I would need this morning. One black suit, the one my mom had worn ages ago to my bat mitzvah—it wouldn't fit me as well as Miranda's black suit fit the real her, but that couldn't be helped. Hopefully nobody would look too close. After the suit, I stretched on a pair of sleek black gloves—I'd leave no fingerprints. No trace. One official police ID. We looked different, but I pulled my hair into a tight bun, rouged my cheeks red, and plucked my eyebrows thin to make the differences as small as possible. Hopefully nobody would look too close. I just had to get through the police station and into the basement without rousing any suspicions.

And, finally, what I'd left for last: the key to my mom's car, currently parked in the driveway. The mere thought of getting back in the driver's seat made my palms so slick with sweat I dropped my phone. It landed with an ominous crack. I considered picking it up and checking to see if I'd broken it, but I didn't bother. I wouldn't need it anymore. I left it there, facedown on my floor, most likely cracked beyond all repair.

The morning was so beautiful and serene and normal I actually burst into laughter as I stepped outside. Birds twittered, soaring over me like they had somewhere to go besides flying into windows and breaking their sorry little necks. Wind rustled the perfectly manicured lawns; each of which was greener than the last, as if our street were competing in some sort of Miss Green Beauty Pageant.

I was laughing again.

I turned for one last and what might be one final look at my house. No, not my house, I told myself. Not Julia's house. Lucy Black's house. Lucy Black, rest in peace. She'd lived a quiet life, and she'd fallen in love, and then she'd disappeared like she'd never been.

Two of my neighbors were in the process of leaving for work, kissing their beautiful families goodbye. Neither of them spared me or my mom's car a glance. I took a few deep breaths, pushing back nausea, before climbing into the driver's side and revving the engine.

My physical reaction was instantaneous—chilly beads of sweat clung to my forehead and upper lip, my throat closed halfway, making me gasp for every molecule of oxygen, and the skin on my hands felt shiny and tight. I went to shift the car into drive. The dying fish in my chest, which was somehow still flopping, had invited a number of his dying fish friends to a party in my stomach. I thought I might throw up.

I could do it, though. I could drive. I had to. I forced out thoughts of Aiden dying behind the wheel, of my wrist cracking like an egg. I closed my eyes for a second, just for a second, and saw eyes staring back at me, shocked eyes, scared eyes, boring through a cracked windshield.

My eyes popped back open. I could do it. It was a short ride.

And I had no choice. It wasn't like I could ask Michael for his help with this. He'd done all he could for me. This last part was all mine. I knew the way to the police station by heart; I'd memorized the directions from Google Maps—three different sets of directions, in fact, just in case any roadblocks or anything should pop up—and programmed them into the car's GPS. But it turned out I didn't need either of the alternate routes; I just drove right on into the parking lot and parked in the middle, not too close, not too far away. I didn't want to draw any extra attention to myself. I expected to hear sirens blaring as I walked in the front door, even with the sunglasses obscuring half my face; to have a cage clamp down on me from the ceiling; to be swarmed by cops enraged by the thought of me, stupid little me, pretending to be one of them.

But there was none of that. I simply squared my shoulders, nodded at the cops on duty, flashed Miranda's ID and presented it for a scan, and walked through the office. I scanned the interior: an entryway and waiting room out front; then a large room filled with desks, filing cabinets, and assorted other office things; a hallway that must lead to the bathrooms, the chief's and deputy chief's offices, and interview rooms branching from the sides; then a stairway to the basement, where they kept the holding cells. From what Miranda had said, my brother wouldn't be in the regular holding cell with the drunks and hookers and vagrants. There was a more secure holding cell, down another flight of stairs, near the water heater, where they were keeping him.

I nodded at a few of the officers at their desks sifting through mountains of paperwork, keeping an eye out for Michael's dad. His dad was hopefully still in Berkeley with Aria for the day, but that could always change. Anything could change. If he was here, all I could do was duck behind my sunglasses and pray. "Morning, Officer," one of the cops said, smiling absently.

I tried to smile back as I nodded. "Morning," I said. I held my arms by my sides as I walked through the room. Were my arms too stiff? I swung them a little. No, now I looked too carefree. Somebody else nodded at me. I nodded back. Oh God, they were on to me.

"If you want some coffee, Officer, there's some in the kitchen," someone piped up from behind me.

I gave a wave of my hand. "Thanks, maybe," I said. "I'm just here to see the prisoner."

Thankfully, that didn't set off any red alarms. I continued through the office, each step as loud as a bomb, and made it into the hallway. I exhaled heavily in relief. One room down.

Then a hand clamped around my arm. "Julia?"

TWENTY

I was caught. It was over. Everything was going to come out. I might as well be dead.

I might as well be dead. My hand was already by my side. I lifted it so that my fingers grazed the bulge of the gun in my suit jacket. If I ended it now, I wouldn't have to deal with the fallout. I couldn't deal with the fallout. It would be worse than the days before I became Lucy Black.

"Julia?"

My captor was Michael. Life whooshed back through me like a cool breeze, rendering me so weightless I might have floated away save for the stabilizing hand on my arm. "Michael, what the *hell*?"

His lips opened again; I stood, frozen, as he moved them in what appeared to be exaggerated shapes. "I should be asking you that," he said. A vein ticked in his forehead like the countdown clock of a bomb. "What the—"

"Shut up." My eyes moved frantically back and forth, but nobody was gaping at me in horror or pulling their gun. We were hidden from view in the narrow hallway, but it was only a matter of time before somebody took a stroll for some of the aforementioned coffee. "We can't talk out here." I tried to pull him to the side. He resisted at first, but I slowly dragged him through a doorway that turned out to lead to the handicapped bathroom, a small, dank, mushroom-smelling space packed with boxes. It was so claustrophobic I could hardly breathe; just standing there we were pressed right up against each other, our elbows nearly brushing the stacks. And yet I couldn't help but let out a dry chuckle. In times of woe I always seemed to find myself in handicapped bathrooms.

"Did you follow me here?" I finally whispered, my voice shrinking even further at the sound of footsteps in the hallway outside.

"Yes, I followed you," he said vehemently. "But what I want to know is—"

I shoved him. His back hit the wall, and his mouth dropped open in surprise. "Do you have any idea how important this is?" I hissed. "Do you have any idea what you might have screwed up?"

"Breaking your homicidal maniac of a brother out of prison, where he rightly belongs?"

I saw red. Literally, my vision flashed red. I couldn't see anything but blood and heat and rage. I might or might not have shoved him again. I couldn't be held responsible for what the red did. "I don't want to break him out of prison," I said, my face so close to his I knew he could feel my breath on his nose, hot and spiteful. "I need to talk to him. He's planning on talking to the police later today. On telling them the whole truth and nothing but the truth, so help him God."

Michael was silent for a moment. "He never confessed, did he?"

"Not that I know of," I said. I knew he didn't. Otherwise things would have worked out very differently. Otherwise the police actually would have had something to crow about. "I thought he was as good as dead until just a few weeks ago." Tears sprang to my eyes. "I need to tell him goodbye. Privately."

Michael sighed. "This is really hard on you, isn't it?"

"No," I said. "What's really hard on me is having a stalker who followed me here from my *house*."

From the shock on his face, you'd think I'd slapped him. "It's not like that," he said.

"Oh yeah?" I snarled. "Because it looks that way from over here."

"Listen," he said heatedly. "Alane called me. She said you were acting really weird and you practically spat in her face. She was worried about you and she asked me to make sure you were okay.

"You know I have study hall first period, so I skipped and went to your house. But as I was going to pull in your driveway, I saw you skulking around in that outfit and getting in the car. I've never seen you drive before. What else did you expect me to do?"

"Stay out of this," I said. That could've applied to anything, I thought. To kissing me. To traveling with me to Elkton. To ever speaking to me in the first place. "You would've been better off if you'd never gotten tangled with me in the first place. You know what you should do?" I didn't wait for him to answer. "You should turn around and walk away and pretend you never met Julia Vann or Lucy Black or whoever the hell I'll be tomorrow."

He grabbed my hands. I tried to pull away, but he kneaded my palms with his thumbs. Despite myself, my shoulders slumped. "Never," he said. His Adam's apple bobbed in his throat. "I'll help you, Julia. I'll help you say goodbye to your brother." He was speaking so quietly I almost couldn't hear him, and I wondered, for a moment, if I was imagining it all. "He's done a terrible thing, but he's still your brother. If Aria killed someone, I wouldn't stop loving her."

Tears choked me. It was a few seconds before I was physically able to speak. "Are you sure?" I asked. "You might end up worse than grounded for life. This is probably illegal. No, this is definitely illegal."

"I've already run off with you, picked my way around dead cops," he said. "I don't think anything could be worse than that."

I had so much to do, and so much to think about, but I was too busy dissolving into a warm glow I thought might be happiness. I wasn't entirely sure. It had been a while since I'd felt anything but stressed or afraid or tense, and there was so much on the line it felt almost obscene to be happy.

"You have no idea," I said, but I didn't have time to talk him out of it. To talk him away from me. My brother would be talking this evening. "My brother is downstairs. How did you get this far, by the way?"

"My dad," he said. Duh, Julia. "Everybody here knows me. I've had the run of the place since I was five. They probably just think I'm stopping in to bring him food or something. He'll be back at work tonight." He eyed me up and down. "How did you get in, anyway?"

"I stole an ID and put on a black suit," I said.

"You stole an ID? From that cop yesterday? Won't she, like, notice?"

"Don't worry about that," I said. "We have to keep going. We have to keep the element of surprise." The element of surprise. More important than oxygen, or nitrogen, or whatever makes my mother's pills work so spectacularly quickly.

"Of course," he said. "He's just downstairs. You just want to talk to him, right?"

"Yes," I said. "I only want to talk."

I eased back into the hallway first, checking to make sure no cops would see Michael and me emerging from the bathroom together. I nodded at one walking back to the office area, steaming cup of coffee in hand, and stretched, killing some time. When the officer was gone, I pulled

260

the door back open, and Michael slipped into the hallway after me.

A stroke of luck: there was nobody in residence in the regular holding cells, and therefore no cops guarding them. A further stroke of luck: Michael knew where the key was, he said, that unlocked the heavy metal door that led down to the secure holding cell. I had assumed the key would be somewhere obvious. But now I was glad he was with me. The retrieval took Michael only a couple of minutes. And there wasn't supposed to be anyone downstairs; they were short on men as it was, and there was no way out of the basement aside from the one door, so where would my brother go? I slipped through, held the door for Michael, then shut it firmly behind me, resolutely listening for the lock to click shut. It was a heavy door. I hoped it was soundproof.

Now only a flight of stairs and another barred door stood between me and my brother. Emptiness gnawed at my insides. So this was it. I only needed a second or two with him. And then that would be it. There would be no more miraculous escapes, or do-overs.

I cupped Michael's cheek. His chin was a paradox, rough as sandpaper yet somehow smooth and soft at the same time. I traced his jawline with a finger. "I don't think I've thanked you yet," I said.

"For what?"

"For loving me," I said. I stood on my tiptoes and pressed my lips gently to his. There was no paradox here: they were

261

only smooth and soft, silky against my own. "And for everything that comes along with that."

His hands held my hips as I lowered myself down. His touch ignited small fires beneath my skin. My one regret: I'd never get to see him naked. I was sure he'd have a beautiful body. Swimmers all had beautiful bodies. "You don't need to thank me," he said. "That's not what love is."

Really? A new complication. I would think it would be nice to thank someone for loving you. It wasn't like they had to, after all. It wasn't like it was easy to love someone like me. I parted my lips, ready to ask, then clamped them shut. I wouldn't need to know what love was anymore. "Let's go," I said instead.

We went.

I pushed the second door open cautiously, my fingers tense against my holster, into a small, spare room. I took another step in, Michael so close on my rear I could feel the heat of his body radiating into me.

There wasn't much space to move into. There was only a short hallway, with an empty folding chair propped against the wall, and then the cell door. It looked almost like a movie set's idea of a jail cell: barred door; long, low cot; combo sink and toilet so shiny silver I could see my reflection in it. And my brother. My heart skipped a beat when I saw him sitting on the edge of the bed, his head in his hands, whispering to himself. He lifted his head when I came in and jumped to his feet when he saw it was me. We reached the bars at the same time; I wrapped my fingers around two of them, and he wrapped his fingers around mine.

"Ryan," I whispered.

"You came." His hands were firm around mine, strong, even the left one that didn't close all the way. "I knew you would."

My vision shimmered. "Of course I came," I said. I cleared my throat. "What do they know? What did you tell them?" I jerked my head back at Michael, just slightly, a tiny bit, to remind my brother that we weren't alone. I didn't have to remind myself; I could feel Michael's presence in waves of heat, a being that warped time and space around it. He didn't belong here, not in the same room as my brother.

Ryan cleared his throat in response. He got it. My heart squeezed, wrung itself out. He got me. Nobody would ever get me like he would. Not even Michael. "Nothing," he said. "I mean, nothing they didn't already know. I said some things when I woke up from the coma, but then I . . ." His face sank. "I talked to Dr. Spence."

I rubbed his fingers with my thumb. "I know," I said. "It's okay. He won't be talking to anyone." I smiled tightly at him, trying to look reassuring. "The police were ready to make your recovery public, weren't they? Bring you to trial? But you talked to Dr. Spence. And he broke you out to give himself time to prove your version of the story."

"I never meant to hurt you," Ryan said. His eyes shone. I

could see myself mirrored in them, reflecting over and over, Julia into infinity. So many of me. "I would never, ever hurt you, Julia."

But he did. He did hurt me. He got me into this mess, and he would have to get me out. I released my smile, let it bound free. Let it reassure him. "It's okay," I said. "I forgive you, Ryan. I love you." The words came out without any hesitation. "I love you. You know that, Ryan?"

"I love you, too, Julia."

I sniffed. Tears were welling over, blurring my vision. "And I promise you I'll do everything you asked me to," I said. "I'll tell the whole truth. I promise you that."

He smiled. After all this time, it still struck me as guileless, innocent . . . trusting. He might not have trusted anyone else, but he trusted me. I was his sister, his other half, and if he couldn't believe in me, then what could he believe in? "Thank you," he said. "That means everything to me."

I pulled my hands back, away from his, then pressed my face into the bars. Though Michael was here, I couldn't stop now; I was past the point of no return. "I love you, Ryan," I said, and kissed him hard through the bars. I tasted iron. I smelled blood.

He was smiling still, with bliss this time, as I pulled back. "Remember that," I said tenderly, lowering my hand to my side. "I might not know what love is, but I know I love you."

"I know," he said. "I love you, Julia."

"I love you, Ryan," I said, and my voice never wavered. "I love you so much."

I pulled back, wiped the tears from my eyes, and shot him in the head.

Before the dust settled, before the recoil finished shuddering my arm, I whirled around to Michael. "Don't move," I said. "If you move, I shoot."

There didn't seem to be any danger of Michael moving; he appeared to have turned into a statue, his back melting into the wall, his jaw practically on his chest. His lips were moving, like he wanted to say something, but nothing came out. I could see his love for me harden into cracked bits, like drying mud, and fall in a shower to the floor.

I wiped my eyes again, smearing him across the room. "I promised my brother I would tell the whole truth," I said. "So here it is."

Re: Ryan Vann, age 17

Noor and I pored over the records of the shooting for three hours last night, side by side in a dim, dusty records room, our eyes straining to read each line of type and examine each model of the room.

Noor was finally convinced of my interpretation. "I have a friend who will help you when you get there," he said. "Another officer. One who's not opposed to taking 'gifts' in exchange for his help." I appreciated Noor's frankness. "His name is Joseph Goodman. I'll give you his card."

I went in to see Ryan early this morning, the earliest the police would let me. "I believe you," I said. "And I'm going to help prove it."

He sucked a breath through his teeth, like my words had hurt him, but then he nodded. "Thank you," he whispered, and turned away.

If what I'm beginning to suspect is correct, Ryan Vann is not the most dangerous person in his family.

I need to go to Sunny Vale.

TWENTY-ONE

I remember everything.

Once upon a time I got sick of waking up early to take my yappy little dog for walks and of spending half my allowance money to buy its stupid food. When my brother asked if he could take the dog apart to see what it looked like on the inside, I said okay. As long as I got to watch. And when we got caught, he took the blame.

I remember everything.

Once upon another time there was a fire. It wasn't a big fire, not a house, not a school. It was the tree house of a girl who had made the grievous offense of making fun of how close my brother and I were. I wanted her dead. No, I wanted her to burn.

He lit the match and touched it to the tree, but we stood together to watch it burn. And when the girl's mother spotted us through the trees, once again, my brother took the blame.

I remember everything.

I haven't been entirely honest.

Take driving. It is true that I didn't drive after Aiden's accident. It is also true that I didn't drive for a while before that, even though I'd taken driver's ed and passed the written exam and had done my requisite six hours with an instructor and many other hours with my mom and dad.

The California provisional permit allows you to drive at age fifteen and a half, as long as you're accompanied by someone twenty-five or older. For my brother and me, that meant we were required, officially, to drive with one of our parents in the car. What that meant, unofficially, was that, starting at age fifteen and a half, we would often just drive, the two of us, one of our parents' licenses pocketed just in case. We'd switch off and go for long cruises down deserted roads, fantasizing that everybody in the world but us had been cleared out by a plague or a nuclear attack or face-eating aliens. It wasn't that we wanted anything like that to happen—not exactly, not explicitly. It was more planning for a just-in-case, pondering what might happen if everyone else on the planet should just up and vanish. Not painfully—I can't stress that enough. Just dissolve into the air, or sink through the ground, or give one last exhale and disappear.

The day it happened was one of those crisp fall days where the air snaps between your teeth and the leaves are such brilliant shades of red and yellow you just want to tell the sunset "Why bother?" I was driving, and Ryan was in the passenger seat, flipping our father's license over and over between his fingers.

"It was a meteor," I said, starting our game. The country road ahead stretched long and bright, with no houses to mar the beauty. "It struck in the Midwest, triggering the eruption of the Yellowstone supervolcano. Ash blanketed everything from Nevada to New York. This strip of coastline is the only clear place in the US.

"Of course," I hurried to add once I saw Ryan raise a finger, "the meteor strike and ensuing eruption and all the ash caused a dramatic change in climate. Nobody could buy food. Everybody in the urban areas died or fled overseas or south. Only those of us used to working the land were able to eke out a spare existence."

Neither of us had ever done so much as water a vegetable plant, but this was all hypothetical. How hard could it be to grow some potatoes or something, anyway? Just enough for the two of us. We had no plans to feed anyone else should this hypothetical world ever actually come to be. "Naturally," I continued, "once the ash cleared, within a year or two, everything settled down. There was no more humidity and no more fog. It was a balmy seventy-two degrees, dry and warm, every day of the year, in Elkton, California."

"Seventy-two is too warm," Ryan said.

"No one cares."

"You care."

"Fine, I care. It can be seventy-one."

"Sixty-eight."

"Seventy, and that's my final offer."

"Deal."

I sighed and focused on driving again, but was immediately distracted by something moving by the side of the road. No, not something. Someone. A runner, spandexed, red-bearded, old. Maybe forty. Panting. "Do you see that?"

Ryan looked. "That guy?"

"Yes, that guy. What else would I be pointing at?" My heart sped up. "He's ruining everything. How can we live in this empty meteor-world when he's here, chugging through it?"

Ryan squinted at him. "Go faster," he suggested. "We can leave him behind and pretend he wasn't even there."

My heart sped up again, to the point where it practically vibrated in my chest. "That's not good enough," I said.

"Are you sure?" Ryan said. His voice was tense, alert.

I nodded and lifted my hands from the wheel.

Ryan reached over and jerked the wheel. One motion, one second, and our car slid off the side of the road and plowed into the runner with the stomach-turning crack of a butterflied chicken. I didn't hear the man cry out. Maybe he didn't. Maybe he just bounced off the hood of our car, his head twisted in the most wrong kind of way, and slipped bonelessly down the hill beside the road.

I turned to watch, and Ryan jerked the wheel again. "Go, go, go!" he was yelling. With one last glance over my shoulder, I placed my hands back on the wheel and went, my heart pounding against the inside of my ribs with every pump of the gas pedal. I didn't remember driving home, but somehow we made it without spotlights zeroing in on us from above or sirens wailing behind us. My brother was good with cars, and so as soon as we pulled into the garage he suctioned out the dent in the hood and polished off the drying blood the runner had left behind. The windshield had cracked, but the next day he fixed that, too. I wasn't sure exactly how. Somehow he was able to fix everything but me.

We found out later that the jogger died. I hadn't been surprised in the least; no human head could turn that way, unless they were part owl. His name was Joe Johnson, a generic name for a generic thirty-five-year-old insurance salesman, doting husband, loving father to two young boys and a Labrador retriever generically named Fido.

His death hadn't been what stopped me from driving, though.

No. It was the thrill that pumped through my veins as I watched his lifeless body tumble off the road. It was so easy, and the payoff so great. I couldn't be tempted, because someone could catch me, and then I'd go to prison. That was what convinced me I could never drive again. The thrill was what convinced me I was beyond fixing, that my brother or I or anyone else could never make that part of me normal, whole, the way he'd suctioned out that dent.

Joe Johnson was the first. That is not a lie.

I'm stalling. To get straight to the point, I am a liar. A good one, yes, but a liar nonetheless. And no matter how good a liar you are, the fact of the matter is, the truth will always come back to haunt you. And no matter what happens in this room, whether I have five minutes left to live or five hundred years, I know it has come back to haunt me now.

My brother and I were born hand in hand. We grew up leaning on each other, sometimes Ryan holding me up, sometimes me him. On chilly camping trips, we'd huddle together in our tent for warmth. We'd watch movies together on the couch, and I'd fall asleep on his shoulder, feeling safe and warm no matter how bony that shoulder was, with his arm tucked behind my back.

It was only natural our relationship would develop. We were everything to each other emotionally, mentally, spiritually. It was only natural we would become everything to each other physically as well. It was only natural. It was only natural. *It was only natural.*

He kissed me for the first time when we were fourteen. Sure, we'd kissed each other plenty of times before that: when we were little kids playing at being a married couple, on the cheek like dutiful siblings, tentative good-night pecks in front of our parents. But this kiss? This kiss was the real thing.

I'd spent all day at band practice, learning the wonders

of the clarinet and the horrors of a splintered reed. That was back when Ryan was in band, too; he'd taken up the trumpet, though, and as brass and woodwinds practiced separately, I didn't see him until we met up for the walk home. We strode along the side of the road together in a comfortable silence, my clarinet case tucked against my chest, his trumpet case swinging by his side. Light from the setting sun filtered red and orange through the autumn leaves rustling overhead. "So how was practice, Dizzy?" I asked.

"What?" His eyebrows, thick and heavy as caterpillars, bunched together quizzically.

I sighed. "Dizzy? You know, Dizzy . . ." I couldn't think of his last name. "Dizzy something. The famous trumpet player." It came to me. "Gillespie! Dizzy Gillespie." I sighed again. "Never mind. The moment is gone."

"You killed it," Ryan agreed. "I would counter with a famous clarinet player, but I don't think there are any."

"Of course there are!" I went to name one, but my mind was blank. "There are lots. I just can't think of any."

Ryan smirked. "Yeah, okay."

"I would hit you, but I wouldn't want to hurt my baby." I clutched my clarinet case harder against my chest for emphasis. "Anything exciting happen at practice?"

Our feet crunched over dead leaves. A chilly wind whisked by, and I shivered, goose bumps popping up on my arms. "Kind of," he said finally. "Esther asked me out."

"Esther?" My mind went blank again, and then I remembered: Esther, a tall girl with arms too long for her body, who liked to braid her hair into intricate styles all over her head, who had pale blue eyes that sparkled in the shine off her mellophone. Nobody liked the mellophones. They were always off beat. Only failed trumpets switched to the mellophone. "What did you say to her?"

He shrugged. I watched his shoulders slope up, then down, so easily, as if he wasn't tipping the earth off its axis. As if he wasn't changing the way things had always been. "I said maybe. It felt weird."

My breath came in shallow gasps. "It *is* weird. Neither of us has ever gone out with anyone before."

There went his shoulders again, up and down. "Maybe we should," he said. "We're going to have to do it someday. Marriage, kids, the rest."

I darted a glance at him. He was staring off ahead, squinting as if into the sun, though it was actually setting behind us.

"Why?" I dared to ask, then held my breath.

He turned to look at me, still squinting. "What?"

"Why do we have to go out with other people?" I said. My heart pounded through my entire body. "Aren't we enough for each other?"

The crunching slowed, stopped. "Are you saying . . ."

"You are everything to me." The words burst from my chest. "I don't need anyone else."

"But . . ." He studied me as if through new eyes. I looked right back at him. It was physically painful; every nerve in my body screamed for me to look away, but I held fast. "Are you saying . . ."

"Kiss me."

A heart-stopping yearlong moment passed, one where everything might have stopped and fallen dead around me, but then he leaned over, let his trumpet case fall, and pressed his lips against mine. I drank him in for a few seconds before he pulled away. He looked stunned. "Was that okay?" he said.

I responded by pulling him back down to me, my hands traveling over the sculpted muscles of his back.

His trumpet was never the same. I went back to the side of the road the next afternoon to see what I could salvage and found it dented, dinged, tarnished, as if it had aged a hundred years in a day.

We moved slowly. It was necessary, of course, to keep it hidden from our family and friends and society as a whole; as much as I wanted to kiss him in public, to press up against him in the food court or against my locker at school like the other kids, I knew nobody would accept it. I didn't understand why it wasn't okay. We were two people who cared about each other. Why should anyone concern themselves over the blood in our veins? It wasn't like we were making them take part. This was America. Land of the free.

By the next school year, though, people were growing suspicious. Liv included. She'd broken up with her boyfriend. On the prowl for a new one, she'd set her sights on

Ryan and, by extension, on me. "You've never had a boy-friend, have you, Julia?" she asked, her eyes narrowing into slits. "But you're so pretty. Are you a lesbian or something? Because if you are, that's totally cool, you know. Even if you have seen me in the changing rooms at Forever 21. Just tell me."

So I sent Ryan on that disastrous date, and I let Liv fix me up with Aiden. I remember the first time Aiden and I kissed; we were in his car, me tucked against the passenger-side door, Aiden practically straddling the gearshift. "How was that?" he'd asked huskily, his hamburger breath gusting against my face.

It was all wrong. His teeth had knocked against mine. His nose had stuck me in the cheek. His lips were chapped and dry. "Great," I said, my stomach roiling.

I met Ryan at the front door. "I can't do it," I said. "I can't fake it. I can't be with someone who isn't you."

"I can fix that," he said.

Aiden and I went out a few more times. I cheered him on at soccer games, let him parade me around on his arm, endured his kisses, which always mysteriously tasted like various sorts of meat, even when the only thing I'd seen him eat all day was salad. But one day, as Aiden was driving me home from school, the brakes snapped. We crashed.

I sat in the passenger seat, bruised and reeling, my wrist screaming in pain, as Aiden bled to death two feet away. My ears rang so loudly I didn't hear my brother wrenching open my door before he pulled me out. I sagged onto the ground.

Shock waves rippled through me like I was the epicenter of an earthquake. "Did you do that?" I asked, dazed, steadily refusing to look over at Aiden.

"You weren't supposed to be in the car," Ryan said miserably. "Liv was supposed to drive you home today."

I could hardly hear him over all the bells clanging in my head. "Liv was sick," I said. "You almost *killed* me."

I sank into his chest. He rested his chin on the crown of my head, staring over me into the car behind. "But I didn't," he said. "And now you're all mine. For good."

The rippling waves of shock turned into rippling waves of anger, fiery and hot in the pit of my stomach. I shoved him with my good arm; taken by surprise, he stumbled three steps back before catching himself. "You almost killed me," I said. "I almost died. I don't think you get that."

He blinked. "Of course I get that," he said. "But you didn't die. You're still here."

I whirled around. "But I almost died," I said. "And now I'm angry." Neither Ryan nor I spared much thought for the boy actually dying in the car behind us. Neither of us was particularly concerned.

In revenge, I started dating Evan Wilde a few months after Aiden died. My big, dumb football player, the first to die in the band room.

The band room.

Now, that's a subject I don't want to go near.

But I promised Ryan I'd tell the whole truth, and so I *will* tell the whole truth. I owe him that, at least.

277

Evan and I dated for about four months. I let him slobber all over my chin in front of my brother, and in exchange, he boosted my image. Liv was beyond excited to go to all the football parties and hang out with the popular kids. We hadn't ever been unpopular, as in nobody had ever actively made fun of us or ignored us, but we'd been off to the side. Invisible. But with Evan by my side, I walked under a perpetual spotlight. Some of the little band freshmen, flutes and clarinets, mostly, took to following me around, basking in my newfound glow, a rarity in band kids. I knew them in passing—thought two of their names were maybe Penelope and Sophie—but otherwise didn't pay much attention. Most of my attention was dedicated to counting the times the muscle in my brother's jaw throbbed or judging the shade of red to which his face deepened every time he saw me and Evan together.

We lived in the same house, sure, but I did all I could to avoid Ryan during the day: I'd come home and shut myself in my room, only emerging when my parents were around. He'd knock on my door, stick notes through the crack, but I wouldn't budge. He'd almost killed me. He'd almost *killed* me. I wasn't talking to him until he realized how big a deal that was and begged for my forgiveness.

So it wasn't a shock when he cornered me at school that fateful afternoon, just as I was coming out of the band room, in the hallway behind the room lined with all the instrument closets. "Julia. We need to talk."

He backed me against the wall next to the clarinet

closet, pinning me in with his arms. I squirmed, trying to break free, but he pressed the length of his body against me. "Let me go."

"No." He searched me with his eyes, and when he spoke, his voice crackled with intensity. "What the hell are you doing with Evan Wilde?"

"He's my boyfriend." I wanted to cross my arms for emphasis, but there wasn't enough space. "Now let me go."

"No." He leaned down and kissed me. I resisted, keeping my lips stubbornly still, but that only lasted until my insides erupted into flame. I threw my arms around him and drew him closer, closer, closer, until even the air molecules between us were squeezed out.

"The instrument closet," I panted, and cracked the door behind me. We stumbled through.

We were so busy we didn't even hear the footsteps outside. I drew back to take a breath and looked over his shoulder to see two pairs of eyes and two mouths, all round as Cheerios, staring through the small window in the door. Those two annoying freshmen, I realized—Penelope something, Sophie something.

By the time I'd composed myself and made it out the door, Penelope and Sophie were already running down the hall. "Wait!" I shouted after them. "Stop! Tell anyone and I'll kill you both!"

But it was too late. They were deep in whispers with Elisabeth Wood, who would rush to tell Irene Papadakis and Nina Smith, who would eventually tell her boyfriend,

Danny Steinberg, who would nudge his best friend, Erick Thorson, and snicker about it. About us.

Erick Thorson was on the football team with Eddie Meyer, who was starting quarterback beside Evan's running back. Evan would rush to Liv's ear, asking her if what he'd heard could possibly be true. All this would take place in approximately an hour.

Mr. Walrus was a mistake. Mr. Walrus shouldn't have been there.

I turned to my brother. "I know how you can get me to forgive you for almost killing me in Aiden's car," I said, my voice deadly calm. "Run home and find my old backpack. The pink-and-purple one. Get Dad's gun and put it inside. Run home, and bring it back to me."

He nodded, already backing away. I know his mind was racing as frantically as mine, but he trusted me. He'd do anything I told him to.

"I'll be in the band room," I said. "Waiting."

You have to understand—I didn't want to kill anybody. Well, that's not entirely true. I would think back to Joe Johnson, and smashing into him with my car, and the thrill that coursed through my veins. I wanted to kill people; I liked how it felt, but I knew enough to know it was wrong. That doing it again could get me locked away forever. I only did what I did to protect myself. I didn't have any other options.

Most of it did depend on luck, of course. It was only a matter of luck that Penelope and Sophie and the others all had gym class last period, and their phones were tucked away in their gym lockers with their real clothes. If they hadn't all been in the same gym period, and if Penelope and Sophie hadn't been running late, without even time to stop and send a frantic mass text, it never would have been contained.

Luck. Good luck for me. Bad luck for them. It's all a matter of perspective.

But it was preparation, too, of course. I forged assorted notes (which, when found later, were blamed on Ryan) and stuck them to their gym lockers—emergency notes from club advisors: *Don't change into your school clothes, just go directly to the band room. You'll have plenty of time to change and gather your stuff later. This is an emergency.* The roof of the instrument closet fell in, or there was a fire in the locker room out at the football field. Crises that had to be dealt with right away. And I glued the alternate exits shut before anyone showed up. Superglue did the trick just fine.

And then I made my dramatic entrance from the instrument closet and stood in front of the room, an empty music stand before me, surveying all the people on the risers. Everybody had their own distinct shade of horror on their face.

"You're here because you heard a terrible rumor about me," I said. It should have taken Ryan about fifteen minutes to get home, maybe ten to find my backpack and get the gun, then fifteen to get back. It had taken about that long, maybe even longer, to figure out the chain of gossip and gather everybody together. I was just glad they'd all come. "And I wanted to talk to you about it."

"This isn't French club," Nina Smith said, still confused.

Evan's face was glowing and red, a planet all its own, or a dying star. "Can we talk in private?"

"We don't need to talk in private," I said. Now that Ryan and I had been together again, I couldn't face the thought of Evan's hot-dog breath or clumsy fingers on me. I'd already given his varsity jacket back, stuffed it symbolically into his locker while he was in gym. "Not when—"

And that was when Ryan burst through the door. He already had the gun in his hand.

You know what happened from here. I carved my name into the music stand as it all went down, knowing this was the end of life as I knew it.

First went Evan. Then Liv. Then Eddie. Then Elisabeth Wood, Irene Papadakis, Nina Smith, Danny Steinberg, and Erick Thorson piled into stacks like firewood by the superglued doors. Then Mr. Walrus, then the trembling Sophie Grant and Penelope Wong, trapped under our teacher's sweaty bulk.

When it was over, in our twelve minutes alone, Ryan dropped the gun to his side. The barrel released an acrid scent into the air. Somebody, Evan, maybe, or Eddie, had left pink spatters of brain on the blackboard. Distantly, somewhere outside, we heard shouting. People had clearly heard the shots and screams. It would only be a matter of time before the police showed up.

I think he knew then what I was going to ask him to do. I could see it in the way he searched my face. Like he knew he was never going to see it again. I was looking at him the same way, my eyes roving over the scar on his forehead from when I'd thrown that glass at him when he dared to have a crush on someone else, memorizing the slope of his nose, the golden shimmer of his hazel eyes. He was the only one. There would never be another. There *could* never be another. We were suitable only for each other. We were both born defective, lacking the same empathetic center in our brains. Or perhaps we were both born stronger. Maybe we'd gotten a glimpse in the womb of all we would need to do over the course of our lives, and had steeled ourselves, ripping those parts of our brains out right then.

"One last time," he said. He didn't have to specify. I rushed to him and we tangled together, desperately, as the blood of our classmates soaked into the carpet. His lips tasted like blood, though it might have been my imagination.

Time flew by. We pulled apart, panting, after eleven minutes that felt like eleven seconds. "Are you sure you can do it?" I asked.

You can tell me I'm a sociopath. You can tell me I feel nothing. But I promised my brother I'd tell the truth, and I'm telling the truth now when I say that I felt something then. Grief was tearing through me, a rip through the very core of my being. But he had to do it. There was no way for both of us to walk out of there, and I couldn't bear to see him in jail. Better a sweet memory than that.

"I have to," he said. "For you. For us."

He always got me. I bowed my head. I didn't want to see it happen, but I couldn't avoid the sounds: the quick intake of breath—the last one—before pulling the trigger, the single, sharp gunshot, the nanosecond of silence that hung in the air before the thud of his lifeless body hitting the ground.

Or the thud of *him* hitting the ground. Not his body, because he didn't die. I hadn't checked; I hadn't thought it necessary, and I couldn't bear it. I'd simply squared my shoulders, taken several deep, shuddering breaths, and strode out the band room door into the waiting arms of the police. Everybody who knew about my brother and me was dead. I would be okay. I would start over.

And I *was* okay until I saw Spence lurking, telling me with his mere presence that things had changed. But now my brother is dead for good, and our secret is safe, and I'll never have to worry again.

TWENTY-TWO

I was very studiously not looking at Michael as I finished my story, though I really should have been. I was pointing a gun at him, after all. What if he dove at me, or screamed and tried to run?

He wouldn't. I knew he wouldn't. Was that love? Knowing what someone would or wouldn't do before they did it?

"Did you ever care about me?" Michael said flatly. "Or were you just using me to get to him?"

"You don't understand," I said. "He wanted to tell." I remembered meeting my brother in the backyard the night Alane had slept over at my house to keep me safe. I'd wrapped my robe around myself, trying to shield my body from the chill of the night, but it didn't work.

"I can't do it anymore, Julia." I could hardly believe the changes the past year had wrought in him: the stiff left side, the stumbling

speech. "I can't keep pretending. I won't do it without you. Tell the truth with me."

My breath caught in my throat. Tell the truth? I'd go to prison and be scorned and mocked as the incestuous twin. I'd be reviled by the entire country. My parents. Alane. Michael.

"I can't," I said. "Remember? We decided you would take the blame."

"You *decided* I would take the blame." He crossed his arms. "We didn't decide I would keep taking the blame. You made it look like I killed Dr. Spence. I liked Dr. Spence." A muscle worked in his jaw. "I don't want to tell them without your blessing, but I will. I'll give you some time to think about it. I want us to do it together because we've done everything together, but I'll do it myself if I have to."

"No." The word came out reflexively.

"Of course not," he said. "Why would you sacrifice your new life and your precious new boyfriend?"

He knew about Michael. "Why should both of us go away when—"

"I've spent the last year in solitary, Julia, relearning how to talk and eat with a spoon and wipe my own ass." A fine spray of spit settled over my face, and I flinched. "All alone. By myself. Not answering any of their questions. Protecting you. And you've spent the last year gallivanting around with your new friends and hooking up with some new boy. I don't think that's fair. I mean it, Julia. I'll tell." He stepped back, melting into the darkness. "I'll give you some time to come around. I know you will. I have faith in you."

286

He shouldn't have. My voice shook as I spoke next. "Yes, you were very helpful. But I swear, I wasn't using you."

"But you want to keep this a secret. And you've told me."

He'd picked up on it. My hand was shaking now, too, not just my voice. Because I'd killed so many people to protect my secrets. Evan. Liv. Eddie Meyer. Elisabeth Wood. Irene Papadakis. Nina Smith. Danny Steinberg. Erick Thorson. Mr. Walrus. Sophie Grant. Penelope Wong.

Dr. Spence.

Miranda.

My brother.

There was real fear in Michael's eyes because he knew exactly what I was thinking. If I didn't want everything getting out, he had to die.

"I could make it look like a battle," I said, my voice deceptively calm. The way I framed Dr. Spence's death as my brother's doing. The way I'd crushed my mom's pills into Miranda's hot chocolate and left her there in the back of the parking lot—she wouldn't be waking up anytime soon. "You snuck in for some thrills, to talk to the killer with me. Ryan got free, grabbed your gun, shot you. I wrestled the gun away and shot him. I'm traumatized, yet again. Nobody could prove otherwise." I was very, very good at this.

"Julia," Michael said. "Please."

I looked at the gun. I looked at him. I looked back at the gun. I didn't hear anyone coming; the room must indeed have been soundproofed. But eventually someone would come down to check in. I couldn't stand here forever and keep us suspended in this nebulous state between action and inaction, no matter how much I wanted to.

I had to kill him. If I didn't kill him, what was the point of everything I'd done so far? Why were the eleven dead? Why had I staged those deaths? And why, why, why had I killed my brother, my only? If I didn't kill Michael, they would all have died in vain. All my secrets would get out. I would be hated. Hunted. Even if I made it away, started over as someone new, I would forever be looking over my shoulder.

And yet . . . and yet.

There was the determined set of his jaw when he told me he'd go with me to Elkton. There was the glow on his face when he stirred the sauce for his lasagna and poured me a cup of hot chocolate straight from his heart. There was the graze of stubble as he kissed me, and the catch in his voice when he told me he loved me, and the way my mom described the glow on my face when I realized I had his love held tight in my fist.

The epiphany struck me like a firework. *This* was love. Love was not shooting somebody even though you really should. Love was leaving someone free to destroy your life and stomp on the ruins because you couldn't bear the thought of ending theirs. Love was putting somebody else's needs over your own. I couldn't shoot him, because I loved him.

I tucked the gun into my waistband. "Give me an hour to get away," I said. "That's all I ask."

He said nothing. I avoided his eyes as I turned my back, exposing myself to him, and walked toward the door. I almost hoped he would stop me, but he didn't. I couldn't look at him. I didn't want the last expression I'd see on him to be one of horror and loathing.

I expected at any second to feel someone's hand clamp around my shoulder and tell me I was under arrest. I had my gun just in case—I'd sooner shoot myself than fall victim to the same system that had held my brother. But nobody did. Nothing happened. I nodded goodbye to the cops in the office, still working through their mounds of paper, climbed into my mom's car, and drove off into the figurative sunset.

TWENTY-THREE

Once upon a time my name was Julia Vann. Then, for another, wonderful time, it was Lucy Black. For a brief flash I was Julia Vann again, but that burned out faster than a sparkler on the Fourth of July.

Now my name is Ariella Brown. I wanted to name myself after Alane, or after one of Michael's sisters, but I'm not stupid. I won't do anything that could possibly help them find me. The *A* is enough of a tribute.

Ariella Brown lives in New York City. The city is a big place, and it's easy for someone to disappear.

Especially when no one is looking for her.

I've Googled *Julia Vann* so many times I'm starting to worry the police will track me down through it, even though I'm filching off a neighbor's Wi-Fi. The eleven-year-old cancer victim Julia Vann is still dead, and the volleyball-playing Julia Vann ended up deciding on UCLA and the scholarship (and seems happy there, even with a recent shoulder strain), but nothing new turns up about me. I'm assuming the cops want to keep everything that happened, motives and all, a secret. No one wants to admit they were outsmarted by a stupid teenager.

I was surprised by one thing I found, however. I'd Googled everyone associated with the case, from Spence to Joseph Goodman, and that included Miranda. I'd expected to find her obituary, maybe a tribute featuring stunned relatives and friends with no idea why she'd descended into drugs. But I'd apparently misjudged, hadn't given her enough of my mother's pills. I found a snippet on a state college website a few months ago talking about their incoming candidates for a master's degree in social work, and Miranda was among them. I'm not unhappy she survived. I wish her well.

I didn't Google my parents. Ariella Brown doesn't have parents. I can only assume that Mr. and Mrs. Black are happier not being parents anymore.

Miranda apparently didn't talk, and Michael didn't, either, at least not that Google can tell me. I wonder, sometimes, if the love Michael once felt for me was enough for him to keep my secrets. If he, too, claimed amnesia. If he let some big, fat crocodile tears slide down his cheeks and then moved back into his life, like I'd never been there at all.

Google tells me he's done quite well for himself in this last year. He made it to states in the butterfly, finished fourth, and will be coming out to NYU in the fall to study history and swim. His oldest sister, the one he thought of as more of a distant aunt, lives out here—I've walked past her building once or twice, maybe even seen her, though I don't remember her face that well. Sometimes I wonder if he's coming out here to become closer with his sister, to see what he's missed out on.

Or maybe it's because of Alane, who will be attending Columbia. After I vanished, Alane threw herself into her studies and graduated as valedictorian and captain of the show choir, which she led to a fine showing at regionals. I watched their video online; her voice was richer and fuller than I'd ever heard it before, with a thread of melancholy in it that brought tears to the judges' eyes. Sometimes I fancy I'm the reason for that, too.

They're together now. Alane and Michael. One of Alane's comments online celebrating their one-year anniversary tells me that they leaned heavily on each other after I left, which soon progressed into something more than friendship. I love them both. I hope they love each other.

I like to think that they're being pulled to New York because of me, because they're in my orbit, that I'm Saturn and they're my rings.

I know that's ridiculous. The city is a big place.

I'll probably never see them again.

ACKNOWLEDGMENTS

It's impossible to thank everybody who influenced this book or my writing in a few pages, so before I start in on the specifics: thank you, all of you, who have championed my book on Twitter or talked over a plot point with me or helped me somehow with this whole book thing.

Merrilee Heifetz, you are wise and wonderful and the best agent anyone could ever ask for. Sarah Nagel, you found me and let me cry on you and are just generally amazing, really. Michael Mejias, I don't know where I would be today without you. Thank you, thank you, thank you. Thank you to everybody else at Writers House, too, and to Kassie Evashevski and the rest of United Talent for handling the film side.

Chelsea Eberly, thank you for being the best editor I could possibly have ended up with—the way you "get" my writing and my book never ceases to amaze me. Michelle Nagler, thank you for acquiring me and championing me through every step of the process. And thank you to editorial assistant extraordinaire Jenna Lettice, as well as to Aisha Cloud, Jocelyn Lange, Nicole de las Heras, and Christine Ma.

Thank you to the friends who supported me throughout this whole process, especially those who let me steal parts of their lives or our friendships in my writing: Christienne Damatac, Shimmy Edwards, Eleni Axiomakaros, and Kim Holmes. My colleagues at Lippincott Massie McQuilkin have been incredibly supportive of me and my writing, especially Kent D. Wolf; I couldn't ask for a better workplace.

Thank you to the critique partners and beta readers who helped make this book and my writing better: Annette Dodd, Brenda McKenna, Lucas Hargis, and Dahlia Adler. Fearless Fifteeners, I'm thrilled to be on this ride with all of you and glad to have you on my side. And thank you to all the teachers and librarians throughout the years who helped this dream come true, especially Emily Franklin, Mary-Sherman Willis, and Naomi Fletcher.

Finally, I don't want to imagine life without my weird and wonderful extended family—grandparents, uncles, aunts, and cousins—and my siblings, Rebecca, Adam, Noah, and Sam. I love you all, and I'm so glad our relationships are nothing like the ones in this book.

Turn the page for a sneak peek at
Amanda Panitch's next nerve-fraying thriller!

She's done with the past. . . .

But the past isn't done with her.

NEVER MISSING NEVER FOUND

AMANDA PANITCH

author of *Damage Done*

PROLOGUE

I didn't choose to join the illustrious society of missing girls. I didn't grab an application, dot my *i*'s with hearts (it was third grade, okay?), and sign my name with a flourish in my newly acquired cursive. I was taken.

My breath puffed into clouds and the cold cut through me clean, like a knife, and yet when the car idled to a stop next to the sidewalk, I chose *not* to get in. It didn't matter. I was a short, skinny little kid, and it was easy enough for the man to get out of the car, tuck me under his arm like a football, and whisk me away.

And I didn't choose Pixie. If the woman upstairs had given me a choice, I would have asked for a nice girl. A girl to stroke my hair when I cried and make up stories with me to chase away the dark. I wouldn't have chosen this skinny girl with the rat face and ever-darting eyes. Still, after a month of scrubbing floors and crying into my dirty mattress—my only friend the dim, flickering bulb swinging overhead—I took the girl she gave me.

I made almost no choices in that basement. None that mattered. I secretly chose to call the woman upstairs Stepmother, after the evil stepmother who made Cinderella scour the fireplace until her knuckles bled, but it wasn't like that turned me into an actual Cinderella and sent me a fairy godmother to sweep me away. Stepmother chose the clothes Pixie and I wore, the chores she'd make us do, the food we ate, and the times we woke up. The only real choices we had were how much food to eat and what time to go to sleep, and as eating too little or going to sleep too late made us painfully hungry or tired the next day, they weren't real choices at all.

At the end of my time with Stepmother, I made one choice. That choice mattered. That choice changed everything—took my path and Pixie's path and untangled them in one swift rip.

After so long without the ability to choose, making choices feels . . . I don't know, like a superpower. Five choices can change the world.

Or at least myself.

CHAPTER ONE

In the first issue of the Skywoman comics, the good citizens of Silver City are in trouble. An eeeeevil villain has diverted the course of a fiery meteor and has, for no good reason, decided to plop it right on the city itself. Everybody's weeping and tearing at their hair and pounding the ground with desperation, but there's nothing they can do (like go to another city, apparently).

Until Skywoman shows up in a swirl of baby blue and gold. She swoops through the air and forces that meteor back on track. Then she decapitates the eeeeevil villain for good measure. Everybody cheers and kisses the ground they were just beating.

In the basement, every time I closed my eyes, that's

what I pictured: Skywoman, sailing down from the sky, smashing the bars of the basement's window in one great sweep, and lifting me out by the nape of my neck, as if I were a kitten. She never came. Because she isn't real.

The theme park bearing her image is, though.

I think it would embarrass her, honestly.

The employment office of Five Banners Adventure World, home of Skywoman and the League of the Righteous, is more trailer than office, plunked at the far side of the vast employee parking lot, where it creaks on its wheels every time a gust of wind blows through. I sit in one of the trailer's tiny cubicles, my dignity cupped in my hands as I speak to one of the park's assistant managers, who doesn't look a second older than me.

"I just love working with people," I lie as enthusiastically as I can manage. "Making people happy makes me happy. I love to problem-solve." Did I hit all the buzzwords the job listing mentioned? "I don't have any retail experience, but I've done some babysitting." I thrust my hands out in front of me and unfurl my fingers, revealing my dignity, the gleaming and golden center of a flower.

The assistant manager, who wears a lime-green polo so bright it hurts my eyes and clashes with her blond hair, smiles. "You sound like you'll be a great fit here, with your zeal for helping people," she says. "Congratulations, Scarlett. You've got the job."

"Yay," I say.

"You look like a medium-size women's shirt," she says,

apparently not much impressed with my display of zeal. That's fine, because my zeal stems mostly from a desire to pay for my gas and car insurance. It's not like I really use my car to go anywhere, but I need to have it, because as long as I have it, I *can* go somewhere if I want to. Without it, I'm trapped. "What size pants are you?"

I tell her, and she stands. "Great, I'll be right back," she says. I wave a silent goodbye to my dignity as she goes. Anyone who works at Five Banners Adventure World over the summer needs to be prepared to exchange her dignity for the allotted two lime-green polo shirts, two pairs of khaki pants, a brown belt, and a name tag that screams SCARLETT! in bubble letters. Bonus points for knowledge of Wonderman, Skywoman, and the gang, the group of superheroes around whom the park is based. I love comics, so I win all the bonus points.

It's worth the temporary loss of dignity to be here, surrounded by Skywoman and Wonderman and their crew. I spent so many years imagining them that the thought of seeing them walking around every day, of talking to them— well, the people dressed up as them—is so exciting. What I really want is to be one of the girls who get to wear the Skywoman costume, but you're required to put in a season of work at the park before you can transition to the Costumed Character Department. This is my one season. And then I'll get to make kids' days, smile wide and tell them that nothing will ever hurt them. That's not true, of course, but it's a good thing for someone to believe. At least for a little while.

The assistant manager bustles back in, her arms over-flowing with tacky clothing. She dumps them in my arms and grabs a set of forms off the desk. "You just have to sign here," she says, pointing out the signature lines with a pointy crimson nail. She flutters lashes coated so thickly with mascara I imagine it must be a struggle for her to open and close them, like lifting miniature weights with every blink. "To say you received each part of your uniform, that they're all in good condition, et cetera, et cetera."

I run my new shirts through my fingers. They stink of industrial detergent and the fabric is rough against my skin. My fingers tingle with the ghosts of old calluses. "There's a stain up by the neck here," I say, and Stepmother's voice echoes in my skull, *r*'s rolling with her Eastern European accent. I was never able to pin down exactly what country she'd come from, just the general area. *Not good enough, girl. Do you know what happens to girls who are not good enough?* "And a thread's ripped out here."

The assistant manager snorts. "If that's the worst you get, you're lucky." Her name tag screams MONICA! "My first year I got a pair of pants that were ripped right through the crotch. I had to sew them up myself, and my supervisor told me they looked unprofessional. My pay got docked for that."

I check both my pairs of khakis for rips through the crotch. All the crotches are intact, thank goodness. Though if I have to sew them up myself, my sewing will be perfect. Perfect, neat, *good* little stitches. Maybe I can teach this

Monica how to sew. She'll marvel at my talents, ask me how I got so good.

I've been quiet for too long. I should probably express sympathy or something. That's what a normal person would do. Like my sister. "That stinks."

"It's cool," Monica says. "Everything else is great here, really. Job is great, people are great, lots of fun perks." Her voice sounds rote, memorized. This is probably the speech she gives to all the new peons. "Do you have any questions? Orientation is next week."

"I think I'm good," I say, and I stand. "I just show up here for orientation?"

"Yeah. It'll be in the arena, inside the park, but there'll be signs pointing you there from here." She hands me a stack of papers, glossy brochures and forms emblazoned with the dual insignias of Skywoman and Wonderman, who are positioned front and center on the top brochure. As they should be, of course. They're the heads of the League of the Righteous, or LoR for short. They can save anyone. Or so I thought when I was little. Before I turned eight.

They couldn't save little Scarlett. Or Pixie.

I shiver, a trail of cold water rushing over my spine.

To distract myself, I think hard about Skywoman's first epic battle with her archenemy, the Blade. The Blade murdered Skywoman's parents back when Skywoman was simply Augusta Leigh Sorensen, setting Augusta on her heroic path in the first place. Skywoman unleashed her lasso made of clouds, which swirled over her head under its own power.

Even after so many years, Pixie has a way of working herself into every facet of my life. She's there when I eat breakfast, when I sit down to do my homework, when I feel the sun wash warm over my face. Always reminding me she'll never get to do any of those things again.

I swallow hard and concentrate harder on the battle going on in my head. The Blade's always-sinister yellow eyes, flashing like a cat's. Her claws shearing through Sky-woman's lasso and then lunging at Skywoman's throat.

"Are you okay?" Monica asks. She smiles sympathetically at me, as if she knows exactly what I'm going through. She doesn't, of course, but I appreciate the effort, and so I try to smile back.

"Yeah, sorry. Just got dizzy when I stood up. Guess I should've eaten breakfast."

"It's the most important meal of the day!" Monica chirps. "You got everything?"

I pile my uniforms, my forms, my brochures, my everything, into a precarious leaning tower in my arms. "I think so," I say. "Thanks. I guess I'll see you next week?"

She goes to shake my hand but drops her arms and laughs when she registers my leaning tower. "No problem," she says. "See you next week."

My first job. I've chosen Five Banners, and Five Banners has chosen me back. This is the second choice I've ever made that has meant anything.

. . .

I dump my papers and uniforms in the passenger seat of my car. The air feels warm and humid, and it smells like wet leaves and pavement; it must have rained while I was inside filling out forms and working my way through my assorted interviewers. Roller-coaster loops stretch high up in the distance. The rain couldn't have been that bad, because every so often the tracks loose a roar and a faint shriek that translates to a successful ride. If there had been thunder or lightning, all the coasters would have closed and all the people who wanted to ride the coasters would have gone to ride the massive line at Guest Relations instead, with its hills of yelling and loops of children's tears and the splat at the end when the Guest Relations rep flatly denies your refund request.

Because no refunds. No refunds ever. On anything. That's Five Banners' corporate policy.

By the time I get home, my forms have scattered all over the floor and my uniforms are in a crumpled heap in the passenger-side well. I blame the town's traffic lights, which have yellow lights about as long as an eyeblink to try to milk money from all the Adventure World–going tourists. I don't mind so much, though. It's kind of like a game, making sure I stop in time. A good way to distract myself from the fact that I'm steering thousands of pounds of sharp metal and flammable liquid with the touch of my hand.

After pulling into the driveway, I reach down to collect

my belongings, groaning just for the sake of groaning, and jump when something thumps on my window. I look up to see my little brother's face smushed against the glass, his nostrils open wide and his breath clouding the rest of him in fog.

A smile breaks across my face, and I lean over to click the lock open. Matthew scrambles in and immediately starts cleaning up my stuff, beaming the way only a seven-year-old can. If I believed in God, I'd thank him (or her) every day for creating baby brothers.

I take the pile of uniforms and forms from his lap. He grins up at me, exposing a space where one of his front teeth should be.

"Thanks, dude," I say. "Did you just lose that today?"

He kicks his feet. I'd frown very strongly at anyone else who smeared footprints on my dashboard. Matthew can kick all he wants. "Yeah," he says. "Did you get the job?"

"I did get the job." I raise my eyebrows. "And guess what that means?"

He punches the air. "Free tickets!"

"All the free tickets you can eat," I promise.

He scrunches his nose. "I don't want to eat them."

"Oh, really?" I pretend to consider. "What in the world would you do with them, then?"

"You're being silly," he says. A lock of brown hair flops over his eye, and his lips purse like he's still not sure whether to believe me.

"I am," I say. His face splits into a wide smile. "Now

help me carry this stuff inside and we'll have a snack." Food is the way into Matthew's heart. Food is also the way into my heart. It's how you can tell we're related.

Though we've lived here in Jefferson for four years now—the majority of Matthew's life and almost all the time since I called my parents from the police station, my teeth chattering so hard they thought it was static—I still think of this house as "the new house."

It's objectively nicer than our old house in Illinois. Our New Jersey house is a neat two-story with cherry-red shutters and bright white siding my dad pummels with the pressure washer the first Sunday of every month, and a lawn so even and green that, in combination with the red shutters and red door, it makes for a festive, Christmasy mood all year round. It's objectively friendlier than our old house, too, which was located at the end of a very long driveway at the end of a very long street, where neighbors were few and far between; our New Jersey house is smack in the middle of a cul-de-sac, crammed side by side with houses that are crammed side by side with more houses, so close that neighbors can shout from window to window if they need to borrow a cup of sugar or need someone to pop over and watch the kids.

Still, it's firmly part of the After, and anything in the After is new. Even Matthew, though I can't imagine my life without him.

Matthew precedes me into the house, doing a weird sort of dubstep move that works only when you're seven years old and delighted. Sometimes I wish I were seven years old again. And that I'd never turn eight, because eight was when the man grabbed me off the sidewalk.

"I want *cookies* for a snack," he says.

I dump my pile of stuff onto the hall table. "How about celery with peanut butter?"

"Okay, but how about cookies?"

"Okay, but how about celery with peanut butter and raisins?"

"Okay, but how about celery with peanut butter and chocolate chips?"

"That just sounds gross." I wrinkle my nose. "Celery with peanut butter and raisins. Final offer."

He pouts and runs ahead of me. "Fine."

The new Jefferson kitchen is blinding in its whiteness and shininess and sunniness; every time I walk in, I have to blink and tell myself that no, Scarlett, you haven't just stepped through a portal to the future. As my vision clears, I notice my sister at the table, her hands cloaked in oven mitts, sliding the last cookie off a baking sheet and placing it onto a piled-high plate. Wisps of dark hair stick to her forehead, forming crazy curlicues in the sweat.

"Hello, Scarlett," she says, her voice cold and distant. You'd think the sugar would sweeten her tone even a little bit, except she probably hasn't tasted her product. If I'd made those cookies, I'd have eaten all the dough, and it would have been worth it, even after Melody told me how much I'd regret it next time I stepped on the scale. "I told Matthew he could have a cookie earlier. I had to make some for the bake sale tomorrow."

I have to bite my tongue not to ask "Which one?" Melody is sixteen, a year younger than me, and involved in so many school activities it makes my head spin just to think of them: student government (vice president!), chorus (second soprano!), field hockey (varsity!), French club (*la trésorière!*), creative writing club (cofounder!). Even now, during summer, she has all sorts of things to do and baked goods to make. I honestly have no idea how she manages to do all that she does. I can barely manage to hold myself together enough to make it to school every day. Even this new job is pushing it.

"He shouldn't be eating cookies before dinner," I say.

It's too late: a cookie is already half-chewed and half-down Matthew's gullet. Little traitor.

"It's just one cookie," Melody says, turning around to put the baking sheet in the dishwasher. "I think he'll live."

I stare at her back and fantasize about her turning around with a big white smile, a hug, and a "How was your interview?" I wouldn't even care if she got flour and sugar all over me. That could be showered off, but the glow she'd give me would last for days. Weeks, maybe.

"I got the job," I say. Not that she'll care.

"That's good," Melody says, turning back and flicking a sticky curl from her forehead. She rubs her hands together; bits of flour and sugar and whatever else goes into chocolate chip cookies flake off and drift to the floor like snow.

"You'll have something to put on your college applications now." She gives Matthew a peck on the top of his head, and love washes over her face for a moment; it makes my chest hurt just to see it. Matthew doesn't even acknowledge it, consumed as he is with his third cookie. "I have to shower and take these to Sarah's. Can you watch Matthew? Dad should be home any minute."

I deftly pluck a fourth cookie from Matthew's hand. He groans, and I almost relent. Almost. "Yeah, I can watch him."

"Good. Thanks. See you later." Melody sweeps out of the kitchen without a backward glance, shiny sheet of hair swinging behind her.

After I'd made the call from the police station, the cop, the nice one who had wrapped me in a blanket that smelled like old milk, sat with me to wait for my parents. Plural, because once upon a time I had a mother, too. They came as soon as they could; I could hear the screeching of their tires in the parking lot through the open window. My heart thumped as I heard their footsteps coming down the hall, and then they turned the corner and I saw them: my dad, hollow-cheeked, threads of silver winding through his beard; my mom, her face lined and eyes weary, carrying toddler Matthew; and Melody, trailing behind them, hands clasped before her, mouth trembling.

My dad burst into tears and fell to his knees, pulling me into his arms and holding me so tightly I could barely breathe. My mom couldn't stop patting my head, like I was a lost dog. She had this funny look on her face, half disbelief, half astonishment, and she had to put Matthew down and rest her other hand against the wall to keep herself from falling over. Matthew kept tugging on the bottom of her shirt and asking her who I was, but she didn't answer.

Melody just stared. Even when I looked at her and said, squeezing the words over the lump in my throat, how happy I was to see her again, she just stared. Even after I made it out of the hospital, my butt frozen from sitting on cold metal table after cold metal table, and I told her how happy I was to go back home and sleep in my own bed, she just stared, eyes colder than the hospital's tables.

Nothing has changed since.

ABOUT THE AUTHOR

AMANDA PANITCH grew up next to an amusement park in New Jersey and went to college next to the White House in Washington, DC. Amanda now resides in New York City, where she works in book publishing by day, writes by night, and lives under constant threat of being crushed beneath giant stacks of books. Visit her online at amandapanitch.com and follow her on Twitter at @AmandaPanitch.